THE MUSE

THE MUSE

Sylvia Gilbertson

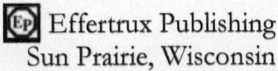 Effertrux Publishing
Sun Prairie, Wisconsin

Effertrux Publishing
P.O. Box 694
Sun Prairie, Wi 53590-9998
www.Effertrux.com

Library of Congress Control Number: 2013940638

ISBN: 978-0-9858427-4-1

Cover design by Cid Freitag

To the memory of

Carl Bocock, my eighth grade English teacher,

who encouraged me to write.

ACKNOWLEDGMENTS

I am grateful to the friends and colleagues who have read and commented on this book and encouraged me every step of the way. You know who you are.

Very special thanks to Laurel Yourke and D.L. Burnett.

THE THIRST

Sylvia Gilbertson

ONE

Ada found Bathsheba in the public library. At six years old, Ada was barely tall enough to peep over the table tops, but she liked big books, and this one felt fat and hefty under her searching fingers. So she crawled up on the chair to look, and that was when she saw the serene and naked queen at her bath. Ada stared. She'd sometimes seen her big sister Emily naked, but never her mother, never a grown lady. Never had she seen such a woman, whose milky body was like a cool star in that dark room, jewelry glinting against her tender skin in dainty points of light. Breathless, Ada touched the image, getting her nose as close as she could to the curves and crevices, the rounded belly, the strategically placed bit of gauze. And then she turned the page and her world cracked open.

The color plates included a pale and scrawny Adam and Eve wearing nothing at all, their guilty eyes gazing at a writhing creature in an apple tree. A whole section featured Michelangelo's powerful male nudes. Then macabre devils leaping up like jack-in-the-boxes, skeletons slithering from dim corners to menace wide-eyed, alarmed girls clothed only in filmy veils. Succulent fruits and vegetables, voluptuous dead deer and peacocks. Ada's little animal heart, drowsing in listless torpor after so many board games, television shows, and censored conversations, nearly popped from her chest. The dark desire seemed to crackle the very scalp off her head. She wanted the book. She wanted to take it home, creep into her room with it, and swallow it whole.

She lugged the treasure off the reference table and staggered over to her mother so they could check it out, though even at that very moment of hope and inspiration the little voices hissed at her— watch out, watch out. Yet the sweet foreign promise of possibility made her bold.

Her mother touched the book as if it were poison ivy. Then she lifted it and peered at it, riffling through the pages with her lips pinched tight and white. She slapped the cover shut and clutched the volume tight against her bosom.

"Ada, this is not a children's book, and we are going to put it back." She marched it over to the first high shelf she saw and slipped it away, hidden from Ada's sight. "And we should talk to the librarian about keeping adult materials out of the children's section, don't you think?"

Ada thought that she wanted that book. She wanted it like the seedling wants the sun. Attacking the shelf where it now lay out of reach, she flopped onto the floor and hammered her heels in a wild protest that surprised even herself. She shrieked and wailed and finally had to be dragged out of the library, followed by the silent and disapproving eyes of other parents whose children had manners instead of embarrassing tantrums. Instead of such an unnatural attraction to the flesh.

Writhing in the front seat of the car, Ada wept all the way home.

Her mother tried to explain. "The library won't let you check out grown-up books. You have to stay in the children's section. Some books are bad for children."

But Ada just howled and kicked her legs in fury. "I want the pictures! I like the pictures!"

"You have Cat in the Hat pictures, and look how nice they are."

"They're not the same," Ada sobbed. "They aren't pretty." And of course they were not, not compared to Rembrandt's Bathsheba. Those bright, flat, red and blue cartoon images had no fire, no bright and beautiful danger to spark a child's soul.

Ada never found that particular book again. It was re-shelved and hidden, lost forever and thus destined to become mythical. A touchstone. The sapphire blue robes draped on ethereal white bodies, the pretty little dogs with their bright living eyes, the beautiful people with their bountiful flesh and muscle, would beckon her like some sensual pilgrim's path. Follow us, they would say. Follow us on the beauty path.

"Ada was just born that way," her mother explained to the relatives as they sat around the table that Christmas. "She's a fussy child. She gets up in the middle of the night and scrawls on the wall with crayons. We finally had to take them away. And what a temper!"

"I do not have a temper!" Ada pouted in her chair, glowering. Her sister knew where the crayons were, but Emily wouldn't tell, even after Ada hit her with a stool. She'd tattle, though, when Ada crawled under the wooden coffee table and scribbled on it.

Aunt Delia, bright as a fire hydrant in her red holiday suit with the big multi-colored Christmas tree brooch that Ada liked, regarded the child with some sympathy, though she agreed that the girl was a handful.

"Lucille, why don't you give her some construction paper to draw on at night? So when she wakes up she'll have something to do. Some children are just more active at night. It's not their fault."

Ada watched her mother's uncertain eyes. "It's not my fault," she said, sensing the moment of weakness.

And in fact it was not. This desire was not anything she even understood.

"That way she won't bug me either," added Emily. The sisters scowled at each other.

That evening, after everyone went home, Ada ventured into the darkened living room with its holiday decorations. The family had a brand-new aluminum Christmas tree that looked like it was made of stiff silver foil. It was decorated with neatly placed bright pink glass globes, each exactly the same. Yet the tree was rendered mysterious and beautiful by a rotating color wheel that turned it blue, red, green, and yellow. Spellbound, Ada crept under the tree and lay on her back while the wheel revolved and the tree silently transformed into an endless pattern of color. In the background a record of plaintive medieval Christmas carols played on the phonograph, whispering of some distant world. She watched the shapes, the shadows, the shifting lights. The music made her melancholy and content. The colors calmed her. She could hear her parents and Emily in the kitchen eating canned peaches, but she feasted on color alone, and dreamed of more.

The next evening the crayons reappeared, along with a big tablet of colored construction paper. If she got the urge to draw pictures in the middle of the night, Ada was to tiptoe quietly out into the hallway and close the bedroom door without waking Emily. When she was done, she had to remember to turn out the light and lean the tablet and crayons up against the wall where no one would trip over them. Wild with anticipation, Ada lay open-eyed in bed across the room from slumbering Emily until she heard the toilet flush next door, the familiar sound of her father blowing his nose in the sink while her mother slipped on her big flannel nightgown in the bedroom. When the flip of the light switch signaled that her parents were in bed, she grew tense and excited, but she waited, waited till the silence settled, then was broken by the lusty snores of both parents. And finally, in love with the loneliness of night, she slipped into the hallway to draw Christmas trees, flying cats, birds with long purple feathers, herself like some foreign orange flame bolting off the edge of the paper.

Though her mother seemed to think that following Aunt Delia's advice might quench Ada's thirst for art, the nocturnal drawing sessions in the corridor triggered an explosion of creation. From crayons Ada went to pencils, from pencils to charcoal, then paints and canvases, and then she reproduced Emily in front of the television, her father sleeping with his mouth open on the sofa. And unbeknownst to her mother, even before Ada was in high school she had found an illustrated book of Greek statues. The marble bodies of Aphrodite and Diana, the proud and naked Apollo and Hercules, triggered Ada's memory of that day in the library, those soft high Renaissance foreheads and mysterious pale faces with their bulging sixteenth century eyes. They were as luscious as truffles or sugar plums, as the spectacular marzipan fruits that she would one day make in her own kitchen instead of her mother's apple strudel, served with expensive white wine instead of instant coffee.

By the time her family realized that Ada was going to be an artist, it was too late to stop her. Skinny idealistic high school teachers scooped her up like a rummage sale find and talked to her about university. An arty friend's psychic mother gave her a deck of Tarot cards, and Ada replicated in full color The Tower exploding under a bolt of lightning, its foundations rent asunder. It made her mother sweat with discomfort. She was prohibited from even mentioning art school and university to her father, who already had to worry about Emily and her crackpot plans to be a medical transcriptionist, even though she had a fiancé with a job. The last thing he'd need to hear was Ada's big ideas. She was stretching her feet too far for her blanket, that's what, getting a swelled head, a little miss getting way too big for her britches.

Too late, too late. Ada had lost her fear and talked only of travel and university and dangerous dreams. She threatened to be the Sutter girl who escaped her blue collar destiny. And now she could check out any book she wanted.

That last year in high school before she got the scholarship, the year she was enthralled by Dionysus, Ada wanted to paint her bedroom with ivy and grapevines. She imagined green tendrils and fat bunches of purple grapes running wall to wall, transforming the cracked plaster into a fecund greenhouse. But like that book so many years before, her mother would not allow it. And truth be told, Emily too would have hated it, even though she'd be married and gone in less than a year and could have afforded to be generous.

So Ada locked herself in the bathroom and imagined dancing naked with Dionysus crowned in grapes and ivy, both of them spilling over with beauty and color, and she was already gone long before she packed her bags and left for university, blonde hair braided and twined with red ribbons, heart and soul intent on ascending the ladder that the masters had climbed centuries before.

Burning and focused as a laser, she blazed beyond them all.

TWO

From the tiny window table where she devoured a slice of sausage pizza, Ada could see the steps of Florence's Duomo, the great and gleaming cathedral with its gaudy stripes. Tourists thronged the square, students flashed by on bicycles, a young priest in a long black habit photographed the bell tower. She could see the doors of the famous Baptistery that Michelangelo had called the Gates of Paradise. And it did not matter that she was living the frugal life offered by a post-graduate grant. That she resided in a closet-sized room in a drafty old house with high ceilings, damp marble floors and inadequate lighting, with a window that looked onto the grimy wall of the building next door. It did not matter, because she had touched the Gates of Paradise with her own hands, sat alone on those cathedral steps to eat a bag of fresh apricots. And because now, finally, she was on the trail of the wellspring from which the masters had drunk. She would dig deep till the water rose around her, and then she would gulp it down. She would soak in it like a scented bath. She would grow so heavy with inspiration that it would finally gush from her like a fountain. She would find her muse. She bit at the pizza, grease running down her thumb.

Someone strolled past the window and did a double take. Ada surveyed him over the top of her rhinestone-trimmed white plastic sunglasses, the sausage-laden pizza hanging in her hand. She liked the curl of his lip and his white teeth. She liked the fit of those impossibly tight clothes over that nice body. She liked the way he seemed thunderstruck at the sight of her. So she crossed her legs in their cheap tight pants and red vinyl shoes and gave him a smoky smile. She did need to improve her Italian. He gave her a rapturous gesture—please, please, might he come in?

Indeed he might.

Cristian Montinelli was an architecture student who wanted to remodel old farmhouses for a living and knew little about Renaissance art. He'd grown up with cathedrals and palaces, marble statues and famous paintings, and he wasn't impressed—that first night he even told Ada that as a boy he'd spray-painted a girl's name on a medieval church. And it charmed her. It even intimidated her, at first, to imagine growing up so surrounded by glory that the sight of it grew quotidian. Could she ever stroll through the Uffizi with Cristian's casual nonchalance? Oh god, another Renaissance portrait, let's get out of here and have a gelato. And when he told her that she was the art he wanted to worship, not that dusty dead stuff in the museums, she was flattered. Though an unexpected melancholy envy curled through her too. For he did not quicken her that way. But yes, she was flattered, and she thought his adoration might be enough.

Later, of course, long after they'd sampled each other's pleasures, after he confessed one night in a torrent of Italian that he loved her, it no longer quite sufficed. Though by then they'd grown so entangled that Ada, who was no poet, strained to tell him what it was like to seek the gods. Like sparkling dust, she wanted to be swept up into the whirlwind of creation and tossed, helpless and roaring, into the sky. Shooting out of herself into some higher place. Touching some kind of greatness.

"Cristian, I am surrounded by beauty here. Look at it. I want to honor the masters in every brushstroke. I want to feel what they felt. I want to be right in their skin, breathing the same air. I want the art to pour out of me like it did from them. I want to learn how that feels."

But Cristian had nothing to say. After all, beautiful churches full of art were scattered across Italy like so many stones. Who needed more of the stuff?

So Ada never told him the rest. She never told him that, like water, the ghost of Leonardo had seeped into her very dreams. Be worthy, he told her, or go home. Or that she believed that when she could duplicate Michelangelo's hand of God sparking life into Adam, she too would be offered a seat at the table of the masters. She too would receive her muse. And she didn't tell him her fear—that the masters would find she was wanting. That they would discover her mother collected stuffed owls and had a velvet painting in the living room. That she would be sent home in shame, an undeserving fraud who would never be given the key. To whom entry would forever be denied. Someone in whose veins flowed only mediocrity.

She did ask Cristian if she could draw him as Lorenzo de Medici, so he posed for an excruciating session where he had to sit perfectly still, back straight and chin tilted, while she examined him with a cold eye.

"*Porca puttana,* there's still something wrong."

"Come on, Ada, can I move my neck now? My aunt will be home soon."

They were in the tiny old-fashioned apartment of Cristian's great-aunt Simonetta. Cristian was from up north in Torino, but while he went to school in Florence he lived with his great-aunt and slept on a fold-out bed in the living room. Ada had met the old lady once and had been invited to visit again, so they'd come by while Simonetta was out at the market and they'd had hot sweaty sex on the floor. Then Ada finished by sketching Cristian as Lorenzo de Medici.

"Stop winking at me," she said. "It's distracting."

Cristian stuck his tongue out. "I want to put my tongue in your ear."

"When I get it right it's going in my portfolio and Professoressa Garavoglia is going to see it and she is going to be amazed. Then you can put your tongue wherever you like." But he looked so nice in his tight shirt with that curly dark hair that she went over and let him have what he wanted anyway, and they were almost rolling around on the floor again when they heard great-aunt Simonetta coming up the steps outside, and only just had time to straighten their clothes before she opened the door.

Later that evening, after a bottle of wine in a little bar on the other side of the river past the Palazzo Pitti, he flattened her against the façade of a medieval building and they kissed and touched again.

"I love you," said Cristian. "I'm going to take you to Rome and show you the Sistine Chapel."

Braids undone, mascara smeared and cheeks pink from Cristian's rough evening stubble, Ada smiled, her eyes a shallow pond.

THREE

By December Ada had finished the Cristian-as-Lorenzo de Medici portrait to her satisfaction, and as promised, added it to her portfolio for the meeting with Professoressa Garavoglia. Ada was ready for the session: to show off her technique, she had copied Titian's *Venus of Urbino* with her own face superimposed on the visage of the languid goddess. She'd reproduced Caravaggio's *Medusa* in the same way, with her own screaming mouth, her own wild eyes on the shield. Easy as it was to produce, such drama was arresting. Perhaps Professoressa Garavoglia would be so impressed that she'd commission Ada to do her own portrait. And Ada would rise to the challenge. The floodgates of inspiration would finally crash open and she would capture the professoressa's soul on paper. It would be the gateway to the rest of her life.

So Ada came in jittery with sweet anticipation. She felt fine in her stylish new Italian clothes, carrying the leather bag that Cristian had bought her from the Coin department store on the Via Calzaioli, and speaking the competent Italian she'd learned in bed and out over the past two months. She was proud to present her work, her admission ticket, to the esteemed professoressa of art.

Rumor had it that Lidia Garavoglia had eaten cats back in the 1940s during the occupation. She'd been there when the Germans blew up the city's historic bridges and all those priceless streets past the Ponte Vecchio. And she had such a chip on her shoulder about it that she'd never been to Germany in all her life. She even refused to go to the Dolomites, because she couldn't stand all those German-speaking Italians up there.

But she knew Renaissance art.

Ada had made sure that the first thing Professoressa Garavoglia would see when she opened Ada's portfolio was a nearly perfect copy of Berruguete's *Salome with the Baptist's Head*, but with Salome sporting Ada's own face and Valkyrie braids. And sure enough, the professoressa sucked in her breath and scrutinized it, mouth slack. But she said nothing. Then she flipped through the rest of the portfolio, which brimmed with more of the same: Botticelli, Titian, even Ada's hero Michelangelo. Some were straightforward, practically flawless reproductions, while others featured Ada's own face or Cristian's superimposed. Ada hoped it would be a treat for the professoressa. That her skill would take the professoressa by delicious surprise.

Lidia Garavoglia pulled on her long cigarette and said nothing. When she looked up, her face was expressionless.

"So, signorina Soo-ter, you are quite the copyist. I see you have mastered various styles here."

"I've worked hard on it."

Lidia Garavoglia blew a stream of smoke out the side of her mouth with a soft hiss. "I see that you have." She met Ada's eager gaze with a hard little squint. "So tell me, what are your plans?"

"I have focused on portraiture in the Renaissance style."

"Portraits like this." Holding up the drawing between two bony fingers, she gazed at Ada's blonde tresses on the Italian master's Florentine model. Her hard black eyes were mean as a snake's. She dropped the portrait back into the portfolio and slapped it shut. "I see. So. Did you think you would set up shop outside the Uffizi, perhaps? In the street with the human statues and caricature artists?"

Ada drew back, mouth open. "What do you mean? Of course not."

"But you are inspired by—novelty art?"

"Novelty. I'm sorry, perhaps I haven't understood—"

"Ah, signorina Soo-ter, I think your Italian is very good, quite sufficient. Yes, I mean novelty as opposed to originality. One can make a fine living that way, if that is one's vocation. There is no shame in that, unless you intend to become a counterfeiter." The professoressa jabbed out her cigarette with a satisfied little stab.

A red flush spread up Ada's face. It beaded into little drops of sweat on the sides of her nose. "I am trying to perfect the technique." Her voice squeaked.

"The technique of what?" Lidia Garavoglia leaned forward, thin red lips pressed tight. "I ask you." She flung her arms out, palms up, in one of her country's weary jaded gestures, and puffed out her cheeks with a little sigh of disdain. "I ask you, signorina Soo-ter, to reflect on what the technique serves. You are young, there is time to reflect. You have come here to work and reflect, no?"

"Reflect? I—"

"It is true that you have good technical skills. A very good eye. And that is an important first step. A vital first step, to my mind. Without that, one goes no further." She handed the portfolio back to Ada and stood, gold bracelets dangling from her sun-spotted arms. "But now you must probe a little deeper. You must explore, you must take risks. Do you understand?"

Ada stayed seated, clutching her portfolio packed with the gifts she had created for this day. "Wait. I don't know if I understand. What risks do you mean?"

"It's not something we can teach." Lidia Garavoglia tapped her heart. "You reflect, signorina Soo-ter, and we will talk again in the spring."

Ada sat there. They eyed each other across the desk. Finally the professoressa expelled a long, exhausted sigh and sank back into her chair. "On your way out, would you ask the girl in the front office to bring me an espresso? Tell her three spoons of sugar."

Ada shoved herself up and snatched the portfolio. Now sweat ran down the back of her neck.

The professoressa drew her fingers together and looked down her narrow patrician nose.

"Child," she said. "I offer you the words of Paul Gauguin. *L'art est la plagiat ou la révolution.* Do you understand? Art is either plagiarism or revolution." She pointed a long skinny finger at Ada. "Revolution is the risk."

FOUR

"**D**rink," Cristian purred. "Come on, you are here in the land of Bacchus and I want you to be happy."

They huddled over a tiny bar table as Ada downed her wine in greedy rage, hands still shaking.

"I sold two portraits last year. I sold them. People paid money for them. I got this damn grant because I'm good at what I do."

He refilled her glass and replenished her plate with salami and bread and olives. Ada tore at the meat and spat an olive pit into her hand. Cristian leaned back into his chair with the hungry look of a man watching a peep show. She didn't know why he loved it when she grew fierce. Maybe he thought she was a change from whiney Italian girls with good manners. Maybe he thought she had not shed any tears over this. Maybe he just wanted her to drink enough wine to flush her cheeks and look sexy. She pushed the food away.

"I'm never going back to that office. Screw her, I'll drop out. I'll open up my own portrait studio and the first thing I'll do is Professoressa Garavoglia as a Renaissance lap dog. Portrait of a bitch."

Ada knew she could transform the professoressa's nose into the long snout of a skinny little dog. Whether or not it was revolutionary. She ripped into the bread and slugged back more wine.

Cristian leaned over and ran a finger down her cheek. "*Bellissima.*" He tried to caress her neck, but Ada pulled away.

"*Porca puttana,*" she snapped.

Cristian put his finger to his lips, though his face was merry. "Not

14

so loud."

The people at the next table exchanged glances. Ada glared at them and finished her wine with a smack.

"No swearing when you meet my parents," Cristian said.

That stopped her. She sank back in her chair and folded her arms.

"What do you mean?"

"Come on, Ada, I had a great idea. Come to Torino with me for Christmas."

Ada closed her eyes and exhaled. Now she would lose the boyfriend too.

"I can't meet your parents."

"Why not?"

She squeezed herself even smaller into her chair. Many a smitten young man had brought her home in good faith, and she'd always disappoint. Of course she knew that lots of artists were pigs, but she wanted to be the kind who could go to a gallery opening and drink the right amount of wine and speak in the right tone of voice, with a smile that bespoke fine china and elegant drawing rooms and vacations in Switzerland. Who could be graceful before a boyfriend's parents. But then she'd eat something with her fingers when she wasn't supposed to, or snort when she laughed, or be morose and forget to speak at all, and that would be the end of it. Parents would see the white and green Corelle ware and that velvet painting over the TV, the family outings to Niagara Falls, the whole miserable package, even if their sons did not.

"Well," she said, "I had plans to walk in the cemetery up at San Miniato on Christmas day. I want to sketch that tomb with the man in the fedora."

"Pah," said Cristian. "Dead people on Christmas day. Come to Torino. My parents will be crazy for you."

The sight of his kind eyes and ingenuous face caught at her heart a little. She almost leaned over and touched his chest.

And all right, she would go.

They stuffed their clothing into backpacks and great-aunt Simonetta packed salami sandwiches and artichoke pie in one bag, fruit and a hunk of sweet panforte in another, and bottles of sparkling water in yet another, and on a clammy gray day before Christmas they boarded the train and headed north.

Cristian, going home to comfort, parents, and his own room, soon fell asleep. Ada sat across from him with her cold feet and watched the dank, fallow winter fields rush past. She had taken out her braids and tied her hair back in a demure ponytail. She'd been frugal with her makeup and conservative with her clothing, opting for a big loose sweater and woolen scarf. No sunglasses, no ribbons. Cristian had seemed bemused by her preparations, though he'd offered no advice.

She gave him a sharp kick with her boot. He stirred awake, eyes dark with sleepy irritation.

"Do I have talent?"

He heaved a big sigh. "We have to talk about this again?"

"Do I?"

"*Sì, sì.* Yes. I liked it when you turned me into Lorenzo de Medici."

"But is that talent?"

"*Dio buono*, Ada. Sure it is."

But it wouldn't stop niggling.

A little later he leaned over and nudged her in the rib with a gentle finger. "I think you're the best," he said. "Isn't that enough?"

Ada closed her eyes and leaned her head against the cold black glass.

FIVE

It was late when they rolled into the gigantic terminus in the middle of the city, its arching doors and massive halls echoing with the cacophony of holiday travel. Damp as Florence, it felt colder, bigger, louder, harsher.

"Ready?" said Cristian, just before they stepped outside. He kissed the top of Ada's head, but she was staring up at the soaring atrium, lips parted like a child's. When he tried to kiss her mouth, she pulled away as if startled.

"There's my mother." Christian pointed her out just before she recognized him and came hurtling forward.

"Look at you." Fernanda Montinelli beamed, holding out her arms to Ada and squeezing her in an unexpected embrace. "Look at this blonde American my son has brought home." She gave Ada a big kiss on each cheek. "And you smell good too."

"Oh, Mamma, don't squeeze her like that, you'll scare her."

But Ada liked his mother's quirky amber necklace. She liked her bright brisk eyes. She liked the hug.

Cristian's father was illegally double parked, so they tumbled outside with no ado, into the slick wintry slush and a street clogged with tiny, aggressive automobiles jostling for position. Ada and Cristian were bustled into the back seat of a rickety white Fiat that now darted out into the churning mess, the city's winter-streaked buildings rising around them.

"So this is the little American." Cristian's father looked at her through the rear view mirror.

17

"I hope you can understand my Italian." Ada had practiced the line over and over in front of the mirror, trying on various facial expressions in an effort to look sincere and harmless, but since they were now bouncing through dark streets like a motorized tuna can and no one could see her, she hoped she at least sounded confident and Italian.

"Mah, Cristian will translate, yes?"

"She speaks fine," said Cristian. "You speak fine, don't worry."

"*Americana!*" his father called cheerfully at her, his big voice filling the car. "You can call me Gianni. We'll get some wine into you and you'll be talking all night long whether we understand you or not."

His mother patted Ada's arm. "I am Fernanda," she said, then she turned back to face the front, her ruddy face serene. "I cannot face backwards," she added. "I will vomit if I do."

Ada never did discover where exactly in the city they lived. Years later, she would remember only a nondescript concrete building somewhere within the sound of traffic, a small elevator, a dim corridor with cold marble floors. Then the indoor warmth, the tiny artificial Christmas tree on top of the stereo and the lavish nativity scene set up on its own big table, decorated with real moss, bits of wood and twigs, and talcum powder for snow, peopled with tiny figures swarming around the manger like some three-dimensional toy Brueghel. The smell of coffee and roast meat and garlic, the sound of clinking glasses and the muddle of voices that sometimes eased into the comfort of white noise. It all offered a fleeting protection from the gray heart of winter that crept round the chilly windows. But it also masked the blue mountains out in the distance. One might never even know they were there.

"So," said Fernanda with a businesslike air, though there was a glint in her eye, "here is your room." And she ushered Ada into Cristian's own bedroom, occupied by two narrow twin beds and decorated with posters of Italian pop stars and soccer players.

"What about me, Mamma?"

Fernanda smacked him on the head and he yelped. "There are two beds in here, aren't there?"

Cristian's eyes widened, and Fernanda seemed pleased. When she turned to Ada, she looked positively crafty. "Otherwise you must sleep on the divan," she explained. "Here you are more comfortable."

Gianni dumped her bag on one of the beds with a huge sigh. Recovering some of his swagger, Cristian dropped his bag on the other bed. Ada stood in the middle of the room, feeling ready to bolt. When she tried to slip into a little wooden chair in the corner, Fernanda briskly motioned her right back up.

"You are hungry and I have made soup and good bread. Maybe an aperitivo first?" Ada stood up to attention. Fernanda then marched over to Cristian, now lolling on his bed like a wriggling puppy, and lightly smacked him again.

"Up!" she said. "And go call Nonno Franco and Nonna Angela, they're waiting to hear from you."

Out at the dinner table, Gianni was already uncorking wine bottles and sorting through various liqueurs. "Start with this!" he called, holding up the Martini & Rossi alongside a plate of olives and cold meats. Cristian had gotten on the phone and was having a loud conversation with the grandparents, and Fernanda busied herself at the stove.

"Sit," said Gianni. "Sit, be comfortable, have a drink. No Coca-Cola here for the American!" He gave Ada a glass of vermouth. "And no ice for you Americans."

He looked like an older, balding version of Cristian. Balding, Ada thought uneasily. She nervously drank most of the vermouth in one gulp.

Cheered, Gianni sloshed more in her glass. "We will teach you about Italian liquor. You can try a few tonight, but not too much, it's not good to mix! You like that? Good with olives, no?"

"Don't get her drunk, Gianni!" Fernanda called from the kitchen. "Ada, say no if you don't like it!"

"I like it," Ada said. "I like it."

"She'll drink anything," said Cristian casually as he hung up the phone. "She likes it all."

"Everything is good here," Ada added in careful Italian. Looking smug, Cristian came over and kissed her on the cheek. She could smell his clean hands and fresh shirt. She drank again, waiting for the alcohol to calm her, and noticed that her glass still bore a little gold packing sticker, faded from many washings.

By the end of dinner, as the grappa-spiked, sugar-soaked espresso arrived, Fernanda had honed in on Ada from across the table. She wanted to talk politics—what did Ada think about liberation theology? About social class? What did she know about South America? Ada did not know who the Italian prime minister was and did not care. She knew nothing about the theological geography of South America and didn't care about that either. And she certainly did not know how to broach the subject of social class with an Italian boyfriend's inquisitive mother. When Cristian surreptitiously pinched her leg and rolled his eyes, she did not know whether he was commiserating with her or chastising her. Still, the vermouth and the wine and the artichoke bitters and the grappa had opened the linguistic portals. She had never heard anyone say the words "self-determination" and "Bolivian lover" in Italian, yet she understood. *La liberazione!* She found herself waving her arms with an occasional fervent "*sì!*".

"I told you," Cristian said to her in English. "I told you they were crazy."

"Ouf!" Fernanda retorted sharply. "Enough of that!"

"'Crazy' I know," said Gianni. "I know that word. Nobody here is crazy."

Cristian rolled his eyes again. "Give me some more grappa."

Ada smacked her fist down on the table hard enough to make him jump. "Nobody here is crazy!" she echoed fiercely.

"And look how good your Italian is tonight!" marveled Gianni. "We are astonished, *stupiti.*"

Cristian stroked her leg under the table. "She is ferocious."

Later, they found that Fernanda had left a cup of honey-sweetened warm milk for Ada next to the bed, with a condom placed neatly beside it.

"I guess we're supposed to use it," Cristian said.

Much later, sobered up and squashed together warm and naked in Cristian's bed, they giggled about Ada's first evening in Torino.

"Where would you rather live?" Cristian whispered. "Torino or Florence?"

"Wherever it's warmer."

"Florence, then."

"All right, Florence."

"My parents like you."

Her throat was full and no words would come out.

"I told you." He wrapped his arms around her.

She lay awake for a long time after he fell asleep. She imagined a little stone apartment in the hills outside Florence. She saw herself wearing pointy yellow shoes with foxy jeans, looking like the young Monica Vitti. She thought about exhibiting her work in crazy little galleries, making a lot of money from Lidia Garavoglia's dog portrait. She would moonlight as a tour guide of secret art sites in Florence. That night she even had fantasies of giving birth to Italian babies. She envisioned fancy European strollers, herself grinding oil-drizzled rabbit meat in a baby food processor. She steeped in those images till the traffic thinned and the cold stars emerged.

SIX

She didn't go back to Lidia Garavoglia in the spring. She did enough to keep the grant money, but she didn't need the approval of a sun-spotted old cow bent on destroying her. Once she passed the professoressa in the street, but they didn't speak. Professoressa Garavoglia gazed at her with an inscrutable expression, a curious softness in her eyes, but head high, Ada sailed past in an electric blue scarf Cristian had given her, as if she had important errands to run.

And in fact she did. She had dates with an Italian boyfriend who had thick curly hair and a nice smile. Who would be an architect and remodel old stone farmhouses, maybe even an old stone farmhouse where they would one day live together and thrive on olives and cheese and Chianti. And he didn't think she needed any more grief from snooty Lidia Garavoglia. He thought Ada was good enough. His parents thought she was good enough too. They thought she was so fine that that they had invited her to spend the summer holiday with them in their little apartment in the Ligurian village of Rocca. And that bitter old professoressa had probably never had a boyfriend like that, with a family like that, people who took her in as if she were one of them already. Who offered her a place in their own warm nest. It felt like serendipity, and one does not turn away from the blessing of Fortuna.

So now, stretching out before her was almost an entire summer on the Mediterranean. She was promised beaches and sea and fried fish, pleasant walks along the promenade at sunset, and gelato and bars at night. And Cristian's enlightened parents were so European, so perfect, that they would put her in a little room with Cristian, almost as if they were already married. In the fall she could still go back to Florence with him. She could try to sell her portraits. She would sell her portraits. And who cared if tourists wanted to buy them. One day the art would explode from her like a geyser, and in the end the professoressa would eat her heart out with envy.

In the meantime, here she was, standing at the window of a train gleaming with heat as it rounded the coast and the soft blue water of the Mediterranean came into sight, stretching out to the invisible purple horizons of France, Spain and Africa. Ada pulled the window down to stick her head out as the hot coastal breeze caught her hair, and the sea seemed to soak into her eyes and mouth and nose in a brilliant turquoise haze. "Oh," she breathed. "Oh."

"You like it?" Cristian asked, pleased.

She liked it in so many ways. She was running out of money despite her frugal year, and Cristian and his family had promised to look after her living expenses for the whole summer. Besides, she needed a break. After she failed to make the appointment with Professoressa Garavoglia, she had received a polite, formal letter inquiring about her progress. She had not responded. Then at the end of the semester she'd received another note from the professoressa wondering about her future plans. She had not responded to that either. Then she'd pretended not to see the professoressa that day in the street, and for a moment she'd had a panicky sensation that the woman was going to touch her. It made her feel queasy, and she was relieved to be leaving Florence. She could not, in fact, remember the last time she'd had a vacation. She'd never needed one before. Her work had been pleasure enough, once.

And now the hot silver train was pulling into Rocca, a mass of crooked pastel buildings perched on the stony cliffs overlooking the sea. Every house had long green wooden shutters and little balconies blazing with geraniums, pansies, and fat succulents. The pungent market square reeked of fish and cheese and sun-warmed fruit splattered on the pavement, but the palm-lined promenade was bright with the odor of iodine and sea. The tranquil Mediterranean caressed the coast with long blue fingers. White sails bobbed farther out, the darker distant water occasionally cleaved by a tiny, steel gray ship gliding past almost invisible against the horizon. Snow was a stranger here, where wild rosemary sprang tough and fragrant from the high cliffs. Tourists and locals sat on the sidewalks under big umbrellas and ate fancy gelato treats brimming with fresh fruit, or plates of fried calamari and whole crisp fish with filmy dead eyes and downturned mouths. On Saturdays the French came in on the train to shop for bargains.

Cristian's family owned the mezzanine floor of a salmon-colored house not far from the station but not within sight of the sea. Gianni and Fernanda's bedroom had a long, narrow balcony overlooking a cobblestone lane with a little broken fountain, its stone water nymph holding a long-dry vessel over a dusty marble basin. Cristian and Ada shared a cramped bedroom with twin beds that they didn't openly push together, for fear of overstepping, though at night they were happy to squeeze into Cristian's bed. During the day they ate Fernanda's meals, swam in the sea and lay in the sun, and at night they went out for gelato and walked the promenade all the way to the end, where the lights winked out and the sea took over. By the time the Fiat plant closed at the end of July and Gianni joined the family for their final month of vacation, they were as sleek and lazy as cats. And Ada had not picked up a pencil all summer. What for, she thought, lying entangled with Cristian on the hot pebble beach. Maybe this was good enough.

THE SCENT OF WATER

Sylvia Gilbertson

SEVEN

On the golden Mediterranean coast, even arthritic old widowers indulged the young people clinging moon-eyed to each other in line at the bank, the suntanned couples kissing and groping on the promenade, the pretty blonde foreigners like Ada necking in public with their horny Italian boyfriends. And Ada had sunk so deep into the indolent, sex-scented summer that she'd have been oblivious to disapproval anyway.

That night they had eaten big plates of mixed grilled fish and drunk a bottle of white wine, and now they sat outside under the umbrella at a crowded bar facing the promenade. Ada's Martini & Rossi glinted in a big thick glass, and Cristian drank a chinotto. She felt comfortable and blurred.

Cristian nuzzled her neck, caressed the little hollow above her breastbone that caught the shadows when she lay on the beach. Her arms felt pleasantly tight from salt water and sun, and she'd splashed on some cheap cologne that seemed to drive Cristian crazy. He'd been proclaiming his love to her for all the world to hear, and it seemed she needed to do nothing more to deserve it than exist.

Ada kissed him with her liquor-soaked tongue and let him run his hands over her. They arched and squirmed together. This brazen display of sensuality made her feel powerful and Italian, like an old-fashioned movie star, and she loved the touch of the cold glass of vermouth under one hand and Cristian's hot bronzed neck under the other. She parted her lips as his warm fingers explored her navel, crept up under her shirt, drifted down onto her lap.

All around them, groups of strutting men and bejeweled women floated in and out, voices musical in the warm night air. Foreigners with backpacks and wrinkled T-shirts ventured to the inside bar in cautious anticipation of gluttony. Italian children wearing starched outfits shrieked and swarmed, bellies full of fruit and sugar. Someone cranked up the disco music across the street. Ada leaned back, her arm outstretched holding the sugar-coated glass of liquor, and kissed Cristian with languid abandon, sweet and delectable as Bathsheba herself.

She surrendered to the heart of summer.

At some point Ada opened her eyes and pulled away with a breathless giggle, only to find herself caught in the dispassionate gaze of the person who now sat under an orange umbrella at the next table. He seemed to be wearing black eyeliner, but he looked away too quickly for her to be sure. She could not, however, help but notice the expensive dark trousers and the white shirt with just one button open, like someone's Victorian uncle, though he couldn't have been much older than she was. Then the hair, a little too long to be fashionable for someone wearing such natty clothes. He was leaning away from her now, sitting back in his chair as if relaxed, though his fingers wrapped tight around his untouched alcohol-free San Pellegrino Sanbitter. He surveyed the promenade like a watchful cat, as if he had never noticed Ada at all.

Suddenly he clutched the edge of the table, slid from his chair and hurried into the bar, leaving the electric red Sanbitter quivering in its glass. Moments later, a rumpled teenage girl threaded through the tables, hands in the pockets of ill-fitting jeans. Homely as she was, she, too, had beautiful eyes, even without makeup. She took in the Sanbitter and stopped. Then she scanned the tables one by one, her gaze flitting across Ada and Cristian without interest. She peered into the back of the bar, then slowly wove her way out of the tables and exited onto the promenade. She continued to the gelateria next door, where the reconnaissance began anew.

As soon as the girl disappeared down the street, the elegant young man with the eye makeup fluidly slipped back into his chair. He and Cristian caught each other's eye for a moment in a brief European stare-down. The stranger broke the gaze first as he reached out to sip the Sanbitter, chest heaving in an almost audible sigh as he leaned back again, still alert. Ada pinched Cristian's arm and they exchanged amused glances. Then she slouched, drinking her vermouth fast, and serenely wrapped her leg around Cristian's under the table.

She'd already ordered another vermouth when their neighbor abruptly burst into action again, this time nearly knocking his chair over as he fled back into the bar. And there came the unkempt girl, this time from the other direction. Once again she spotted the Sanbitter, now nearly finished. She stopped, looked around, made her way back into the bar, and emerged as before. And then she meandered over to Ada and Cristian's table.

"Is anyone sitting there?" She pointed at the half-empty glass.

"There was," said Cristian, as if he had more to say.

"He left," Ada interrupted. "He's gone."

The girl flopped into the empty chair and quickly drank the rest of the Sanbitter. "Which way did he go?"

Ada shrugged, crunching a piece of ice from her glass. "Out." She waved an indifferent hand toward the promenade.

The girl stared at the glass, twisting her mouth and scratching her arm with big-knuckled fingers. "All right." She heaved herself up and left.

"Why did you do that?" Cristian asked as they watched her drift away down the promenade. "Couldn't you see he was hiding from her?"

"I don't know. She seemed like a little turd."

It was the girl's proprietary attitude, the way she finished the young man's drink and sat in his chair as if they belonged to her. Her air of doom and duty. Who wouldn't want to run from that? But this was nothing she could share with Cristian, so she just told him that she thought the girl looked like a little *stronza*, an expression she liked in Italian. That made Cristian laugh and tell Ada he guessed she was right, the girl did seem like a tenacious little jerk.

Then the young man came back and slid into his chair with almost guilty stealth. He noticed right away that his glass was empty—he grew still and impassive, then touched it with tentative fingers.

"She drank it," Ada blurted.

He looked at her, startled.

"That girl," she said. "She came and drank it and went off that way."

Collecting himself, he picked up the glass and shook it, as if he did not know what to do with it, then drained the last few drops himself.

"Ah."

"I told her you'd left."

"Ah," he said again, this time with the barest hint of a smile. "Thank you. Yes, I had left."

She grinned, expecting some token of complicity. Instead, his eyes narrowed in a mulish flash of defiance. Then they went blank, remote as the face of some sixteenth century noble. The face of a portrait.

A sudden fierce voice cried, "Michel!"—and they all jumped. Bearing down on them fast was a very tall young woman with short, spiky red hair and enormously long limbs. Their eyes widened at this Nordic giantess, at the yellow miniskirt and red lipstick. She looked like she might hurl a thunderbolt from her blouse.

Michel himself remained as if pinned to his chair. "Ah, hello, Gisele," he said, his tone conversational.

She stood over him and pointed at the empty glass. "Have you paid for that?" When he hesitated, she blew out her cheeks in exasperation. "Never mind, I'll get it," and she slapped money onto the table. "I'm sick of being blamed for it when you disappear. Let's go." And without the slightest protest, he got up and followed her out.

Cristian shook his head and whistled through his teeth in disgust. "Now that's a real mama's boy."

Ada watched them strut off down the promenade like belligerent peacocks. Her hand itched for a pencil.

"A real mama's boy."

And she slowly unwound her leg from Cristian's under the table.

EIGHT

Ada had met Cristian's grandparents in Torino on Christmas Day. They spoke a mostly unintelligible dialect, but his grandfather, whom everyone called Nonno Franco, had nevertheless managed to communicate a coy invitation to drink vodka with him when Nonna Angela was out. Then, the day before she and Cristian returned to Florence, he'd taken Ada aside to tell her that he approved of her, that she was the kind of woman men wanted to touch, and that he hoped she gave freely of herself. She had thanked him because she didn't know what else to do, and because his tone was kindly, and because she was not positive he'd really said what she thought he'd said. And she never told Cristian.

By summer she had forgotten Nonno Franco. She had let him slip out of her life as if he never existed, as if the fact of him could not possibly affect the landscape of her own fate. Though this is how destiny has its way, in the end, by catching us unawares, slipping in like mist while we sleep in the bed we thought was safe, within the walls we thought were sound.

On that day as every other, Cristian and Ada woke up late to an empty apartment. Fernanda and Gianni liked to have a morning swim before the sun grew too hot, then they would take a leisurely stroll back, stopping at the bakery for a bag of tender and oily coastal focaccia topped with onions or rosemary or soft cheese, which Ada and Cristian would later take to the beach. And during that hour of lazy, unsupervised liberty, Ada and Cristian would fall over each other. They'd grow hot and tangled in the little bed, bumping against the wall and throwing the sheets in a heap on the floor, maybe even rolling right off the mattress and knocking the wind out of themselves as flesh collided with cool tile.

"*Ti amo*," he'd say. "I love you."

She'd feel safe.

They were drowsing together on the little bed that morning, resting from their intimate exertions, with Cristian's mouth on Ada's sweaty neck. The street noises filtered in dim and muffled, as if from some great distance. The city air was ripe with summer and the aroma of eggplant pizza and fried fish. Ada could smell the fertile fragrance of their own bodies wafting from pungent skin and crumpled linens.

She heard a sudden thump out in the kitchen. A door slammed. Quick footsteps clattered in. And then someone pounded on the bedroom door like a scene in an old war movie. Startled, they jumped and instinctively sought to cover themselves.

"Cristian! Cristian!" cried Fernanda from the other side of the door. "Get up now, this is an emergency!"

Alarmed, they scrambled out of bed.

"One second, I'm coming, I'm coming!" shouted Cristian. The panic in his mother's voice made Ada freeze naked and confused as Cristian sprang into action. Somewhere in her brain a photo clicked—Cristian's transformed face and animal body as he leaped to dress—and slapped itself onto an inner canvas. The image was so vivid that at first she did not even hear the confused murmur of voices on the other side of the door.

"Get dressed!" Cristian hissed as he zipped his pants. Jolted, she blindly reached for the first things she could find and forgot her underwear. They rushed out as they were, rumpled, uncombed, smelling of sex, though now the scent of dread poured out too. Gianni and Fernanda were in the kitchen, their faces sharp with concern. Fernanda paced back and forth, slapping her forehead with her palm.

"Nonno Franco has had a stroke," said Gianni. "We just found out."

"I should have called last night!" lamented Fernanda. "Why didn't I call?" She wheeled around the room, beach sandals flopping at her heels, and clasped her hands to her face as if in physical pain. The sight filled Ada with such discomfort that she had to look away. "Ai, ai, why didn't I call last night?"

"Will he be all right?" Cristian's voice dropped just like his father's.

"We don't know. We are going to Torino now, so get ready fast."

"Mamma, it's all right, come on," he said in an unfamiliar, encouraging tone. He hugged Fernanda protectively, and she leaned into him with a little cry. Ada could not envision such a scene with her own mother, who had always shied away from embarrassing emotional outbursts in front of her children. Fernanda's distress seemed almost indecent.

And because Ada had never known such solace herself, she did not see the man Cristian might become in her own time of need. She did not feel proud or comforted or reassured that she had chosen well. She saw only a once doting boyfriend whose attention had faltered. Whose blood relatives had become more important than she was. Who was now discussing travel plans that clearly did not include her. And she did not perceive their reluctance to ruin her summer by dragging her into a family emergency. She saw only the exclusion. Ada folded up, becoming smaller and smaller, until she was no larger than a postage stamp. She retreated to a chair at the little table, drew her knees to her chin, and huddled there while they threw their things together.

During those last frantic minutes, Fernanda came out and knelt by Ada's side. For a moment Ada thought the invitation would finally come, and she looked up with hesitant anticipation. But when Fernanda touched her arm with that rueful expression, Ada knew she was staying behind.

"I am so sorry," Fernanda said. Her voice was distant and tight. "We don't know—if we will arrive in time."

"Please don't worry about me." Though Ada still hoped that the portal would open to her. That she'd be welcomed in behind the gate.

"Of course, you are free to stay as long as you want. Please, enjoy the apartment."

The apartment had no telephone, but she could use the phone booth across the street. Fernanda gave her the number and Ada promised to call.

But Ada did not want to call from a phone booth. She wanted them to take her with them. She wanted them to ask. "I don't need to stay here in Rocca," she ventured.

"No, no, Ada, of course you should stay here, as long as you like. You are absolutely welcome here."

But that, of course, was not what Ada meant.

The men came out with the bags. Ada caught Cristian's eye. He looked distracted and unsettled, his face more like his father's than ever. He hesitated. Ada leaned toward him, unclasping her hands and bringing her palms together on her knees in an unconscious gesture of supplication. Christian's eyes softened, and for a moment Ada thought he would sweep her into his arms, that he would rescue her. Then he reached into his back pocket, pulled out some money, and laid it on the table.

"Telephone me," he said.

Ada curled up tighter in her chair. "All right." She felt like a small, mean little interloper. "I'll call tonight."

"Try again if no one is home. And here, take my key." He tossed his apartment key at her. Ada tried to catch it mid-air and missed. As she scrambled under the table to retrieve it, they were out the door. They hadn't even said good-bye.

NINE

The tattered remnants of their departure fluttered in the air. Crouched in the chair, Ada turned the big key over and over in her hands. The silence settled. On the table lay the abandoned bag of focaccia meant for the beach, and the money Cristian had left her. Ada snatched the bills, crushed them and dropped the crumpled ball on the floor, then smashed it with her bare foot. A kick sent it skittering across the tiles. Hands on hips and jaw set, she eyed it for a few moments before expelling an angry hiss. She stalked over and retrieved it, smoothed the bills, and stuffed them into her pocket with the key.

Fuck you, Cristian.

She had never looked into the kitchen cupboards, which were Fernanda's domain. But now, taking an inventory, she found pasta, sauce, olive oil, vinegar, rice, flour, coffee, bread, honey, sugar, salt, spices, onions, potatoes, garlic, red and white wine, and a bag of breakfast cookies. In the refrigerator were milk, cheese, jam, fruit, lettuce, green beans, prosciutto, chicken, and a big salami. She put the chicken in the freezer because she did not know how to cook it. She was not sure what to do with the rice or potatoes either, though she imagined both could be boiled till soft. All in all, it was probably enough for a few days, then she would have to think about shopping for herself. And for how long? When it was all over, would she be asked back to Torino? Would they come for her? Or was she supposed to disappear?

Fuck you all.

35

She took a shower. She washed off Cristian till she smelled like sweet soap and shampoo, then ate some of the focaccia. She wanted coffee, but that meant she'd first have to wash the dirty coffee pot, so she just drank milk out of the carton. She considered making the beds, but decided that no one would know the difference. Still, she'd noticed that the room, like her pre-shower body, had a heavy odor of sex, so she stripped both beds with the idea of trying to wash the sheets in the complicated little washing machine. She would hang them on the drying rack on the balcony, and then they would smell of sun and sea and she would feel better about sleeping on them. And while they were drying, she would get a coffee in one of the cafés and contemplate her situation.

The washing machine churned and simmered for most of the morning, slow as the Italian summer. It gave her time to steep in bitter and resentful abandonment. Would she now be required to clean up and vacate the entire apartment for them when the summer was over? Would she have to scrub floors and wash curtains like a maid? She thought about getting on a train and escaping, maybe even to Florence, but she didn't have a room there anymore. In the end it was easier to do nothing. She went to the café around the corner, had her coffee, then returned to the apartment and went back to bed on the stripped mattress, where she slept till late afternoon. She woke groggy and cranky, the back of her neck sweating. Fernanda would have prepared some peaches in wine, or cold melon, or a rice salad, or mozzarella with fresh tomatoes and basil and black olives. Ada would have sat with Cristian over a nice meal, then they would have gone out for a gelato.

She flopped back onto her bed. "Fuck." The thought of a long lonely evening settled darkly. As the shadows shifted and lengthened, she dozed off once again into a leaden and stifling sleep.

This time, dusk had settled when she woke famished and thirsty. She struggled off the bed, fumbled out to the kitchen, and stood at the table to finish the focaccia, which by now had stained the bag with grease. And in fact it tasted as heavy and oily as a paper bag, and stuck in her throat.

"Fuck," she said again.

It was unthinkable to stay in that apartment all evening. She'd slept most of the day, and anyway, she was accustomed to being out late. She and Cristian went to clubs and bars on steep crooked lanes and to gelaterias with neon lights and music. They took long walks on the beach to the dim and deserted end of the promenade where the black waves slapped against the sea wall. She knew no one in Rocca but Cristian and his family. Who were supposed to have stayed with her all summer. Whose lecherous old relatives were not supposed to have strokes.

That reminded her that she'd promised to call. Now she would have to spend money in a telephone booth, cramming endless coins down the indifferent slot. She didn't even call her own family in the United States, but she was expected to call his. She crushed the greasy bag and hurled it against the wall, strode over and kicked the bag back to the other side of the room. Crumbs flew across the floor.

She fidgeted in the phone booth across the street while the telephone rang in her ear. No one was home. Slamming the receiver down, she decided to go spend Cristian's money and worry about finances tomorrow. Surely she deserved one evening of pleasure.

Before she left, she pulled her portfolio from under the bed. Sitting cross-legged on the floor, she went through it till she found the pencil and charcoal self-portraits she'd taped to the walls of her room in Florence. Ada as Medusa, Ada as Aphrodite, Ada as the calf-eyed Madonna. She stuck them to the hard cement over her bed and felt some unaccountable desire to weep.

But Ada did not weep. She left her hair unbraided and put on a low-cut red shirt that Cristian liked. And then she went out to the promenade alone.

TEN

As a young undergraduate, before she turned serious about her art, Ada had enjoyed a wicked reputation. She and her friend Bobby went dancing and drank cheap beer as they trolled for men. She'd point out the dark-eyed types they both liked, he would growl deep in his throat, and she would punch him and tell him to behave. On Ada's twenty-first birthday, they'd even run an Alice in Wonderland caucus race around the parking lot in their underwear, and would have stripped naked if friends hadn't coaxed them inside out of the snow.

Now Ada slogged through the musty world of Renaissance portraiture and Bobby struggled with plans to open an art gallery, but had she been back in Buffalo, they would have gotten drunk together. She missed Bobby as she sat in an unfamiliar bar downing a whole bottle of white wine by herself.

The flirty waiter brought her two shots of yellow limoncello on the house. Ada drank the free liquor thoughtfully as various members of the wait staff swaggered past her table, casting furtive glances her way. She could stay and perhaps drink for free till the evening wound down. And for a while, Ada let herself slip into a winey fog, downing with stoic indifference everything that was put before her. But she was not going to sit there all night, hot-eyed waiters notwithstanding. She shook off her torpor, stood up with a delicate lurch, and ambled away down the promenade.

And now, left to her own devices at last, she slid back into her slow undergraduate strut.

Ada knew she was drunk because walking felt like moving through water. And because she had not been in such a state for a long time, she considered going back to the apartment and calling it a night. Then she remembered that she hadn't made the beds, and that the freshly washed sheets still hung out on the balcony. Crumbs littered the table and floor, and the dirty coffee pot needed to be emptied and cleaned. She had slept too much already. More importantly, she felt resentful. It wasn't her apartment, why did she have to take care of it? She didn't want to be their housekeeper.

She decided to go to the Casa Bianca discotheque, where Cristian wouldn't take her because he said it was noisy, tacky, and expensive. She would spend his money at the Casa Bianca. Taking care to walk with sober deliberation, Ada wove her way onto a side street and up a flight of slippery stone steps into a little alley where the red, white and blue neon sign flashed excitedly. She could already hear the music thumping from within. Skinny Italians in tight clothes stood outside smoking cigarettes and gesticulating. Ada stuffed her hands in her pockets and sauntered up another short flight of steps to the dirty armored door.

When she pushed it open, music and strobe lights bombarded her. A big, cold-eyed man with slick hair took her money—twenty thousand lire. It would have been enough for a grocery trip, and she felt a catch in her heart as she handed it over, but then the moment passed and she stumbled in. She realized that she'd spilled wine on herself—there was a wet spot on her shirt in the middle of her stomach. She rubbed at it half-heartedly.

Cristian had been right—the club did have a cheesy American theme. Three walls were covered with giant electric American and Confederate flags. Wild-eyed illuminated Lincolns and Washingtons glared down between them, interspersed with stick-like figures in cowboy hats chasing buffalos and mustangs. Presiding over it all was an enormous psychedelic image of the White House that covered the entire fourth wall, sputtering with enough light to trigger an epileptic fit. Red, white and blue strobes churned in frenetic abandon across a dance floor that was still half-empty—the Casa Bianca would not begin to fill until nearly midnight, and the crowds would not leave till dawn.

Ada took a deep breath. She stood, eyes closed, palms out, head back, and opened to the music and the lights, the fragrance of pot and acrid cigarette smoke, the promise of sweating bodies on the dance floor. She let it flow straight in from her crown, down her spine and into her belly and hips, where it blossomed and made her remember sex with Cristian that morning. Except that now she was being filled with color and sound. She wanted to hold a pencil in her hand again. She expelled that breath in a river of dark longing.

She went to the bar for another glass of white wine. She downed it in three sweet gulps, threw the plastic cup to the floor, and turned to face the music.

The vibrating bass made her feel talented and sexy. She wanted to wiggle her hips and so she did. Now she rubbed the wet spot on her stomach with affection—it was a fine tanned stomach with tiny golden hairs where her jeans swept past below her bikini line. It was a stomach she was happy to reveal. She would lift her arms high and her little shirt would pull up above her navel, her jeans would slide down her hips.

With the confident abandon of the young and intoxicated, Ada merged onto the dance floor, sure that tonight she would twirl like an angel. For a few minutes, in fact, she was so moved by Dionysus that the god himself seemed to have settled in her groin. And like so many mortals who find themselves caught in his fierce and tangled cords, Ada rejoiced, mistaking the snare for possibility. She whirled and stomped, and the little silver chain around her ankle tinkled.

She danced very close to someone. Then she lost track of time, and suddenly the dance floor seemed more crowded and her forehead grew wet with sweat. She backed up into someone else and they undulated, pressing together for a few intimate moments. Someone's hands were on her hips, creeping around to the front, and she stayed close. Then she was somewhere else again, dancing alone as the whole world spun past in a blur. Fuck you, Cristian. She leaped, arms wide, into the freeze frame of the strobe.

She saw someone she liked. He was dark like Cristian, but not as tall, with longer, curlier hair and blacker eyes, and was wearing an enigmatic little beret like Che Guevara. Ada was gripped by a sense that they should talk, that it was important for them to talk. She strutted over to him, cocky in her red shirt, with the odor of wine wafting from her pores.

She was delighted and amazed to learn that he was Mexican and spoke English.

"But you have curly hair, how come you don't look like an Indian?

Can I try on your hat? Do you want to dance?" She reached up to swipe the hat, but he stepped back, and no, he did not want to dance. Ada wavered a little, then came at him again.

"So what's your name? Are you sure you're not Bolivian? Come on, give me the hat." This time she got it and slapped it on her own head. "Do I look like Patty Hearst? Bang bang! Up against the wall!"

He snatched his hat back and moved away from her.

"You think I'm a North American capitalist dog?" she demanded. "Is that what this is all about? You're some kind of racist, are you?"

The Mexican boy hung on to his hat and turned his back on Ada.

"What kind of Mexican comes to Italy anyway?" She sidled up to him. "Come on, give it back."

It wasn't until he slapped her hand away that Ada realized the cute Mexican didn't like her. She might even have offended him. She backed off in a huff and decided she would have just one more glass of wine, which she downed in a single breath. She stood off to the side, plastic cup in hand, and watched the Mexican ignore her in favor of a thin dark Italian girl with lipstick and a cigarette. Ada hated her. She looked like an anchovy, skinny and flat, with a snooty, sophisticated, European attitude that seemed especially loathsome that night.

"Anchovy!" she called out, but no one heard. By that time she knew she was too drunk to be quiet. Maybe that last glass of wine had been one too many.

She leaned against the wall, threw her cup to the floor and stomped it. The Mexican and the slippery little Italian girl never once looked at her. She talked to someone, grabbed someone else's forearm in an urgent desire for conversation, and felt vaguely patronized by a patient face and accommodating smile. Sound and color seemed to blare and encroach and spin at her. It began to feel very late. Perhaps it was time to walk back to the apartment and get some air.

"Fuck Mexico," she offered, though no one was listening. "Fuck Italy. Fuck boyfriends. Fuck stupid clubs." She decided that she was done with the worthless Casa Bianca and its ignorant décor. She was never coming back. "I'm done with you all," she called. The world tilted around her in a loud and hazy bubble.

She went out the door and stumbled on the stairs, but someone grabbed her and pulled her upright, then helped her to the bottom.

People around her were laughing—were they laughing at her? Ada gathered herself with some dignity and walked away with dainty steps. Then suddenly her foot trod on nothing but air, and her knee buckled, then her leg, then her arms were flailing, and the next thing she knew she was tumbling down that first, forgotten flight of steps and crashing into the street with a thud.

ELEVEN

Ada sprawled at the bottom of the stairs, breathless as a gasping fish. The little knots of locals outside the club gazed down at her with disapproval. Someone made a coarse comment and people laughed.

Ada heard none of it. White stars were exploding around her head and she seemed to be hurtling into blackness. She opened her eyes and saw a pale freckled leg near her nose. Someone touched her shoulder.

"Hallo, hallo, are you all right?"

Ada tried to pull herself up but moved sideways instead. "I'm fine, I must have tripped." Her wrist unexpectedly collapsed and she slumped down again, then someone had grabbed both shoulders and was trying to pull her up. All she could see was a confusion of legs and someone's bright red toenails sticking out of pink leather sandals.

"Are you drunk? Are you all right?" She found herself staring into a set of intense, deep-set blue eyes as she tried once again to balance herself, this time on her elbows.

"Her knee and elbow are bleeding," said another voice, tinged with a hint of distaste. People clattered by, slowing to watch the scene at the bottom of the steps. Stunned and fuzzy-brained, Ada heard their chatter as if from afar. She caught a whiff of their tobacco and then, when her head lolled sideways, the disconcerting odor of dog shit.

"Ow, ow," she gasped.

"Here, let me help you. You've hurt yourself." Once again someone tried to haul her up, this time by grabbing her under the

43

armpits and pulling. Ada attempted to cooperate, but her legs were butter.

"Ow," Ada said again, louder, and suddenly, distressingly, found that she had burst into hot tears. "I can't walk! I broke something. Ow, ow, ow!"

"She's drunk," said the other voice.

"I'm sorry! I'm sorry!" Ada wailed.

"You're hurt," said the first voice. "Michel, we can't just leave her here. It's not safe." The blue eyes peered into Ada's face again. "Where do you live? Where are you staying?"

"It's too far," Ada wept. "I can't do it, I don't remember."

"Take one arm, Michel, don't just stand there. We'll take her to my place till she's sober."

They lifted Ada to her feet. She saw the torn bloody flap of her jeans fluttering at her knee. There was a stinging sensation in her elbow and an ominous queasiness rose in her stomach. Now someone grabbed her by the waist, and she tried to help by hanging on tight.

"That's good, hold on and we'll get you fixed up so you can go home."

"Ow, ow, thank you, I'm sorry I'm sorry," Ada blubbered. "I feel sick, I want to throw up."

The grip loosened almost immediately. "She's going to be sick. Are you going to be sick?"

Ada panted and cried. "I don't know, maybe not yet, I don't know, that fucking club poisoned me. Help, help."

"Oh come *on*, Michel, let's just get her home, it's only a couple of minutes. Don't be such a baby."

They dragged her along again, and much to her relief, she was not sick in the street. She even staggered on between them with almost no help, after the shock of the fall wore off. But then, when they entered a building and began to ascend what felt like an interminable flight of steps, Ada began to cry and snivel again every time she had to bend her knee. They gamely pulled her up three flights, then a door was unlocked and Ada and her benefactors stumbled in.

Ada woke on an orange sofa with a pillow under her head and a light blanket over her. Everything was dark and silent. Her head pounded and she felt battered. When she turned to one side, she felt a big bandage on her knee under her jeans, and a smaller one on her elbow. She groaned. They would have had to take her pants off to get that bandage around her knee.

Ada fell back limp against the pillow, hair wet and sweaty against her neck. The room had finally stopped spinning, but now thirst overtook her. She curled into a lump, face to the cushion, but could think of nothing but water. She tossed back and forth as perspiration beaded on her forehead. Finally she raised her head. It throbbed. But she pulled herself up to sitting and looked around. There must be a sink somewhere. She stood on bare feet and wondered what had happened to her sandals. Across the room, narrow French doors opened to a balcony illuminated by a street light. In the other direction, she could discern a closed door, perhaps the way out. Then a darker area off to the side. She began to creep that way, hoping to find a bathroom or kitchen.

She stepped on someone's warm arm. Ada leapt back as if scalded, heart racing. She had nearly trampled a person lying on the floor not six feet from her sofa. The shadowy figure, now stirring, stretched out before her like a ghost.

"I'm sorry," she whispered. "I'm looking for water."

A pair of liquid eyes blinked open, the gleam of light on dark water. "There's a bottle on the kitchen table," he whispered back, pointing to the dark area.

"Thank you. Sorry. I'm sorry." She carefully picked her way around him to a tiny kitchen with a bottle of sparkling water on the table. She popped off the plastic cap and drank furtively without even bothering to look for a glass. The water slid down her throat with a cool, carbonated, calming bite. She sighed and sat for a minute. The kitchen smelled of soap and incense. Ada drank again, letting the crisp water fill her mouth and then her gullet.

When she padded back out to the sofa, she gave the person on the floor a wide berth. He lay motionless, too still to be asleep. She dropped back onto her temporary bed and huddled against the cushion. Eventually she dozed off, pricked by the uneasy awareness that she was not alone.

The next time Ada woke, she had been dreaming of ominous, disembodied voices. Now sun streamed though the French doors and traffic swished and whirred outside. As she stirred, the dream voices shifted to reality, though at first she understood nothing through the fog of her pounding head.

"Ow, ow, shit." She flopped over onto her back. Her knee and elbow burned and she was desperately thirsty again.

She was hearing an argument, or at least one side of it. ". . . never have money, you do it on purpose, what if I did that to you?" A cupboard door slammed. "And don't look so innocent. You spend days at a time here, I cover for you over and over." A softer voice responded in an inaudible murmur, and Ada could hear the sound of footsteps in the kitchen, water running. ". . . not just the money," said the louder voice—a woman's voice. "You just take advantage. I'm not your mother." The footsteps came out into the living room, and Ada closed her eyes and feigned sleep. Then she heard the door slam and the sharp sound of someone briskly descending the stairway in the outside corridor. Silence ensued.

Ada lay as still as she could for a few minutes, then cautiously opened her eyes. Thirst made her tongue feel huge and cottony, and she pictured the bottle of sparkling mineral water on the kitchen table. She breathed in and out, listening. Perhaps she'd been left alone. She rolled off the sofa with a little more grace than the first time, and when she stood up she was careful to watch for the person on the floor, but saw only an abandoned orange cushion. When she looked to where the dark area had been, she glimpsed kitchen cupboards and a sink with a window over it, draped in a delicate lace curtain. She neither heard nor saw any movement. She could think of nothing but the taste of cold water. She tip-toed back over to the little kitchen, trying not to make any noise, trying to be invisible. If they had left her alone, she planned to have a drink and then slip out before anyone returned.

But when she poked her head through the door, she saw the little table and someone seated on a small blue painted chair, hands folded in his lap and head bent. He became aware of her and looked up. Their eyes met.

It was the young man with the makeup from that afternoon some days before. It took Ada a few seconds to realize it, because now he wore no makeup and was dressed in jeans and an old black T-shirt. He seemed abstracted, as if recently deep in contemplation. If he recognized her, he gave no sign.

"Hello." She hesitated. "Good morning."

"Ah, Sleeping Beauty," he murmured, a hint of indolent rebuke in his voice. "Good morning." But he gave her a sweetly enigmatic smile that took the sting from the words.

Ada stood poised in the doorway, waiting for him to invite her into the kitchen, but he just sat there, looking at her with an odd formality, as if he were the butler. So she did the only thing that seemed reasonable—she walked over and held out her hand, and when he took it, perhaps because he didn't know what else to do, she shook it firmly.

"Hello," she said. "My name is Ada."

Now he rose from his chair, hand still in hers, and inclined his head like a courtier. They continued shaking until Ada twisted her hand away.

"*Molto piacere*, Ada." The words ran off his tongue in an unfamiliar musical cadence. "I am called Michel. Would you like to sit?"

Relieved, Ada plopped into a bright yellow chair. "Thank you." Michel sank back into his own chair, and they sat there in silence for a few more uncomfortable moments.

Ada spotted the bottle of water from which she'd slaked her thirst during the night. "Could I have a drink?"

As if chastised, he swiftly pushed the bottle over to her.

"And a glass—might be—in the cupboard?"

Now he looked completely nonplussed. "A glass," he repeated, as if this were some vague philosophical concept. Then he motioned dismissively. "Oh, just drink it from the bottle. I don't know where the glasses are."

So she popped the plastic cap and swigged gratefully. "Good," she said. "I was so thirsty. And you know what, I drank it from the bottle last night too."

Now his expression changed, his shoulders straightened, and his eyes brightened with sudden recognition. He remembered her. Ada waited for him to say something, but instead he grew watchful.

"You're an American."

Ada hated being marked as an American. She guzzled the water, replaced the bottle smartly on the table, and changed the subject. "I think I saw you at a café the other day. You were drinking a Sanbitter."

He leaned back with a thoughtful air and folded his arms across his chest. He looked different without the eye makeup. "I do like Sanbitter," he said, as if just realizing this fact.

"Remember? I was at the next table, with my boyfriend."

She was sure he remembered. He must have. Yet he seemed to be waiting for Ada to tell him her version of the story, and he gazed at her inscrutably, arms still folded.

"I helped you lose that girl."

The downstairs door buzzed open and banged shut. Quick footsteps echoed up the stairs, then she heard someone at the door and the turn of the key in the lock. Michel looked like he was steeling himself for an injection.

"Well, you helped me lose one of them, anyway."

And then the door opened and his face became a mask.

TWELVE

Ada knew her immediately by the spiky red hair, the lipstick, and the long pale legs. She rushed in, a white paper bag in hand, which she tossed roughly onto the table.

"So now you have your breakfast," she snapped.

Michel peeked into the bag and poked his hand in. "You got three of everything."

"Well, there are three of us, yes?" She threw a big green mirror cloth bag onto the floor. "How are you feeling?" she asked Ada.

"Better, I think." Ada held out her leg with its torn jeans and the fat bandage on the knee beneath, and she twisted her arm around to reveal the similar bandage on her elbow. "They don't hurt too much. But I feel like I've been hit in the head."

"You look like it too. Do you remember anything?"

Ada sighed. "Yes. Yes. Thank you for helping me."

She clucked and made a dismissive gesture. "Someone could have stepped on you." She bustled about the kitchen.

"Gisele, meet Ada," Michel offered. "We've been having a nice chat."

Gisele ignored him. "Coffee?" she said to Ada.

"Thank you. That would be really good."

"Michel is hungry," Gisele added. "Michel wants his breakfast, he needs someone to go out and buy it for him."

"Look," Michel said with the air of an excited child. "Apricot-filled croissants, butter croissants, chocolate-filled croissants. Look, Ada."

"Leave them alone, will you? I'll put them on a plate and make some coffee. Can you wait that long?"

"I'm just saying they look good. Thank you, Gisele, they are going to be so good." He lay the bag down tenderly.

She rolled her eyes and turned back to Ada. "So you like that American bar?"

"Last night? It was the first time I ever went there. I hate it. I hate that place."

"Ada is an American," Michel interjected, as if this were an amazing fact.

Gisele, stuffing a coffee maker full of fragrant espresso and pressing it in with a spoon, turned to Ada. "You're an American?"

Ada threw up her hands in surrender. "That's me. An American."

"Pfft. You speak good Italian. I myself am German, but I've lived here a long time." She jabbed a thumb at Michel. "Don't even ask what he is."

Ada looked at Michel, but his expression was mild and vacant.

"A lot of Americans go to that bar," Gisele added.

"I didn't see any. I saw a Mexican."

"And you are staying at the hostel?"

"No, on the via Cavour. I was with my boyfriend and his parents, but now they've gone back to Torino. They had a family emergency. They're coming back in a few days. I just talked to them on the phone last night."

Gisele broke out in a sneering laugh. "Michel, did you hear that? A family emergency."

Michel's face went blank. Gisele deftly lit the gas under the coffee maker, one hand on her hip.

"Michel has some experience with family emergencies," she said dryly, turning to look at Ada. She tossed her head over at Michel. "Don't you?"

Michel folded his arms tightly over his stomach, face placid but jaw jutting stubbornly. "Families," was all he said.

"My boyfriend's grandfather had a stroke." Ada imagined rushing into the hospital with them, nestled within the family fold. "They wanted me to come, but I didn't feel right about it. I didn't want to intrude, even if they insisted. I told them I would stay here and look after the apartment. But I was so upset yesterday that I tried to get it off my mind by going to that stupid bar. People kept saying 'Oh what's wrong, you look so sad, let me buy you a drink,' and I didn't know how to say no. I never drink. I didn't know it would affect me like that –"

Gisele pulled out a big, ornate plate and began to arrange the croissants.

"Don't you touch them yet," she told Michel. "He's greedy, he is."

"I didn't have dinner last night. And now it's noon. You'd be hungry too."

Gisele sighed irritably and laid out napkins, sugar and milk, even a liter of orange juice with fancy little juice glasses.

Michel turned to Ada with an expression of harmless curiosity. "You're staying on the via Cavour? Is that what you said?"

"The corner near the meat market, that small building there. The balcony looks out over that little side street with the dry fountain." Ada liked that fountain with its pensive nymph, brittle leaves whispering around her feet at night as she and Cristian returned from the promenade. "And I really need to get back. I don't even remember if I closed the doors to the balcony. What if someone tried to break in?"

"Nicer than a hostel," he mused, as if approaching a delicate subject.

Gisele ignored him. "So," she said in an efficient German cadence that made everyone sit up straight, "you will have some breakfast now."

Ada's head and stomach were not ready for croissants. And all the talk of apartments reminded her that she was now responsible for someone else's property. She checked the pockets of her jeans for her money and the key.

"Wait," she said. Her front pockets felt flat and empty. She stood up and dug her hands down into the back pockets. She found a crumpled twenty thousand lire bill and nothing more. Sharp unease prickled through her. She checked pocket after pocket all over again.

"My key," she said. "Maybe it fell in the sofa." She hobbled back to her makeshift bed, the bandage impeding her gait, and groped under the cushions. She shook out the blanket, dropped down on her belly and looked underneath. No key. "I can't find my key! The key to the apartment!" She sprawled back against the sofa, the swaddled leg stretched out in front of her, and pounded the floor in frustration. "Ow." The bandaged elbow stung.

Coffee bubbled up in the machine. Gisele clicked off the gas.

Michel sauntered out to the living room and stood watching, arms folded and expression meditative. "Maybe it's at the bar."

"Shit! *Porca puttana*! I can't believe I lost the key."

"Coffee is ready!"

"Eat now or starve," said Michel blandly. "I'll go with you to the bar to check later if you want."

"Michel!" Gisele cried impatiently. Ada heard her filling cups with coffee and milk. She looked up at Michel from the floor. "What if I don't find it?"

He smiled sweetly with something akin to affection. "Then it will be an adventure. It'll be fun. So let's eat."

They discussed the problem over croissants and big cups of strong coffee with milk.

"Ada and I are going to look for the key, then maybe break into her apartment," Michel announced, croissant in hand, as if they were going to buy fruit at the market. Gisele gave him a sharp look. Ada said nothing—it was the first she had heard of such a plan. All she really wanted to do was find the key so she could get in and change her clothes. Then she wanted to sleep until the hangover faded. She probably needed to make the beds and wash the dishes. And in the end, she needed to call Cristian, and she didn't want to tell him she'd lost the key within 24 hours after he'd given it to her.

"I need to get in somehow, key or no key. All my money is in there too."

Michel looked interested again. "We look for the key, then we break in."

Now Gisele seemed distracted. She lit a cigarette and smoked it in tense little puffs. "You be careful."

But Michel seemed positively cheerful. "That smoke stinks," he commented brightly, popping the last of his breakfast into his mouth. He'd also eaten two of Ada's croissants and asked Gisele for extra coffee and milk. Ada had never seen anyone eat so many croissants at one sitting.

"It'll be easy." He licked his fingers one by one, eyes narrowed with pleasure like a satiated cat. "Easy to break in."

"Well," Ada said doubtfully, "it is on the first floor. But I never tried to climb that balcony."

Now Michel's smile was of heartbreaking beauty, bursting with innocence and optimism. "I will climb it, Ada."

"Ach." Gisele heaved a great sigh. She placed her hand on Ada's arm. Cigarette smoke tickled Ada's nose and she could see the pale red freckles on Gisele's face and shoulder. "Be careful," she repeated.

"First I want to finish the coffee," said Michel. He gazed at the empty plate, then cast his eye around the kitchen. "The croissants are all gone, Gisele?" His tone was almost intimate now, and in response Gisele let her gaze linger on him.

"If you come back for dinner," she said, "I'll make lasagna and a fresh fennel salad."

"Ah, I hope I can." His tone was fervent and longing. He turned to Ada. "Maybe we can all three have lasagna tonight, to celebrate a successful break-in."

Gisele stubbed out the cigarette in her empty coffee cup. "Fine." She was not looking at either of them now.

THIRTEEN

Ada was placid as a duckling as she followed Michel back to the Casa
Bianca. He sauntered with the prowling strut she remembered from
the bar. Though his shirt was wrinkled and he'd apparently forgotten
to comb his hair, he might as well have worn a smoking jacket and
tie. Trailing behind, Ada watched him parade past the sidewalk cafes.
She watched the eyes on him. And now, lame as she was, she preened
too, following in his wake with her chin up and mouth proud.

The Casa Bianca was closed. Ada diligently checked the steps
where she had fallen, though Michel hung back, hands stuffed in his
pockets, watching her with languid disinterest.

"Let's just break in," he said. "That key is gone for good."

"Maybe they have a lost and found."

"But they're closed till late tonight. And it doesn't matter, you'll
see." He gave her a radiant smile.

She remembered the flash of those eyes in the dark, the glitter of
light under water, now shrouded. Those eyes belonged on paper.

"All right," she said. "See if you can break in."

They made their way to the via Cavour and stood on the little
cobbled side street by the fountain. Workmen in blue overalls
surrounded it now, busily pulling up the street to expose the
underground water line, its odor of dark moisture beginning to rise.
The apartment was up a half flight of smooth stone steps behind one
of the old, heavy, green-painted wooden double doors that dotted the
whole town of Rocca. The apartment above it had its own entrance
up a longer flight of metal stairs. The Montinelli apartment had a

narrow balcony overlooking the side street off Gianni and Fernanda's room. The sheets were still hanging out on the drying rack and the tall wooden shutters hung loosely in place, closed but not locked. Michel paced back and forth below the balcony, sizing the distance with the confidence of a prowling cat. He turned to Ada with a little flourish and winked, as if they were co-conspirators. Then he reached up and grabbed the wrought iron bars.

"This will be easy." He hoisted himself up with surprising strength and agility for someone so slim and full of croissants, using one arm to grab the top of the railing and one leg folded against the bottom of the balcony for balance. He swung up his other arm, pushed off with his leg and vaulted gracefully over the top.

Ada jumped and waved her arms. "Woo! You did it!"

He pulled open the shutters with a dramatic sweep of his arm. Ada did a little crippled jig—they were in. "Go in and just turn the lock!" she called. "Turn the lock on the front door bolt!"

He gave her an unexpected waggle of the hips and smiled without showing his teeth. "Welcome to my home," he said. "Please go around to the front." He disappeared inside.

Ada rushed to the front and limped up the stone steps to the heavy green doors just as he turned the inside lock and pulled them open. She burst into the kitchen, waved her arms and hooted. She wanted to jump up and down and hug him, but he was still half a stranger, so she hugged the door instead, stroking its beautiful opened lock. She still didn't have a key, but she was in. She had her house back.

"Well, thank you," she said.

With the excitement over, though, there seemed nothing left to say. Ada lingered by the door while Michel drifted toward the far wall and avoided her gaze. An invisible moat widened around him.

"Why don't you and Gisele come over some time, and I'll make you dinner." But all Ada knew how to cook was her mother's green bean casserole with canned mushroom soup, and she regretted the stupid words as soon as they were out of her mouth. Michel's expression grew even more pensive and remote.

"Or I could buy you a drink," she added, with a little more confidence.

"I know a better place for dancing than the Casa Bianca." His face was unreadable. "If you're ready for that again."

And despite the chilly distance he'd set up, despite his tepid tone, it felt like a come-on, or at least something built to look like a come-on. He casually ran his hand across his hair, and she noticed for the first time a thin gold coin hanging from his ear. She registered the tantalizing charcoal beauty of his unadorned eyes. She thought about how he'd leaped over the balcony and opened her door, and she wanted to walk down the street with him again. She wanted to watch him move. And what harm could there be in friendly companionship? In going out for a few hours of music and dancing? Cristian would want her to enjoy herself. He knew she was here alone.

So Ada narrowed her eyes till they sparkled and lowered her voice an octave. "I'm always ready to dance."

But Michel scarcely seemed to react. He did not return her smile. And now she felt as coarse and loud as her beer-swilling uncles, like trailer trash at the opera. Had she misunderstood? As the uncomfortable silence deepened, he wrapped his arms around himself, fists tight, and avoided her gaze.

"Anyway, thank you," Ada continued, mostly to fill the silence.

He took a breath. "Gisele said she is making lasagna and fennel salad tonight."

"That sounds good." Was he inviting her?

"You could tell her how we broke in."

"I could!" Ada responded enthusiastically. "And maybe I can bring something to thank her. For last night, you know."

"You could bring her some candles. She likes candles."

Ada had been thinking more of a paper plate of *pasticcini*, the fancy little petit-fours that Italians customarily brought when they were invited to dinner. She could make a good impression with miniature cream puffs and tiny chocolate-glazed cakes studded with almonds and fresh fruit.

"She likes purple candles," Michel added.

"Purple candles."

"And she usually makes dinner at eight."

They eyed each other.

"All right, then. At eight."

Michel sauntered off like a hired locksmith done with his service call. Ada leaned against the door he'd opened and watched him disappear down the street. She'd seen trained dancers walk like that.

She craned her neck for a last glimpse, then he was gone.

Yet the scent of the unknown future lingered, so dense and fragrant that it was almost liquid on her tongue. It slipped through the cracks of her will, infused with dangerous promise. And floating in its wake were the first misty edges of the stranger in herself, the creature yet unborn. Ada felt a startling desire to draw herself nude, with a snarl on her face and a spear in her hand. Crashing into deep water.

FOURTEEN

Ada wandered the apartment naked, toothbrush dangling in her hand, and did not call Cristian. She needed aspirin and a shower, but first she had to remove the bandages, check the bruises, delicately examine the scabby scrapes and discolored skin and scrutinize them in the mirror at various distances and angles. She practiced dancing, doing can-can kicks and swinging her arms above her head flamenco-style, then twirled like a dervish, watching her white hips wiggle between their tan lines. She imagined dancing naked with a dark stranger.

Finally she showered. It melted her into a dreamy languor, and it was some time before she remembered to wash her hair. Then she stood half-entranced under the spray until all the hot water was gone. She emerged into a steamy bathroom and sat on the toilet seat, eyes closed, for at least twenty minutes, swathed in towels and feeling too dim and drowsy to move.

She'd have to make the twin beds if she wanted to sleep in one of them. With that in mind, Ada let the wet towels drop to the floor and wandered into the bedroom, feeling clean and sun-kissed. She in fact felt beautiful enough to venture nude onto the balcony to fetch the sheets from the drying rack. But once she'd tossed the linens onto the mattresses, the process of making the beds seemed more challenging than anticipated. And now it occurred to her that Gianni and Fernanda's bed was big and inviting and ready for an occupant. Ada stood in the doorway and contemplated it. No one would ever know if she had a nap in their room. She cracked open the shutters on the balcony to let in a sliver of light and the tranquil voices of the workmen repairing the fountain outside, then carefully slipped under the coverlet, lay her wet head on a crisp white pillow, and slept till late afternoon.

She woke hungry and disoriented in the unfamiliar bed. Stretching out diagonally, she wiggled her toes under the coverlet. The extra space felt good after being squeezed into a twin bed for so long. She kicked her legs and flailed her arms, taking up as much room as possible. She threw off the coverlet, stuck her legs straight up in the air, and grabbed her toes. The injured leg looked bad but no longer hurt much. She wondered if she should paint her toenails like Gisele's. How she would look walking beside Michel with painted toenails.

In the kitchen, she rummaged for something easy to eat. The potato chips, smaller and oilier than their American counterparts, were still a comforting reminder of dinners back in Buffalo, so she ripped open the package and stuffed herself, washing it all down with a bottle of water. As she pulled the last few chips from the greasy bag, Ada realized that although now she could lock the apartment from the inside, she could no longer lock it from the outside. How would she explain that to Cristian? Probably now was not the time to tell him. He had other things to worry about. Anyway, perhaps she would go back to the Casa Bianca and they would have the key. A lot of things could happen—there was no need to let him know just yet.

Ada wandered into the room she had shared with Cristian and again considered making the beds. But she was still hungry. She should go out and buy herself a tiny snack, a chocolate bar and an *aranciata* to drink, then she would feel stronger and more ambitious. She would be able to get organized and make the telephone call.

When she looked at herself in the long floor mirror, Ada saw that her hair had dried at crazy angles, flat on one side and sticking out in all directions on the other.

"Shit." She had been feeling beautiful, ready for a snack, ready for a surprise visitor. Now she would have to soak her head to straighten this mess.

As she ran the flat half of her hair under the kitchen faucet, Ada imagined the salty Mediterranean and the slick feel of skin under water. She decided that she needed to maintain her fine summer tan. Tomorrow she could go to the beach and take her top off. Maybe she could go with Michel. If he went to beaches. She thought about Gisele's pale freckled skin—she wouldn't spend much time in the sun. But Michel was coppery dark. He probably didn't even need to lie on the beach. Still, perhaps he would want to if Ada suggested it. They could spend a friendly afternoon together and eat artichoke pizza. A perfectly harmless idea.

When she straightened, Ada flipped water all over the tile floor, soaking the crumbs of the focaccia that she'd scattered the previous morning. Using a damp bathroom towel she'd left on the floor, she rubbed her head till it stopped dripping. But water had already dribbled onto the tiles, creating little puddles, and when Ada splashed through them, she left a trail of footprints in her wake.

She went out to get her snack and forgot Cristian's telephone number on the kitchen table. By the time she remembered it, she was waiting in line with her chocolate bar and orange drink. She should probably call soon, but perhaps not now, when she was hungry and distracted. So she bought extra snacks, strolled back to the apartment, and sat on the stone steps out front to eat. Cristian never snacked between meals and no one in the family sat on the steps, but Ada thought it was pleasant to feel the warm stone against her butt and the slanting sun in her eyes. She leaned against the unlocked door, chewed her chocolate, swished down the *aranciata*, and lounged.

Later, she slipped on a tight little emerald green top that showed off her hair. Perfect for dinner at Gisele's. Then she preened and primped before the mirror, proud that no one would ever guess her father was a janitor, her mother a part-time cleaning lady. Janitors and cleaning women had daughters like Emily. They drank cans of beer in front of the television and ate green jello salads with marshmallows. Tonight, those people would scarcely recognize their offspring in her rhinestone sunglasses and studded jeans. With her new international acquaintances. They would not understand the language she spoke. They would not comprehend how the very idea of capturing these unfamiliar faces on paper was as erotic, hair-raising, voluptuous as any intimate touch of skin against skin.

Ada stared at her foreign face in the mirror with hopeful disbelief.

She dawdled too long with her reflection, and by the time she rushed out the door she was already late. Only as she rounded the corner to Gisele's apartment on the via Garibaldi did Ada remember she was supposed to call Cristian and had once again forgotten the number. It was too late to go back now. After dinner, she thought, she would go right home and get it. Maybe she would call after dinner.

Gisele lived in a newer, larger building than the little salmon-colored house on the via Cavour, with big glass doors and a lobby with a doorkeeper's desk, but no one was on duty. The only way in was to buzz the right apartment from the cluster of names displayed next to the doors. Gisele had said she was German, so Ada found a Hartmann on the third floor and gave the button two sharp taps, as if she were sure of herself. And without any response on the intercom, she was buzzed in. She peered upward as she climbed the steps, half-expecting to see them staring down at her from the landing, but there was only silence. She had to explore the doors, each one heavy and double-bolted, till she saw a little gold plate with the name Hartmann on it, etched in elaborate script. No one was waiting to greet her, so she rose on tiptoe to look into the peephole and tried to rap with confidence. There was a long silence.

Just as she was thinking she'd come to the wrong apartment, the door flew open and Gisele towered over her, mouth half-open as if she were about to speak. She looked past Ada into the empty hallway, then back at Ada.

"Ciao, Gisele." Ada tried to sound bright and assured. "Sorry, I guess I'm a little late."

"Oh, that is only relative." The words came out like nails. "Well, come in."

Inside, a soft bloom of incense and sound enveloped Ada. The orange sofa gleamed under an Indian spread in hues of violet, sepia and green. A little coffee table that Ada did not recall from the night before was sitting before it, covered with a lace cloth. Purple candles flickered on every surface, even the windowsills. It reminded her that she had forgotten to bring a dinner gift. Fine shards of a broken mirror in the form of a starburst, or a comet, had been glued to a pale apricot wall, illuminated by an orange Chinese paper lantern hanging from the ceiling. The scratchy phonograph played some old boudoir song by Leonard Cohen.

From the kitchen came the heady aroma of good food. And Gisele herself smelled like something tasty, as if she too had come fresh from the oven. She wore a big green cotton apron that was longer than her short skirt. Her pale forehead looked flushed, but her lips were red and shiny.

"It'll be ready in just a few minutes. Let me see that elbow." Ada held her arm up like an obedient child, and Gisele inspected the scrape with efficient, if not exactly gentle fingers. "Remember to keep it clean. How is the knee?"

"Much better. A little stiff, that's all. It's going to be fine."

"Mmmph. Are you ready for wine or would you prefer water tonight?"

"Wine would be good, thank you."

"So come, make yourself comfortable. I'm just chopping the fennel." She headed to the kitchen and Ada followed. It was clear that Michel had not yet arrived.

The little table was covered with another Indian cloth, adorned by another purple candle, plus a bottle of red wine and three glasses. Gisele had set out thick, toast-colored cloth napkins and pale ivory plates, as well as a platter of salami and other cured meats. The table was surrounded by three chairs—sky blue, yellow and green. A brick red one stood in the corner, with Gisele's green mirror cloth bag hanging from the back. Big bulbs of white and green fennel lay in luxurious abandon on the cutting board.

"So—you are back in your apartment?"

"I am! Michel climbed the balcony and let me in." Ada peered around the kitchen. "I thought he was coming tonight."

"Ha!" Gisele poured wine for Ada, but none for herself. "Well, we shall see, yes? He may have forgotten completely. Or he may be sitting in a bar somewhere. He may even have gone back up the hill."

"Up the hill? Where the big villas are?"

What locals called "the hill" lay at the summit of a narrow, twisting road that rose from the seafront to a clutch of pastel-colored architectural gems perched above the town. The villas had splendid terra-cotta roofs, opulent Etruscan tiled patios, and swathes of security fences and protective hedges. With their giant windows overlooking the sea, they were the summer homes and estates of Prada-toting ladies and tanned, handsome men who sailed yachts. Was Michel someone's slinky driver, some signora's Egyptian-eyed doorman, some debutante's special interest?

Gisele barely looked at Ada, though she sniffed and curled her lip. "Yes, up the hill. That's what I said."

"But what does he do there?"

"Do? He lives there, that's what he does, when he's not down here slumming with the rest of us." Gisele chopped the fennel with fierce little jabs and loaded it into a cobalt blue bowl.

"He lives there? By himself?"

Gisele laughed deep in her throat, as if truly amused. "Oh no, he has a family, all right. They're even crazier than he is."

Ada took a swig of wine and mulled this information. "I've never been up there. I've never seen those houses up close."

"Well, don't expect an invitation." Gisele wiped her hands on her apron and brought the bowl of chopped fennel to the table. "I'm not waiting for him. If he comes, there's plenty of food." Her eyes were a hard blue veil, but her mouth was melancholy under the lipstick. Still, before she went to the oven to bring out the lasagna, she gave Ada a friendly look. Ada took another nervous gulp of wine. Somehow her glass was already half empty.

"So," Gisele said briskly as she served them, "now we eat to celebrate your unlocked apartment." Ada held up her glass of wine and Gisele raised the entire bottle in a toast.

"To unlocked apartments. To being rescued."

"*Cin cin.*"

They had barely finished their first helping when the door buzzed. Gisele jumped up like a rabbit.

"Finally." When she returned to the kitchen after buzzing him in, she whipped off the green apron to reveal long white legs. But she sat with cool nonchalance, poured herself a glass of wine, and resumed eating as if she expected no one at all. Seconds ticked by and a certain breathlessness afflicted Ada. She expected the door to open at any moment, but there was no sound. She tried to catch Gisele's eye, but Gisele was bent over her plate shoveling food into her mouth. Her red hair seemed to stand on end, electrified.

Then she heard a soft rap and the sound of the door opening. "Hello, Gisele?"

But it was a girl's voice.

Now Gisele jolted away from her food, shoved her chair back and threw her hands up as if in surrender. "Good God," she murmured, then leaned forward on one elbow and gave a great sigh. "In the kitchen, Marion," she called.

And there at the doorway was the slovenly teenage girl who had been searching for Michel that day. The girl's gaze fixed on Ada, and though the expression did not change, Ada knew she had been recognized.

"I'm sorry to disturb your dinner."

Gisele slouched back in her chair and folded her arms. "What is it, Marion? Michel's not here. I don't know where he is."

Marion scratched her elbow, then her neck. She was dressed in the same ill-fitting clothes, with the same dark, uncombed hair pushed behind her ears. Her beautiful black eyes were marred by bushy, untrimmed brows, her cheeks by patches of acne.

"Well," she said after a moment, her voice doubtful. "Our mother is looking for him. You'll see him, won't you?"

"I don't know, Marion, I have no idea."

"What are you eating?"

Gisele sighed. "Oh, come and sit down if you're hungry."

"I don't want to disturb you."

"So sit. Have a piece of lasagna."

"Lasagna, that looks good." She sidled into the kitchen, then settled into the third chair with a firm plop. Gisele filled a plate for her and brought out one of the green bottles of sparkling water. Marion snuffled, wiped her nose with the back of her hand, and gently sniffed at the food. "Good," she said.

Ada tried to look friendly when Gisele made introductions, but Marion gave Ada a sidelong, non-committal look and did not return her smile. She turned back to Gisele instead. "I can't stay long," she said, mouth full. "Our mother's sick today. She is having a bad week. She was sure I would find Michel here."

"Well, he's not here. You need to tell her that most of the time I don't know where he is. I'm not the person to ask."

Marion jerked a thumb at Ada without actually looking at her. "Is she a friend of his?"

"She's a friend of mine." Gisele didn't skip a beat. "Don't be so nosy."

"I just need to find him. He's got a family to think about, all right? I can't go home till I find him."

"Marion," Gisele said, more gently now. "You can't be expected to walk all over town looking for him. Maybe he doesn't want to go home. Can't your mother understand that?"

Marion swallowed hard, her eyes glistened, but her jaw grew tight and pouty. "What do you know? Anyway, it doesn't matter what he

wants, what matters is what he's supposed to do. What he has to do."
She grabbed the bottle of water and sloshed it into the wine glass.
"You set the table for three people."

Ada imagined a rich, querulous old battleaxe, a nasty snob like
Professoressa Garavoglia who made unreasonable demands on her
children and probably even punished them by withholding money.
With the resentment of the penny-pinching laborer, the scholarship
student who'd arrived in Italy with only one pair of shoes, Ada
concluded that wealth was wasted on affluent parents and an
affliction to their neurotic, undeserving offspring. Still, she didn't like
Marion any better than she had that day the girl sat in Michel's chair
and drank his Sanbitter.

"You set it for three," Marion repeated after draining her glass. "Is
he here? Is he hiding somewhere?"

"That's enough. He is not here. Why don't you just relax and
enjoy the food?"

Marion pushed back her chair and stood, wiping her mouth. "I
did. I'm fine. I have to go. You tell him if you see him." She headed
toward the door and Gisele rose with a sigh, all gangly arms and legs,
and accompanied her out. Marion did not deign to look at Ada as she
left, though Ada could feel the force of her brooding presence, the
exquisite awareness, the suspicion. She was glad when she heard
Marion shut the door and thump back down the stairs.

Gisele returned to the table. "Well, that could have been worse.
The last time she sat here for an hour. She thinks I hide him. Or
that's what his mother thinks, anyway." She poured herself a full glass
of wine, took a long swig, and let out her breath like a deflating
balloon. "He'll never show up now. She'll have to go home without
him. And I need a cigarette."

The conversation faded, straining to survive. When Gisele left the
table to chop fresh fruit for dessert, Ada wandered into the living
room, empty glass in hand. The phonograph was quiet now, and even
the candles seemed small and chastened. She sat on the orange sofa
and idly admired a big, expensive camera on the shelf beneath the
coffee table. A fat photo album accompanied it, swirls of black
sequins glued to its cover. Ada touched them delicately, then slipped
her hand under the cover for a discreet look. It was a full page close-
up of Michel, glaring at the camera like a fashion model. The next
page contained two black and white profiles of him, indoor shots.

Then outdoor shots, artistic poses with mirrors and odd settings. Page after page. He stared at the camera in some of them, seemed oblivious in others. Sometimes he wore fancy clothes and eyeliner, other times he was disheveled, as if he'd been buffeted by the wind or just escaped a fistfight. His body was displayed with a certain passive abandon, as if he enjoyed the camera's lascivious eye, but his expression was always inscrutable. Feeling breathless, Ada replaced the album before Gisele returned.

By the time she escaped to the fresh air of the street, Ada's mind felt clearer. The evening had been a mistake. Now, though it was late, she wanted to get the telephone number and call Cristian. She wanted to hear his voice. She would tell him about her drunken adventure yesterday and the strange people she'd met. He might even remember who they were. And when he heard her voice, maybe he would miss her enough to invite her to Torino.

Even if she had lost the key.

THE TASTE OF WATER

Sylvia Gilbertson

FIFTEEN

Ada pushed open the big unlocked wooden door and lurched back in alarm to find the lights on and Michel reading a book at the Montinelli kitchen table.

"You!" she cried. "*Che fai qui?* What are you doing here?"

He answered in impeccable English. "The door was unlocked." He gently shut the book.

She kicked off a sandal and it skidded toward him. "You knew I was at Gisele's!" She kicked off the other sandal to smack against the wall next to his chair.

"I did know." He looked a little wary. "That's why I had to let myself in."

"And I met your sister."

"Ah." He seemed polite and thoughtful.

"You're supposed to go home. She said your mother's sick."

All expression washed from his face. "I see."

Ada kicked the door shut hard enough to make it rattle on its hinges. Michel jumped and gave her a hopeful look. Her head felt big and tight, her stomach like a washing machine. She wanted to grab him by that nice hair and give him a shaking. He leaned back in the chair and tossed his head in a wanton gesture. As if daring her to touch him.

"Well, I don't know anything about your family problems. I'm just telling you what I heard. You missed a good dinner and you were supposed to be there, not breaking into my apartment."

"I don't think I told you I would be there. And anyway, it seemed better for me to be here than to have gypsies rob you."

"Gypsies? What gypsies?"

He waved his hand vaguely. "Oh, you know how they are, appearing out of nowhere at the strangest times. They'll pick your pockets. You won't even know till it's too late."

"I can't believe I'm having this conversation."

He placed his book on the table, ran both hands through his fine hair, and displayed his smooth neck again, as if striking a pose. The long line of his throat and the curve of his jaw stopped her. He would be beautiful on paper. She could almost feel his body writhing out of her pencil.

He lowered his head and gave her a cagey look. "I thought you might want to go dancing."

They surveyed each other across the room. Michel squirmed in the chair and ran languid fingers down his thigh, his expression remote as a painted god's. And the dawning idea of grappling with the challenge of that canvas, of piercing it and trapping the thing behind it, filled Ada with the reckless courage of a warrior, or perhaps a courtesan to fickle royalty.

"I love to dance." She was careful not to sound flirty this time.

"So, fantastic, yes?" It seemed that he, in turn, was taking care to look friendly and harmless. "I hoped you would want to go."

So, carefully, the deal was sealed.

They took a taxi. Ada had never traveled by cab before, and she sat stiff and alert in the back seat. As she watched the dark streets roll by and turn rural, she imagined being a movie star in dark glasses, traveling to a secret party in the hills. Michel sat far away on the other side, gazing out his window in apparent calm. She could sometimes see his profile in a streetlight or glimpse the flash of an eye under black lashes. No makeup tonight.

They came to a little coastal town perhaps a half hour from Rocca and drove up a dark, narrow cobblestone street flanked by creaking old buildings. When the taxi stopped, Michel hesitated before pulling out money for the fare. Ada sat firm and demure, determined not to pay one lira for this ride.

It was a private club with an unmarked door. "I have a guest," Michel said to a man in a silver suit, and they were admitted to a smallish room spackled with slow, shifting lights. Old-fashioned crystal chandeliers, vestiges of a courtly past, still glittered from the high ceilings. Their dim mellow glow illuminated a swirling mass of people. Someone in a scarlet ball gown floated past like a ghost. A long-haired woman in a suit and tie waltzed past the tapestried walls with a long-haired man in a suit and tie. Music breathed in from some unseen place, as if traveling direct from a spellbound Alexandria, from red-walled cities in the desert, the spice markets of Istanbul. Perhaps from the very earth below Florence, before the city itself came to be. In a burst of ancient memory, Ada felt her child's hands on that fat book in the library. She saw the blossoming eruptions of color and flesh. And she wondered how Michel had known to bring her to this place.

"This is beautiful." It didn't matter if he heard the quaver in her voice.

"It is."

She envisioned a huge canvas of these people, intertwined fabric and jewels and limbs. She saw them strung together like pearls on a strand of music, and then Michel and herself being threaded skin to skin on that erotic necklace, limp as dolls in the ravishing presence of beauty.

"I want to get in there and dance."

Their eyes met and he dropped the shield. It was like the explosion of a camera flash, the white light of a bomb. She threw out her arms, and Michel broke into a huge child's smile, as if he'd received a wonderful gift.

"So let's dance," he said.

They moved through the swaying crowd till they were surrounded, and then they let themselves be swept into the current of moving bodies that spread like bright watercolors across the floor. They joined the living palette, centuries upon centuries crowded together in such fleshly proximity that the body itself was transcended. And the true Dionysus, the god distilled to his essence of ecstatic death and rebirth, slipped in to join them, great and implacable in his dark demands.

"Thank you." Ada mouthed the words silently. A small smile curved Michel's lips before he shut his eyes and danced on alone.

They stayed till very late, though they hardly spoke and never really danced together. They passed each other among the pulsing throng, and once lightly clasped hands, but they were planets moving in separate orbits. Other people touched them and danced around them, some close enough for Ada to smell a bosom heavy with perfume or glimpse a tiny diamond tie clasp glittering against silk. Once she saw Michel sandwiched between a slim, dark-haired young woman with a high forehead and big earrings and a tall, handsome man in a lime green suit. Michel had raised his arms in abandon, eyes closed. Ada was jealous, but then she was swept up into another whirl of nameless dancers and forgot about him. She even forgot to drink.

They returned to Rocca shortly before dawn. As they approached the town, Ada could see the dark expanse of the Mediterranean, then a curve of shadowy land stretching north and west towards France and Monte Carlo glimmering in the distance. A faint sheen of future light rose from behind the hills on the inland side. Michel squeezed over on his side of the cab, gazing out the window. He looked a little rumpled, but he breathed evenly, one hand lying motionless at his side. Ada lifted her hair off her neck and leaned against her own window to feel the cool glass on her skin. She couldn't keep her eyes off Michel, but being sober made her shy.

"I'd like to paint that place," she finally said.

He turned to look at her as if distracted.

"The people in the club. They had Renaissance faces. Did you know that I'm an artist?"

He caught his breath. "No," he said after a moment. "I don't know anything about you."

"Well, if you would like to have an early morning Sanbitter, there are six bottles of them at my apartment."

"Hmm." He was now polite but distant. "A little refreshment would be nice."

"You can see my portfolio. And my self-portraits. Ada as the Medusa. Do you want to see that?"

He thawed a little, shifting to squeeze less tightly against the window. "I'd like to see a Medusa."

This time Michel produced money for the cab with even greater reluctance. Ada hopped from the back seat and ignored the transaction. He was the one with the villa on the hill who went to members-only clubs in the country. He could pay. But she was surprised at the peevish glare he shot her as he ducked from the taxi, and how he pushed past her to bound up the steps to the Montinelli apartment and throw open the door as if he lived there. Ada entered to find him pacing the kitchen with a tense, coiled gait. As she closed the door, Michel leaned against the wall to face her, his arms folded and expression belligerent.

"You want that Sanbitter?" she asked.

He set his jaw and shrugged.

She tried again. "You want some wine?"

"I don't drink alcohol."

Was he pouting about the cab fare? "So what can I get you, Michel?"

His face grew tight and stubborn. Then he blinked and took a long breath, and his expression changed. "You should have some wine," he said. "I'll have a Sanbitter, and could I have a glass of water too, please?" He ran his hands absently down his hips and up to caress his own belly, then caught himself like an embarrassed cat. "Please, you have some wine."

His book was still on the kitchen table. Ada picked it up and saw that it was a Gothic romance, in French. A silly sentimental women's novel.

"You're reading this?"

His face brightened. "Yes, I love trashy romances."

"You're like my sister." Ada had never met a man who read dumb romances.

He snatched the book from her. "I know, I shouldn't read it. I don't like it that much anyway. I should probably just throw it away."

She laughed and turned it into a joke as she fished white wine and crimson Sanbitter from the refrigerator. "No, give it to me and I'll send it to my sister. Except she doesn't read French. She barely reads English." But Michel gently placed the book on the floor by his foot when he pulled up a chair to sit.

He relaxed when Ada served him the bitter little aperitif and poured herself a big glass of wine. She tore open another bag of greasy potato chips, which seemed to please him no end, and they sat opposite each other to munch and drink. Gray dawn was leaking in from behind the window. Ada was tired and didn't want the wine, but drank two quick glasses anyway. Michel watched her drink without comment. Nursing the Sanbitter as if every drop were laden with rich syrup, he occasionally dipped his finger in and licked it off slowly. He looked at her once with a blank expression she could not decipher. It was like sitting across from the Sphinx. She poured herself a third glass of wine.

"Last glass," she said. "Or I'll be drunk."

He leaned forward then and tapped her hand with light, cool fingers. Scarcely breathing, Ada reached up her thumb to graze his skin.

"You forgot my water." He moved his hand away.

Ada pushed herself up and kicked the chair away. She shoved the water it in front of him. "Here," she said. "The sun's coming up and you know what, I'm tired."

"You never showed me Medusa." He didn't touch the water.

Still standing, Ada took another slug of wine. She couldn't tell if she was getting drunk or was giddy with fatigue. "Medusa," she said. "You sure you want to risk it? You know what'll happen."

A vague frisky look came into his eyes. "I don't mind a risk."

"It could turn you to stone."

"Solid rock."

She was sure she had him then. "Well come on, let's go find it. It's the Caravaggio, you know what I'm talking about? The Medusa on the green shield." Michel sat inexplicably glued to the chair, but alcohol ran in Ada's veins now, and she was feeling smarter and sexier by the minute. "Up," she said, and was only mildly surprised when he obeyed.

She led him into the room she shared with Cristian, the little beds still stripped and her underwear tossed on the floor. "Welcome to Medusa's lair. There's a little preview on the wall. What do you think?" She didn't bother to look at him—she knew how people reacted to her Renaissance self-portraits. "I think the portfolio is under the bed. Hold my glass, will you?"

Michel waited with her wine glass in hand while she fetched the portfolio, the same one she'd presented to Lidia Garavoglia, plus some minor pieces and unfinished work. She flopped cross-legged onto the bare mattress and spread it out before her. Michel just stood in the middle of the room, looking like he'd been slapped. What was wrong with him?

"Come and have a look," she teased. "Are you scared?"

"I am not scared of anything." He knelt on the floor beside her as she pulled out Caravaggio's Medusa, whose wild and wormy hair now framed her own howling face. He carefully took it from her and studied it.

"Did it turn you to stone?" She ran a light hand down his forearm and leaned closer.

"I guess not." He held the corner of the drawing with two slim fingers and let it drop to the floor like a piece of waste paper.

The gesture rattled her. Her hand fumbled at the portfolio and she spoke too fast. "And here I am as Flora, and Venus too, and one of the de Medicis. You know this painting? It's in the Uffizi. And this is Berruguete's Salome with braids." A nervous giggle burbled from her throat.

He leafed through the drawings, silent.

"And here I am as the Madonna. No child."

No comment.

"Well, there they are." Ada's voice trailed off. It suddenly looked like a pitiful pile, and she riffled through the portfolio for something else, the thing that might make him speak.

"Let me see that." He pulled out an old sketch of St. Casimir's in Buffalo that she'd once done in a fit of pique at her heritage. Flames shot from the dome of the cathedral, curling into the suggestion of two eyes and a mouth. The mouth was hers, but she'd never got the eyes right. She'd never even finished it. It was childhood trivia, long ago left behind so she could focus on mastering technique. Botticelli and Raphael had taught her how to get the eyes right, and now who cared about childhood angst in Buffalo.

Michel held it in both hands, lashes dark against his grave face. "Istanbul on fire," he said. "And part of your face."

"It's old," she explained. She couldn't stop the apologetic tone. "It's the big Polish church in Buffalo. My mother's church. It doesn't have frescoes or anything. It's just Buffalo."

"A long time ago we had a fresco in our apartment."

"What do you mean, you had a fresco in your apartment?"

"A fresco. Of Greece. My mother paid someone to do it. Later we moved and it had to stay behind. But it didn't matter, she was sick of it by then."

Ada thought of the velvet painting of the flamenco dancer in her mother's living room. The print of the poker-playing dogs in the dingy front hallway. She could not imagine growing sick of a fresco in her house.

Michel tilted the glass of wine at her, lips melting into a small, perhaps rueful smile. "I don't drink, but I will have a little sip anyway for you."

"To frescoes," Ada said, and Michel took a delicate drink of her wine.

She reached for her glass so that their fingers touched, and he did not let go when she pulled it over to her. "No makeup tonight," she said, moving her face closer. His eyes might have widened, but perhaps she imagined it. Then his expression went blank. She came close enough now to feel his breath, to break into his energy field. He didn't back off, and now she could even see a bit of dark stubble on his face. Less than she would have expected, and softer skin than Cristian's too. "I noticed you that day. And now here you are."

Now he did look her in the eye, though his expression remained opaque. "Yes," he murmured, "here I am." He slowly let go of the glass, and his fingers slid across hers and down her wrist. She could see the flecks of gold in his eyes, could have brushed her lips across his nose if she'd moved any closer.

He breathed a tiny sigh. "The sun is coming up. I guess it's time to go."

She thought he was teasing. "I guess *not*."

But now she felt him preparing to coil away from her, like a wary cat slowly backing off into the shadows, eyes fixed on hers.

"My mother has been ill, and she will be worried." His tongue rolled over the words as if eating fat pralines. Like an afterthought, he took his fingers off her wrist and pulled his hand away. He was a tide gliding out to sea, back into darkness. As if he sensed her incredulity, he added, "And I have appointments later today. Probably I should get some sleep." He was still inches from her, but his body was taut now, poised to flee.

"Appointments?" Ada snatched away the wine, sloshing some of it onto the mattress. "Are you serious?"

"I have important responsibilities." Except for his hand, he hadn't moved away, not physically. But he had a weird breathless look, and stared at her as if transfixed.

"What are you talking about?"

He didn't answer, but she could see his chest move up and down, and the lump in his throat as he swallowed. He laid one hand on the bed as if to pull himself up, but the rest of him didn't move.

Ada slugged the wine down, tossed the empty glass on the mattress, and stared right into his veiled eyes. "If you were a woman, there'd be a name for you."

"What would it be?" The words came out in a whisper.

"A prick tease. Ever heard that expression, mister big shot fluent English speaker? A prick tease."

He held her gaze and flinched only a little.

"I want you to stay. Tell me you don't want to."

"It doesn't matter."

Though his voice was toneless, Ada heard something else echo from him. It curled out, licking up and down her body, wrapping around her thighs and belly, probing her. She could smell the desire on him, almost taste it like a mouthful of sizzling water. Even as he started to back away. Even as the shields began to lock into place.

Engulfed by a white hot instant of rage, she grabbed him by the hair and pulled hard. He gasped but did not protest, and in fact went almost completely limp. She shoved her other hand against his chest and felt his heart thrumming under his shirt.

"You don't want to go anywhere," she said. "Do you." She swung her feet onto the floor on either side of him and yanked his hair again. Now he gave a little squeak and his shoulders slumped. "You're jerking me around. I'm not going to let you jerk me around. And I don't know how to say that in Italian, but I think you understand me just fine."

"Ada," he stammered, his voice barely inching out, "would you give me one of your drawings? Not the Medusa."

"*What?*" Surprise made her let him go. He fell back on his butt with a thump, then huddled with his knees folded in front of him. He ran his hands across his face and into his hair. Then he sighed and lowered his head onto crossed arms.

"Please, could I have the cathedral?" he murmured into the floor. "And all right, I'll stay."

The drawings still lay on the floor beside him.

"Yes," she said. "You can have any drawing you like, Michel."

He shook his head. "Only the burning church."

Ada laid her hand on his head and felt soft hair under her fingers. His breathing seemed labored. "Okay, that's fine, you can have it. And I'll give you the Medusa too."

He drew his head up and looked around. "Where do you want me to stay? There are no sheets on these beds."

"There's a bed with sheets in the other room."

"The floor is fine. I sleep on the floor at Gisele's but I need a pillow." He fetched the drawings from the floor and busied himself with carefully rolling them into a little tube. "I need a rubber band for this, so it can be transported without damage."

"Let's do that later, all right?" She bounced off the bed and pointed to the door. "That way, come on." She had the disconcerting sensation of being a babysitter trying to convince an unwilling child to sleep. And when she took him by the arm and led him to the room with the big bed, he was as uncommunicative and morose as a boy with a bad attitude. Ada knew he'd been in Gianni and Fernanda's room before—it was where he'd broken in—yet he stood in the doorway as if blocked at an invisible checkpoint, watching her arrange the rumpled linens of the unmade bed. She switched out the light and closed the shutters to block out the rising sun, but still he lingered at the doorway. She had to go over and nudge him so she could close the door, leaving them in perfect blackout darkness.

"Come on," she whispered, reaching up to feel for his face in the dark. She touched an ear, the curve of his jaw, and a little excited vein beating near his throat. She could hear him fumbling with her drawings, rolling and unrolling them in his hands, so she ran her fingers down his arm till she touched them and gently pulled them away. "We'll wrap them later." She spoke more firmly this time, and set them on the floor by the door.

He smelled of musk and clean soap, even after a night of dancing. And his invisible presence felt taller, less ambiguous, less hesitant than the physical person actually there beside her. Just a trick of the dark, perhaps. But he followed her without protest—perhaps by then he was too exhausted to do anything else.

Ada stripped without hesitation and slipped under the coverlet, though even in her sleep-deprived, slightly winey state she understood that the outcome of this encounter rested on fragile ground indeed. Michel fumbled on his side for what seemed forever, then finally got in bed.

"Time to sleep," he said brightly from the very edge of the mattress.

Ada rolled toward him till her hand touched his chest, still covered by a shirt. Now it seemed he had stopped breathing altogether. "Okay, Michel," she sighed. "Time to sleep. At least take your clothes off and get comfortable." She heard him sit up and slip off his T-shirt, then there was the sound of the zipper on his jeans and his clothes falling to the floor with a soft plop. He slid down again, as far away from her as he could get. Ada pondered his invisible back for a few moments, and the wine made her reach out and touch him once more. He was thinner than Cristian but better muscled. She wished she could see his dusky skin, but the room was too dark. Outside, traffic intensified as the day dawned. She thought that they were probably both tired.

"Sleep well," she whispered in his ear, and kissed the back of his neck.

"Thank you," he said in a small voice, but he did not turn or reciprocate. So she just pressed her naked body against his back and wrapped an arm around him. He let her stay like that and they both fell asleep.

Hours later she woke disoriented. The room was still black, but the noisy midday hum outside left her confused. She reached out, half-expecting Michel to be gone, but he was still there, sprawled on his back now and breathing softly. She crept off the bed and gently opened the shutters a crack so that a few shafts of light filtered in. As she climbed back in, his eyes flew open and he shot up on his elbows.

"Sssh," she whispered. "I just opened the shutters a little."

"I can't stay, I can't. I'm sorry." He flopped back down, making a small sound in his throat. Ada placed her hand on his collarbone and he flinched.

"Sssh," she said again, and snuggled up next to him, though he felt like a mass of nerves.

"Oh." He spoke aloud now, with a great intake of breath. "Ada." And to her surprise he curled up close, releasing his breath in a long shudder and burying his face in her neck. She put her arms around him, but it was confusing, like cradling a child who was becoming inappropriately sexual.

"Were you dreaming?" she asked.

"I forgot where I was."

"You're here in the apartment on via Cavour." She reached up to touch his hair again. "You have beautiful hair, Michel."

He jerked and started to pull away, but Ada gripped his shoulder hard. He stopped struggling.

"What are you going to do?"

"What do you mean, what am I going to do?"

"With me." He'd pulled his face away and was looking at her yet beyond her. "With a tease like me."

"Call your bluff, maybe?"

"Are you going to make me do something?"

"You want me to make you do something?"

He said nothing. His face was inscrutable.

"You know what, Michel? I think I want to draw you. Maybe I'll just keep you here so I can draw you while you're sleeping."

There was a long silence. She'd thought he would be flattered.

"Of course," he finally said. "You are going to hold me hostage to art."

"But before that, I'm going to pin you down and kiss you. What do you think of that?"

His body grew limp but he looked her in the eye. "It doesn't matter what I think. I can't stop you."

So she kissed him on the face, neck, arms and chest. "How about that?" she said. He sank back on the pillow in passive abandon, eyes closed and brow slightly knitted. Ada nipped him on the neck and waited for a response. He swallowed and did not open his eyes. She touched the black lashes on his cheeks, ran her hands down his smooth body, and he squeezed his eyes shut tighter. But he expelled a shaky little breath. He was beautiful and warm under her fingers. And because he did not say no, it didn't matter that he had not said yes. She didn't need to care what he wanted, if he was willing to be consumed.

And he was, so she did.

"You just remember," she whispered in his ear afterwards, "I'm not going to be hunting you down in bars after this. You understand?"

"That's good news," he said, cautious.

She leaned back to get a good look at him. He gazed at her out of narrowed eyes. "And thank you for taking me to that place last night."

His lips curved in a tiny smile. "You're welcome."

"Do you want to go back to sleep?"

"All right."

"You don't make a lot of decisions, do you?"

He sighed and turned away, pulling the coverlet over his shoulders. "What do you think this was? I'm going to sleep."

SIXTEEN

Ada woke with the sensation that she'd been drugged and spent the night in some surreal painting by Hieronymous Bosch. The pillow next to her was cool and empty now, and her drawings of St. Casimir's and the Medusa were gone too. Fierce yellow sun poured through the kitchen windows, driven by a hot inland breeze. Could it be mid-afternoon already? Ada fished her wrinkled clothes from the floor and went outside to sit on the stone steps. She didn't smoke, but it felt like a cigarette moment.

"Damn," she said out loud. "Damn." She wondered if he'd liked her body as much as she had liked his. She thought maybe he had—after all, there were some things men couldn't fake—but still, who knew how indiscriminate he might be. Perhaps he let Gisele jump on him too. Maybe he was just a little slut. Maybe he liked to lie back and let women have their way with him.

Or maybe it was something else.

Still, she knew she had to call Cristian if she didn't want to be discovered squirming with a slinky stranger in his parents' bed. But it was hard to think about Cristian—like restless moths, all her feverish thoughts fluttered around Michel. What he was going to do with her ghostly face over St. Casimir's in flames. Whether she would draw him as Adonis or Eros, or perhaps some dark incubus. Whether he'd break into her apartment again. The tantalizing knowledge that he could.

Ada was careful to leave the balcony shutters open a crack when she ventured back to the telephone across the street. She closed herself into the booth and struggled with a fistful of coins, dialing the unfamiliar number and hoping that no one would respond, that she was still abandoned in Rocca. But this time Cristian himself answered on the second ring. It was dark by then, and little clusters of loiterers in tight shirts stood around smoking cigarettes and ogling women. Cristian's deep and musical *"Pronto"* sounded like a dream, like the voice of some ghost from the distant past. And it had only been—what?—two days? Three days?

"Ciao," she said. "I've been trying to reach you."

"Ciao, Ada." His voice was warm but he sounded distracted.

"Is everything all right?"

"Well, we have a funeral to plan now."

"Oh! I'm so sorry. Can I—" Her voice trailed off, because she didn't know what else to say. Ada had friends—Bobby first and foremost—who had the gift of compassion and easy empathy, but she only knew how to succor cats. She felt speechless and stupid, and fumbled with her Italian as if she'd forgotten all her grammar.

But Christian seemed not to notice. "You stay there and don't worry. It just happened this morning and everything is upside down. All the relatives are on their way—you don't want to be here now."

"If you need me to come—" But now she was hoping he did not.

"No, no, no, you stay there. My parents need to take care of things in Torino, but I'll come back to Rocca as soon as it all settles down."

"Well, all right, I miss you. Tell your parents I'm very sorry."

"Yes, yes. They were sad to spoil your vacation. My mother felt bad about leaving you without enough food."

"I'm fine. Tell them I'm fine and not to worry. I'm sorry about your grandfather."

"I have to go, Ada, someone's at the door."

"I'll call in a couple of days."

"Wait till next week. After the funeral."

As she hung up, Ada felt ambivalent nostalgia for Cristian. She missed his broad shoulders and curly hair and playful hands. But she was thinking about the other one too, his smooth chest and indolent eyes, the way he let her touch him and take pleasure from him as if he were some boundless erotic wellspring. The taste of him had left her craving more.

When she curled up in the big bed that night, Ada grabbed the pillow Michel had slept on and wrapped herself around it. She'd bolted the front door from the inside, but the balcony doors were left open. The fountain below the balcony had been repaired, and now water poured from the nymph's vessel, splashing onto cool wet marble. The occasional step of a solitary person resonated on the cobblestones below the window.

Waking in the hour before dawn, Ada wondered how one would draw the sound of babbling water. The color of sound dangled before her, inaccessible. Its ineffable whisper curled round her head. The soul of water. Or something else she could not quite grasp. Though now she could feel it, like tentative fingers. Like a dangerous lover.

Lips apart, eyes wide, Ada let herself be touched till it spent her. Finally, sleep quenched desire.

SEVENTEEN

A week went by with no sign of Michel.

At first Ada loitered around the apartment, waiting for him to reappear. As time passed, she grew bold enough, or desperate enough, to stroll past Gisele's building, eyes hidden under her white plastic sunglasses so she could examine the balcony window unobserved. But she saw no sign of him or her. Forgetting her rash promise not to hunt for him in bars, she meandered down the seaside promenade and stopped at the bar where she'd first seen him that day. She sat, alert, till the sun dipped into the low clouds hugging the sea, but her vigil only produced the unwelcome shock of seeing the Mexican from the Casa Bianca in a bright turquoise shirt and black beret, accompanied by a skinny Italian girl—the one from the club? Ada slouched, slipping the sunglasses over her eyes.

Later, she finally washed the dishes and made the twin beds, though she'd decided that she was going to sleep in the big bed from now on. She went to the market and bought mozzarella, tomatoes, black olives and fresh basil, and for days she lived on that, a bag of focaccia, and raspberry gelato. She called Cristian once and learned that now some kind of money feud had erupted between two factions of the family. An aunt and uncle nobody liked had come down from the mountains to make trouble after the funeral, something about notaries and deeds and property rights, all bound in the tangled Italian red tape of medieval legacy. Ada had endured the same sort of money dispute in her own family—bitter wrangling over who got the cash and bonds when great-aunt Betty died, who'd siphoned off the account so the deserving relatives wouldn't get their fair share, who'd made off with the log cabin quilt and the silverware. With chilly distaste, she listened to Cristian explain the history of the quarrel. She didn't want to know.

Ferragosto, the culmination of Italy's summer holiday season, was arriving in a matter of days and Rocca was filled to bursting. Ada spent hot afternoons in the local baroque church with its cool stone pews and damp walls, where she sketched the altars, the nave, an old woman in a headscarf who sat there for hours with her rosary. Then she crumpled the sketches and threw them into a garbage bin.

She counted her money again. In two weeks she would have to make some decisions. She watched the fashionable young couples in their expensive clothes and gold jewelry and wondered how it would feel to lead of life of leisure. How it might be not to worry about money.

She went to the free beach, where she could spend a cheap day without renting an umbrella, but she attracted too many strutting Italian boys in Speedos. Their single-minded persistence made Ada rude and short-tempered—she had not realized that Cristian was such an effective buffer. Fed up with the swooning onslaught, she gathered her things and trudged back to the apartment. She was sick of the beach and sick of the sun, which had burned her back and left her skin tight and prickly. As she slogged up the stone steps to the apartment, she decided she would close all the shutters and sit in the gloom eating tomatoes, fresh figs and bread for dinner. She would add up the travelers checks one more time. She would think about the future.

When she pushed the door open and found Michel in her kitchen again, she nearly dropped her beach bag. He was clad in the same faintly old-fashioned clothing he'd been wearing at the bar that first day. His eyes were darkened with eyeliner again. He was drinking one of her Sanbitters and reading the romance novel.

"Hello, Ada," he said, as if he hadn't expected her. "Where have you been?"

She flung the beach bag into the corner, thumping it hard against the floor. "At the beach. What else do people do here?" She slammed the door shut. "I see you've made yourself right at home. Remember that this isn't my house."

"Well, they're still gone. While the cat's away the mice will play, yes? Lots of mice on the beach, I guess."

"And a big fucking rat at my table."

He sighed. "Gisele says things like that. Do you want me to go?"

"I thought you'd left town."

"I had things to do at home. But I'm free now, for awhile."

The sight of him, dressed for a decadent Viennese banquet as he sat at the crumb-strewn vinyl table, made Ada hesitate. She didn't know whether to slap him or throw him on the floor and rip that shirt off him. And perhaps he sensed he'd provoked her, because his demeanor changed. He began to look sweetly ridiculous, like a little boy in a fierce costume. Provoked indeed, Ada bolted the door behind her. Michel closed his book and waited, swallowing hard.

"I was going to have some figs and tomatoes with bread. Do you want some?"

He gave her dazzling smile—was it relief? "Oh! I love figs."

Ada sighed. "Of course you do."

Michel seemed moved by the meager vegetarian repast, popping the fresh figs into his mouth with reverent delight and sloshing copious amounts of olive oil over everything. Ada served white wine for herself and sparkling water for him and they sat across from each other, he in the formal attire and she barefoot in beach gear, trickling warm sand on the floor. Neither of them mentioned their last encounter. Neither spoke much at all. But Ada still felt as if they were sharing a sleeping bag. And after she'd downed a couple of glasses of wine, they both reached for the last purple fig and their hands touched again.

"First me," Ada said, ripping the fig in half with her teeth. "Then you." And she gave him the other half.

"That's how it always is." He gazed at the torn fig, expression melancholy.

After they had eaten every scrap of food, Michel carefully pulled something out of the pocket of his ironed white shirt.

"Are those joints?" Ada asked, incredulous. "You know that word? *Spinelli?*"

Michel frowned and drew them back. "Of course I know that word, we used to live in California. But this is kif. It's better, from Afghanistan. Mixed with tobacco. I brought them for you."

Ada clapped her hands and whooped in disbelief. "You brought me hash!" she crowed.

"Is that good? Are you glad?"

"Well, yes. It reminds me of my Modigliani phase."

Michel's eyes brightened. He gently laid the two joints on the table before her, then fished a little packet of matches from his trouser pocket and placed it neatly beside them. "There." He cocked his head and winked at her. "That's why I came, to bring you a present."

Ada picked them up and sniffed them. "Well, this is the kind of present that people need to share."

They smoked both joints, passing them back and forth across the kitchen table. Unaccustomed to tobacco, Ada felt the nicotine explode in her head before the hashish expanded it out of recognition. The matchbook on the table suddenly became hilarious, and Ada had to stifle a giggle. Michel closed his eyes, lids smudged with black like an Egyptian prince, then blew out long streams of smoke, the little Turkish coin glittering in his ear. His throat was long and smooth, dusky against the white shirt. Ada forgot that she was irritated with him. All she could remember was pulling his head back a week before, and how he let her bare that throat, and later how he let her touch it with fingers and lips, nip it hard with her teeth. They caught each other's eye and held the conspirator's gaze.

"Modigliani." Michel rolled the name off his tongue. He leaned back in his chair, arms folded, and put on a sultry expression.

"Modigliani."

They stared at each other across the table like two bookends.

"Would you have one of his portraits on your wall?"

Ada sighed, staring at the blank cement wall and fancying one of those long-faced visages gazing back at her. "I would sit before it and drink absinthe."

"Too many eyes. I might prefer a landscape."

"In high school I put a Modigliani print up in my bedroom. A nude. My mother got rid of it. I wanted to get rid of her."

"You wanted to get rid of your mother?"

"I wanted to be a changeling and get rid of my whole family."

"I never wanted to be a changeling."

"You had a fresco in your house, that's why. We had pictures of kittens. Dogs playing cards. And a velvet painting of a Spanish dancer."

Ada remembered when her father brought the velvet painting home. He'd been proud of it, and she had been young enough to be

87

impressed by the dancer's bright red dress. She recalled touching it with her child's fingers, the ticklish feeling when she rubbed her check against it. Years later, the velvet painting became the subject of funny stories in bars, making her friends cackle and hoot. The tacky velvet painting with the plastic frame that had so pleased her mother.

"We don't have the fresco anymore."

"But you never had velvet paintings either, did you? Modigliani versus velvet. I copied the nudes, I put them up. I wanted to drink absinthe."

"I would drink absinthe," Michel mused.

"We could smoke opium and drink absinthe."

Michel gave her a sleepy smile. "Contemplating Modigliani."

"An opium den, bottles of absinthe, the walls covered with portraits by Modigliani. We would conjure him and he would rise like a genie from the absinthe bottle." Ada loved the sound of her voice and the marvelous sensation of being profound. She imagined wisps of Modigliani drifting out of a bottle of green absinthe. And she thought about her mother taking down the print of that nude and squirreling it away somewhere, maybe even destroying it. "Your mother doesn't like velvet paintings, does she?"

"No, she does not," he said, but now there was a wariness about him, a blankness.

"You're lucky." He gazed at her, impassive, so she plunged on. "My mother doesn't like Modigliani. And you'd think she'd be happy that I finally settled on Renaissance art, but she doesn't like that, either. Too many naked people. Too much art." The thought of her mother's reaction to naked people made her giggle. "But it doesn't matter anymore, I've been gone for years now. I now focus on portraiture in the Renaissance style. I could stay here or go to New York City. Or France. I'm an artist now." Ada felt emotional, almost teary, as she contemplated her destiny. "I have a gift."

Michel blinked at her like a bored cat, then slowly closed his eyes.

"Are you more like your mother or your father?" she asked.

His eyes flew open.

The hashish made her feel like an oracle. "Like your mother."

"I am not like my father." His words were clipped.

"You see? The truth flows through me."

He closed his eyes again, but his lips had grown tight.

"Is your sister like your father?" she asked.

His chest rose and fell once. His jaw grew petulant. He did not respond.

"Well," she continued, "she's sure not like you."

When he finally opened his eyes, he looked at her with an unexpected languor. "It's not my sister's fault. She should be living with her father. But he is in Paris with a new family."

"She has your mother."

He gave her a strange crooked smile. And something else flitted across his face, something so swift and brief that she was not sure she'd seen it. It filled her with unease.

"Do you like me better now?" he asked. His voice was expressionless but the downcast tilt of his head and the glint in his eye spoke of something more.

"I told you I wouldn't come looking for you."

"So I had to come. You forced me."

"Yeah, dude, I think you like to be forced."

He responded with a sweet, merry smile and stood up with the supple grace she'd seen that very first day.

She would possess him. She would run her pencil along every sinew and muscle. She would freeze him forever on paper.

"Well, Ada, I'm going to walk up to the cliffs to watch the sun set. Thank you for the figs."

"The cliffs? I've never been there."

"Not even with your friend? Maybe when he comes back you should ask him to take you."

"Maybe I want to go with you right now."

He contemplated her for a stubborn moment, fists stuck down into his front pockets. Ada wanted to spring at him, push him up against the wall and sink her teeth into him. But she tried to look fun and non-threatening, someone he might want to take on a long walk. Though she knew that was not what either of them were thinking.

"Well," he said, "I haven't been able to stop you from doing what you want so far, have I?"

Ada couldn't tell whether he was teasing her or offering a reprimand. "No, you can't stop me, not when you come over here and let yourself in and eat my food and then tell me you're going to do something fun I've never done before."

"All right," he said, but there was a bite to his voice. "I suppose you want to change your clothes, so I'll wait."

When they were out the door, she realized that they were heading towards Gisele's. Michel had a change of clothes there, he said, and he needed to change his shoes too. With excruciating kif-induced suspicion twisting her thoughts into a million inventive scenarios in which he was trying to ditch her, plot against her, impart some secret message she could not understand, Ada followed him up to the apartment with the orange sofa.

Gisele greeted her with what seemed ill-disguised surprise and Michel with demoralizing complicity. The dreamy psychedelic music on the phonograph made Ada want to curl into the orange cushions and concentrate, but when Michel disappeared, then Gisele, she grew uneasy. Lolling on the sofa, she told herself that this was fun, though now she kept hearing ominous messages in the lyrics. She thought she detected the sound of an argument behind the bedroom door, but reality was too stretched for certainty. At some point they re-emerged, Michel now clad in jeans and a T-shirt and Gisele's legs poking out of skinny mauve-colored pants, her big feet in a pair of calico walking shoes, and a camera and purple hat in the green mirror cloth bag slung over her shoulder.

"Ready!" Michel called with a cheery innocence that resonated with dark and hidden meaning. How did he act when he was alone with Gisele? Did they talk about Modigliani? And what were they doing in that bedroom? Smoking opium? Had she been undressing him? Distressing possibilities flooded in, but Ada decided to be crafty and nonchalant, even though it had become clear that they were all going for a walk together. Even though her head seemed to hover a foot over her body and the world had zoomed in so deep and close that it was like struggling through webs of transparent ectoplasm. She floated along beside them—or behind them?—while every hair on her body quivered in disturbing response to this suddenly sinister expedition.

The cliffs were one of the attractions that Rocca offered to visitors who wanted a break from the beaches and the jowl-to-jowl life in town. A narrow twisting path ran up from the end of the free beach along the steep, rocky walls that jutted out over the Mediterranean toward Spain and Corsica. Ada had seen people clambering up or skidding down as she and Cristian lay under their blue umbrella or sprawled baking in the sun, their skins toasting under a layer of hot lotion. They had never had the energy to climb up. Cristian did not enjoy long strenuous walks in the middle of the day, and it would be dangerous to try after dark.

Maybe it was dangerous to try it so stoned that the trees themselves seemed to mutter veiled and hostile messages, but if Gisele noticed, she gave no sign. As for Michel, he loped alongside them like a frisky puppy, his visage untroubled and serene.

"Can I use your camera?" he asked Gisele as they approached the path, and she let him photograph them. He snapped shot after shot, some as they walked and some after he made them point their noses out to sea as if unaware of the photographer. Then Gisele took some of him as he shifted his weight from one hip to the other and struck a seductive pose, staring gravely into the lens.

Finally they scrambled up through rocks, dirt, and Mediterranean scrub till they left the beach behind and approached a high, windswept plateau over the town, with maritime pines and evergreen oaks now crowding the path on either side. The glittering blue sea stretched out below, its shadowy purple coast circling north and west, then out of sight in the distant mist. Abandoned olive trees, vestiges of an ancient grove, grew gnarled and dusty in the sunlight. Ada brushed past wild rosemary, rangy and pungent, and tufts of silvery green lavender bristling from the rocky soil. They slipped and skidded on loose pebbles and gravel, and by the time they finally pulled themselves up to the top they were sweaty and grimy, and Ada was glad she'd worn her cowboy hat and slathered herself with sun lotion. Gisele had thrown on a long-sleeved white shirt, despite the heat, and stuck the big purple hat on her head, its floppy brim shading her face. Only Michel was heedless of the sun. He seemed to grow darker by the minute, like an exotic coppery chameleon. The gold coin in his ear sparkled in a brief blaze of light and his black-lidded eyes turned as bright and dramatic as a pale-eyed wolf dog's.

"Take a picture," he said to Gisele. He grabbed Ada's hat and put it on, then threw his arm across her shoulders in a casual embrace. Gisele clicked picture after picture as they grinned and squinted into the light. Michel leaned into Ada, or at least she thought he had, and Ada leaned back into him, enough that she could feel his ribs as he breathed. Gisele finished the roll of film and loaded another. Ada still felt foggy, but the cobwebs were dissolving into merciful patches of clarity. She wondered how much he had paid for that kif.

They sat on the dry and dusty ground and stared out at the sea below them, the sheen of the black pebble beaches and the mottled turquoise water splayed out in a sparkling flat sheet as far as they could see. The compact, white hot sun burned as it made its slow way down to the water.

"Modigliani was born on this coast," said Michel, pointing south to the foamy line of sea.

Ada squinted, watching the shoreline vanish into the southern horizon. "He was?"

"But he was cramped here. He longed for Florence."

Ada thought of the cathedral square, the famous dome. The Palazzo Pitti and the Uffizi like polished gems.

"And Caravaggio died somewhere down there," Michel added.

Ada peered down the rubble-strewn cliff to the rocky beach below. "He did?"

"On this coast. The poet Shelley drowned out there too."

She scanned the tranquil waters, suspicious. "Are you serious?"

He shrugged. "It's just history. And people jump off these cliffs sometimes. Or they fall. It happens."

Ada pulled out her sketchpad. She pictured a beach littered with the bones of painters and poets and unknown failures, a place abandoned by Modigliani, who left his own bones in a foreign land. Her hand cramped on the pencil.

Michel curled between Ada and Gisele, head resting on Gisele's green mirror cloth bag, and drowsed in the sun. Gisele lit a cigarette and peered at Ada's blank paper.

"Do you draw?" she asked. With the high faded, she sounded companionable enough.

"I'm an artist." Ada closed the sketch pad.

"I'm a photographer."

"Professional? Is that what you do?"

Michel lay motionless, eyes on Gisele. There was a tick of silence.

"Pfft." Gisele flipped her hand with disdain. "My parents have an old farm in Tuscany, near Prato. We have an agriturismo, a little bed and breakfast."

"And she takes photos of its guests." Michel's tone was non-committal.

"I'm part of the family business. I can speak to the English people who come, the Swiss, the Americans, the Germans."

"The innkeeper's talented red-haired daughter," Michel

murmured, closing his eyes.

"And your mama likes our place."

"But she doesn't like you."

Gisele caught Ada's eye and gestured, palm out, as if to say—you see what I have to deal with.

"That's how you know each other?"

"They've been to our agriturismo a few times. It's nice, isn't it, Michel? A nice escape from the city. We make good food too. And I know the wild plants."

"She will take you on very long walks on hot days, up and down the hills, taking photos of you."

"Somewhat like today," Gisele retorted, though her voice was affectionate. "Tourists love long walks. They love to feel capable in the woods. Even your mother tried that once."

He opened his eyes and squinted at her. "And so?"

"And so nothing. Even she walked in the woods with me once."

"Once," he echoed. He curled up again, tucking his knees to his chest and clasping his arms around his head.

"My father even gave them the real estate information for their big fancy villa here in Rocca. Your mother didn't mind when I showed her where it was, did she?"

Michel curled tighter, silent. Gisele winked at Ada over his head.

"But now she won't have me there. Now I'm just the innkeeper's daughter."

Michel seemed to be feigning sleep.

"And I'll never go to Washington to become a big shot like her big shot son."

"Washington?" Ada repeated. "Like Seattle, Washington?"

"Like Washington, D.C." Gisele gestured over at him. "Destined for great things, he is. Aren't you?"

Michel did not move or respond. Gisele gave Ada a wry look, though malice glinted in her eyes.

"If his mama lets him go, that is. If she can live without him."

Michel shot up, jaw jutting defiantly. "You talk too much," he said. "About things you don't understand. And you have no manners." He didn't raise his voice, but he leaned back on balled fists and the tendons in his neck were taut.

"And that's why we're such good friends, dear." Gisele reached out to ruffle his hair. He ducked away, pulled himself up and stalked off into the woods.

"Don't worry," Gisele told Ada. "He'll be back soon. And if I were really so mean to him, he'd stop coming over, no?"

"Washington, D.C.?"

Gisele stretched out on the ground, eyes hidden under big sunglasses, and took a long drag on the cigarette. "Our boy is meant for great things," she sighed. "Are you having fun with him?"

Ada thought about that incandescent club, Michel writhing among beautiful strangers, and then later under her own hands. "I don't know him very well."

"No," said Gisele, "that you don't."

And then there seemed nothing more to say. Still fuzzy, Ada watched Gisele's bent legs and elbows shift into sharp triangles. Her sunglasses grew black and mysterious as caves, her hands like big white fish. "Gisele, can I draw you?"

"You do portraits? You could draw me?"

"I do and I could." Ada tossed her head. "I can even turn you into Venus on the half shell if you want." Gisele didn't understand the reference and Ada was glad. Though of course Gisele wanted to be drawn. Everyone did.

By the time Michel returned, Ada was nearly done. Gisele was an easy subject, one of those people any artist could caricature. And Ada liked the look of her cigarette in the hot sun. But Michel gazed at the drawing without comment, then sat by himself under a cluster of maritime pines. When Ada looked back at him, he was leaning against a rough red trunk, arms folded across his chest, one knee tucked close to his body and the other folded up on the ground. He refused to catch her eye.

Gisele pulled off the sunglasses to peer at her portrait. Ada handed it to her with a flourish. "Here, it's yours."

"It's me! Ada, this is good!"

Michel gave a loud cough and shifted in his evergreen outpost.

"Look, Michel! Ada drew me."

"What a surprise." He sounded bored. Gisele popped the sunglasses back on and scrambled to his side, waving the drawing. She scooted next to him against the tree, shoulders and hips touching, her spiky red head close to his, and the conversation now too quiet for Ada to hear.

By the time their inaudible communion was over, Michel seemed mollified. Looking chastened, he sauntered back with Gisele. "Quite a portrait," he commented, non-committal, as Gisele gently tucked the drawing into her bag.

"I could do you too. As Venus on the half shell if you want."

He gave her a speculative look.

"Or Eros," Ada whispered, mouthing the words. His expression did not change except for the faintest twist of his mouth.

"The artist makes the final decision," he said.

By the time they headed back down to the beach, the sun was dipping into the Mediterranean in a last brilliant gasp of color and light. Shadows had grown long and slanted and the air was balmy with twilight. They scooted, half-sliding, down the path, in a hail of dust and pebbles and sharp little brown pine needles. Michel reached the bottom first, bounding down the last few yards to leap onto the beach and race into the dusk, while Gisele and Ada picked their way more delicately. Michel reappeared a minute later, looking cheerful and tousled.

"Will you make me dinner, Gisele?"

"Ach," she groaned. But her voice twinkled.

"Anything you want," he wheedled. "I'll eat anything." He bounced backwards and forwards, dancing around them, as they headed off the beach into town.

"All right, all right," she said. "I'll see what I have."

They both looked at Ada.

"Thanks for coming, Ada," said Michel. "This was fun."

"Come over when your friend is back," Gisele added. "Maybe we can all go out."

Ada stood in the black shadow of a tree in the park and watched them vanish. She wanted to grab that tree and pound her head against it. She wanted to rip the bark off with her teeth.

Instead, she went to the train station and called Cristian.

"I miss you," she whimpered. "Everyone here is an asshole. When are you coming back?"

His rumbly voice was comforting. "Next week, I promise. This has been hard for my mother, but next week I'm coming."

"And I'm running out of money. I'm stuck here spending all my money."

"Ada, have you ever thought of teaching at a language school? Teach English. You could do that anywhere. You could do it in

Florence."

"Why would I teach English? I hate grammar, I'm an artist. You think things are so easy but what do you know, your family even pays for your toilet paper."

Ada knew something about stopgap jobs. It was how her uncle had ended up in the plastics factory. It was how her father had become a career janitor and why Emily had taken that cash register position at the drugstore after she dropped out of technical school. And Cristian's promise of dinner and gelato in less than a week did not assuage her. Fear swept through her, like a wild-eyed cow hurtling down the chute to the slaughterhouse. The thought of teaching verb tenses to ungifted students wrestling with diphthongs they would never master, of being crushed under the weight of letters and words instead of the nurturing silence of form and color, made her kick the phone booth after slamming the receiver down. She stormed out to the impassive stares of a young couple waiting their turn.

"*Figli di papá*," she spat at them. "Spoiled brats."

EIGHTEEN

The apartment smelled like a hippie hostel in Kathmandu. And now the clusters of stubborn ants were back, drawn by the spilled orange juice that Ada had forgotten to mop. Yesterday she'd sprayed them down with window cleaner, but they still made constant forays into the kitchen, where they hauled off crumbs and sent exploratory expeditions to the cupboards. Sitting at the table eating a stale, salami-stuffed roll slathered with Italian mayonnaise squirted from a little tube, Ada glowered at the creatures as they marched across the kitchen floor.

Maybe she would skip town. In Buffalo, that had been a way to avoid paying the last month's rent and cleaning the bathroom. She could just close the door and be gone, and someone else could scrub the floors and exterminate the ants. Someone else could sit here with stale food while other people were having a nice dinner by purple candlelight and doing who knew what else.

Ada ripped at the hard bread with her teeth the way a cat tears off a mouse's head.

Late that night, the shutters open to the sound of the newly pattering fountain and its sweet nymph, Ada dreamed of Michel. He sat at a round table with a man in a lion skin pelt and a beautiful watery-looking woman, long knives in hand and a big red human heart on the table. Taking turns, they sliced and ate it. The dream woke her and she lay skittish and distracted, imagining the scene as a fresco on the wall. She remembered her deck of Tarot cards from high school and considered drawing herself holding the Three of

Swords, the heartbreak card with its fat scarlet heart run through with silver blades. She needed to find that deck again.

Traffic had stopped. The night air hung still and listening, but the living water still sang softly. Ada rolled over and slept.

She was lying diagonally on top of the sheets when something woke her.

"Ada, Ada," came a disembodied voice from some great distance. The sound disturbed her peace and she stirred, head heavy and groggy with sleep. "Ada, I'm sorry to wake you, Ada." Now the voice was right by her ear. She jolted awake and pulled herself up with a gasp to find Michel standing over her. The shadow of Michel, the smell of Michel.

"Jesus Christ! Michel?"

"Your door was locked, so I had to come in from the balcony." He'd backed up, perhaps because he didn't want to frighten her, and stood in the middle of the room, his form caught in the faint light of the street lamp.

"What the hell are you doing here?"

"I need a place to sleep. One of those extra beds . . ."

"A place to sleep? Now?"

He made a helpless little gesture. "Can I?"

Ada flopped back down, stuck her head under the pillow, and growled like a wild animal. Then she picked up the pillow and hurled it at him. He caught it with a slap and held it, wordless, against his chest, like the nymph with her vessel of water.

"Those sheets are clean and I don't want you messing them up and making more work for me!"

"The floor?" he suggested.

"Don't be so stupid. Just get in this bed and shut up."

He relaxed his hold on the pillow. "Well, if I'm not bothering you—"

"Oh for God's sake, Michel, just get in." She pulled the cover up over her shoulder and turned her back to him. He padded over and placed the pillow beside her, then straightened the sheet.

"We'll have breakfast in the morning," he whispered as he slid in next to her. "I'll make it."

"If you're still here."

"And this time I got undressed before you told me to."

Ada turned around and looked at him. He smiled broadly, as if he'd just given her a treat. "See? You don't need to be angry at me, Ada."

"Ok, Michel," she sighed. "I'm not."

"Time to go back to sleep."

"Michel, what are you doing here?"

He was silent.

"Did you have a fight with Gisele?" Maybe they'd fought about her.

"I'm supposed to go home." He scooted a little closer to her. But not close enough to touch.

"You don't want to go home?"

"I don't know."

They stared at each other.

"Well, looks like you're not going home tonight."

"So can we sleep?"

"I'll let you sleep for awhile—maybe."

He sighed and turned away, the sheet slipping from his shoulder. "You're going to do what you want, aren't you?"

"No one forced you to come here."

"So when does your friend come back?"

Ada stared at his smooth back. "I don't know. Pretty soon, I guess."

"Will you introduce me?"

She thought about that. Cristian, meet Michel. Would Cristian remember that day in the bar? Sometimes things like that didn't stick in his mind. He'd remember Gisele, though. She could introduce them together.

"Yeah," she said.

The smooth contour of his shoulder blades reminded her of curved driftwood, softened and polished by the sea. And now it felt as if something were scrabbling and scratching inside her, clawing to get out.

"I still want to draw you."

He turned around to face her. "Why?"

She could not say. She wanted to eat him alive.

"Do you draw him?"

"Sometimes." That seemed to cut the tension. Michel rolled over to gaze at the ceiling.

"Mmm. Is he going to sleep in this bed?"

"No way. This is his parents' bed."

"This is his parents' bed?" He sounded interested now.

"We slept in the little beds next door."

"Ah. But you and I, we're in his parents' bed."

"Yeah, and don't you ever say a word about it."

He looked sidelong at her. "Why, is this a secret?"

"You're fucking right it is. Does Gisele know where you are?"

His face turned petulant. "That's not the same thing."

"Sure it is. You stay over there all the time."

"I sleep on the floor. She lets me sleep on the floor."

"What, you'd rather sleep on the floor? Is that what you're saying? You'd rather sleep on the floor?"

He scooted lower under the sheet and did not respond.

"Hey," Ada said. "I'm talking to you. You didn't seem to mind the bed last time, did you?"

He covered his whole head with the sheet and turned away. "Where do you want me?" His voice was muffled and distant.

Ada grabbed his shoulder and pulled him over on his back again, then snatched the sheet from his face. His eyes flashed wide open for an instant and then he closed them tight. "I want you right here," she said. "I want the sheet off. But I don't want you to tell me you go to Gisele's to sleep on the floor."

"But I do. I do go there to sleep on the floor."

"So why aren't you there sleeping on the floor?"

"I'm supposed to go home," he said, his voice patient. Then he tossed his head with an insolent wink. "But I came here instead."

"And I know just what to do with you."

"I knew you would." His voice sank to no more than a breath. And his face became completely unreadable.

Ada whipped off the sheet, sat on him and pulled his arms up over his head. "You did, did you? You just walked right into the lion's den?"

His arms grew limp and his lips parted. "Maybe."

"And you know what lions do, don't you?"

"I don't know." Ada could feel his slim belly rise and fall under her. "Show me."

By the time they finally shuddered apart, the first drowsy sparrows were cheeping out in the alleyway. The air had taken on a cool pre-dawn moistness, though it still felt electric, excruciating, and her body was now so delicate and sensitive that she could scarcely bear to be touched. She noticed that Michel's eyes were wet.

"When I go home, will you come with me?" His voice was barely a whisper.

"Sure, Michel. I'll be your bodyguard. Rrowr. I'll be your lion."

But it didn't make him smile. "All right. A bodyguard, then."

The dream drifted back, the sliced red heart speared on his knife. The otherworldly companions, their shadowy edges, the odor of risk. And she wondered who really needed a bodyguard.

Shaky and uncertain, she ventured back into sleep and did not dream again.

Michel made the breakfast he'd promised, though it was nearly noon before they ate it. He went through the cupboards and pulled out seemingly unpromising ingredients, then threw them into a frying pan and sautéed them, giving the concoction an occasional one-armed flip into the air and slapping it back into a neat pile in the pan. Then he turned it into a huge, dramatically stuffed omelette. An American breakfast, he told Ada, to make her a happy American.

"You know how to cook," she said.

"Of course I do. I have always known how to cook."

Ada thought perhaps she would like to have him cook naked for her. Maybe just a little white apron. Then she'd have him serve her in bed and afterwards she would have him for dessert with a sweet sauce. She would have him any way she wanted. But she kept her thoughts to herself. Instead she said, "Are you still taking me to your house?"

The question raised the temperature in the room. And the blankness flickered into his eyes again. But when he responded, his voice was still half-humorous. "Oh yes, that's why we're eating all this food, to fortify ourselves."

"Well," Ada said, stuffing her mouth, "this will do the job. We can march to France on this."

He seemed placid now, almost limp. Ada thought perhaps she had worn him out. Perhaps she had stretched him to the limit, and now all he could do was relax. She wondered if there was a bruise on his stomach where she'd bit him. Or if his scalp hurt where she'd yanked his hair. It was nice to see him so loose now, and she liked the way he would catch her eye and then avert his gaze. She liked the complicity. And she did think they could march to France, even to Monte Carlo, fortified by sex and tears and giant omelettes.

He cleaned the kitchen afterwards, washing all the old dishes too, and even wiped the porcelain sink dry with a sponge. Ada spent a long time in the shower and then lingered before the mirror, making her eyes dark and dramatic. She put on a flimsy pink top with nothing underneath and a transparent Indian skirt slung low on her suntanned hips. She struck an aggressive pose and scowled at her reflection, imagining that first encounter with his rich old bitch of a mother.

"I'm an artist." She pointed a finger at the mirror. "So I dress like one." She felt sexy and gaudy and potent.

She strutted out of the bathroom and twirled around for him to see. "You like my outfit?"

He surveyed her, expression enigmatic. "Pink is a nice color."

"Good. I like it too. You're looking a little wrinkled." He was still wearing the old black T-shirt and blue jeans, and it looked as if he'd slept in them. He ran his hands absently down his flanks, as if trying to straighten himself.

"I'll change at home," he said, his tone non-committal, almost bored. "Let's go, then."

Something flickered in his eyes and then vanished. Perhaps she had only imagined it.

NINETEEN

"Via Miramare," Michel told the cab driver in an abrupt, imperious tone Ada had never heard before. As the taxi began its ascent to the villas on the hill, he stared out the open window, oblivious to Ada. Warm sea air blew in, the tangy odor of the fish market filling the vehicle as they stuttered and stopped in traffic along the market square. Ada wanted to nudge closer, but Michel leaned his head against the seat back and closed his eyes, face impassive and still. Ada looked down at her lap and realized that she could see her red underwear through the flimsy Indian skirt. Maybe she should have worn the beige cotton pants instead.

Up on the hill the streets were steeped in preternatural quiet, though a gentle iodine-scented breeze rustled the air and scattered an occasional leaf. Fat, bright purple clots of bougainvillea hung on trellises and clambered up pastel walls behind tall wrought-iron gates armed with intercom systems and cameras. A young woman wearing gold jewelry and a pale, sleeveless button-down cotton blouse walked a little white dog along a sunlit sidewalk. Michel gazed out the window, lips pressed together, hands palm-down on his knees. Ada crossed her legs and fiddled with the folds of her skirt, but nothing muted the bright underwear.

She was going to make an even worse impression than she had planned.

They stopped before one of the gated homes and Michel paid the driver, this time without the slightest hesitation. As they stepped out, the breeze briefly wrapped Ada's skirt around her legs and she struggled to straighten it.

"Hey," she said before they went to the gate. "I don't have to come in."

"No, I want you to." But he didn't look at her. His eyes were fixed on the pale lavender house in its garden of blooming rosemary and potted lemons and oranges, its splash of hot pink roses springing up a wall and the palm tree beside the patio. Ada came up behind him and looked through the tall gates.

"Wow." She thought of where she grew up, her neighborhood of brave and crumbling little homes, the sagging porches with their deformed screens, the peeling wooden steps. The cheesy welcome mats. The scrawny shrubs battling summer drought and winter snow. The people who lived in those houses and their hourly wages, their big televisions. And she their emissary, braless with her underwear showing.

Michel punched a combination on the gate. It opened inwards with ponderous ease, revealing the long, smooth drive to the lavender villa with its tile roof shimmering under the sun. "Home sweet home," he said. "Come on."

Walking alongside Michel, she felt him grow increasingly remote. His gait slowed to a sleek, seductive step. His fine nostrils flared with an unfamiliar arrogance. He loosened and cracked his shoulders as if preparing for a fight, and now his face smoothed into the blank and reckless mask of the performer. He could no longer be touched, though he dripped with a dark allure that made Ada want to wrap her fingers around his hips. Or maybe creep away while she still could.

They stepped into a house of polished tile floors covered with Persian rugs, and art on the walls, portraits and landscapes alongside Oriental tapestries, even a few shockingly incongruous abstract pieces. Thousands of dollars on the walls. And complete silence, as if the place were uninhabited, lost in a cool and endless twilight.

"Is no one home?" Ada breathed.

Michel's attention veered back to her, and with an unexpected gesture he wrapped his hand tight around her wrist. "Someone's home." He straightened his shoulders and let go. "Come into the kitchen and have something to drink and then I'll go change my clothes."

The kitchen was a museum of spotless copper pots hanging over polished granite counters and sinks with cobalt blue ceramic faucets

104

that matched the blue and white tiles on the walls. China teapots lined dusted wooden shelves, and a crystal vase full of purple irises stood in the center of a sleek wooden table. Lemon-colored sunlight slanted through the window, open to the brilliant sea that sparkled down below like a distant gem.

They were sitting at the table splashing juice and fizzy water into glasses when they heard soft footsteps. Michel was on his feet in an instant, alert as a deer, or a rabbit. All bravura vanished, Ada hunched at the table, feeling like a sleazy gypsy dressed in the dime store garb of a two-bit tart.

It couldn't possibly be his mother. She was far too young, though she was dark like Michel, her thick black hair held back with a jeweled barrette, and she had the same exotic eyes. This woman still had the softness, the delicacy of youth, the fertile bloom of rounded breasts and hips, though she was clad in a silky, pale yellow dressing gown that bespoke a certain maturity.

"Michel!" she cried in a tinkling girlish voice. "I didn't hear you. And you've brought a friend, how nice!" She spoke in Italian, but with a pleasant, lilting accent. Ada instinctively smiled at her, but Michel had grown stiff and formal.

"Hello, Mama," he said. "We just arrived. I was getting Ada something to drink and then I was going to find you."

"*Buongiorno, signora*," Ada said, rising but trying to keep the table between her body and his mother.

The woman approached Ada and offered a soft, limp hand for her to shake. "Please, call me Mireille. And you are—I'm sorry—was it Ada?"

"Yes, yes, Ada, I'm a friend of Michel's."

"I imagine you are. That's an English accent, yes?"

"American," Ada admitted.

"American! Well, how remarkable that you should speak Italian at all. My son does like to spend time with the Anglo-Saxons." She scanned Ada's body with a tiny smile. "Yes, of course you're an American."

She casually reached over and took Michel's glass, then wandered to the open window. She sipped his blood orange juice with an absent gesture. Ada looked at Michel, but he seemed oblivious to her. A tense silence settled.

"Ah," said Mireille, gazing out the window. "It's a beautiful day, isn't it? I've missed the sunlight, but it makes the eyes throb sometimes, with the migraine." She turned to Ada with a rueful expression. "I hope, Ada, that you have never suffered from a migraine."

"No, I'm lucky. I don't get headaches."

"Fortunate girl. They are beastly, inhuman. All one wants is someone to bring a cold cloth for the temples, a bit of whispered sympathy."

Michel exhaled, one tight fist resting on the table next to him. Then he drew back and folded his arms tight against his chest.

"This latest one lasted three days, if you can imagine that."

"That's terrible," Ada said.

"Yes, terrible, and it was very lonely here." She clucked softly and gently drained Michel's glass of juice. "Michel's sister is very unsympathetic. Ah, teenagers. She closes the door and watches television, no thought for her mother."

Michel swallowed.

"Well, I must be cautious. I still feel weak. It's waiting behind my eye even now—it may return. I shall have to go back to bed, I imagine." She sighed and eyed the refrigerator. "A boiled egg and black tea might fortify me, stave it off. Perhaps I should do that . . ." Her voice trailed off, her pretty mouth turned down like a child's.

"I'll make it for you," Michel offered, expelling the words as if he'd been punched in the stomach. "You don't have to."

She smiled. "Good boy," she said, her voice warm but a funny glimmer in her eye. "That would be lovely." Now she turned to Ada with gracious boredom. "Please, Ada, come and visit us again some time. I think you are the first American that Michel has brought us for a long while." She did not proffer a hand this time, but instead turned with a dainty gesture and drifted out of the room, a sweet floral scent lingering in her wake.

Ada tried to catch Michel's eye, but he was already pulling eggs from the refrigerator and putting the water on to boil. Ada sank into her chair and watched him.

"Hey," she said.

"This won't take long." He selected a pale pink bone china teapot and set it gently on the counter.

"She looks so young."

He looked over at her briefly, his expression inscrutable, and then placed an egg in a pot of water and turned on the gas. He dropped two teabags in the little teapot. "What of it?" he finally said. "She has had a hard life."

"Just saying. My mother doesn't look like that."

"Will you keep your voice down?" he hissed at her with sudden vehemence. "Just let me get this done."

They didn't exchange another word. Ada sat chastened and resentful while he produced a little Chinese enamel serving tray, a delicate cloth napkin, and an elegant blue egg cup. She guessed the precious egg would be soft boiled, and sure enough, soon he pulled out a tiny silver spoon, which he placed on the napkin beside the egg cup. The tea kettle began to whistle in a shrill crescendo, and he hastened to remove it and tip it into the pretty pink teapot.

He had nearly completed this silent, tense ritual when Marion appeared at the kitchen door, wearing a pair of baggy gray sweat pants and a wrinkled T-shirt, her hair scraggly on her shoulders.

"You're home," she said, as if she were not sure whether she was pleased to see him.

"Hello, Marion," he replied, but he seemed distracted, focused on this suddenly weighty task. Ada thought about his ease with the omelette a few hours before. This was just tea and a boiled egg.

"Are you going to introduce me to your friend?" Marion said with brazen wile, though she refused to meet Ada's gaze.

Michel inhaled with evident irritation. "This is Ada, and that's my sister Marion."

"Are you making something for me?"

"Mama asked for it. She said she's coming off a migraine."

"So what, you could put an egg on for me too, couldn't you?"

"In a minute. This one is almost done and I have to take it up to her."

"Forget it then. I don't want to starve to death." Marion stalked out, giving Ada only the briefest scrutiny before she turned away. Running cold water over the egg now, Michel scarcely seemed to notice that she'd gone.

"Why did she act like she didn't know me?"

"What?" He had placed the egg in the blue glass egg cup and now gently tapped the shell around the top till he could peel off a round piece to expose the soft white egg beneath.

"I told you I met her at Gisele's. Remember? She was looking for you."

Michel looked at Ada with a remote, exasperated expression. "I don't know. It doesn't matter, does it?" Now, amazingly, he fetched a violet-colored bud vase from a cupboard, filled it with water, then plucked one of the irises from the big vase on the table and eased it into the bud vase, which he placed on the tray with the egg. Using a spoon, he scooped out the tea bags from the pink teapot and gave the tea a quick stir. That went on the tray too, along with an ornate little cup and saucer with gold trim.

"There. That looks nice, don't you think?"

"Fabulous."

"All right, then." He took a deep breath and lifted the tray. "I'll be back soon." And he left with the focused, professional air of a waiter, leaving Ada alone in the kitchen. About a minute later she heard quick footsteps and he reappeared, looking frazzled.

"Salt," he said. "I forgot the salt, she likes salt and I forgot it." He snatched a salt shaker and disappeared again. Utter silence descended.

As the minutes ticked by, Ada drifted restlessly toward the kitchen door to peer at the art-laden walls beyond it. She saw handsome leather sofas and armchairs, brocade pillows and an ornate tile floor, gigantic windows overlooking the sea on one side and a flowering garden on the other. She tiptoed out to explore. The house felt uninhabited, like a museum at night. She sat in one of the pale leather armchairs and slouched, then curled up and sat cross-legged, the edge of a dusty sandal touching the buttery leather. The room was cool and airy.

On the wall was a photograph of what looked like a big plantation, with unfamiliar vines and trees, tall tropical palms, and a little girl with shiny dark tresses standing before an iron gate between a stern-looking man and woman. A family portrait for sure. Ada stood up for a better look, her sandals slapping the cool floor.

"They ditched you, did they?"

She whirled to find Marion standing there with a bemused, perhaps mocking expression, a box of crackers in her hand.

"What? I'm just waiting."

"Oh yes, you're just waiting. You'll just be waiting for awhile. You want some gelato? I was going to go get some, might as well get you some too."

"All right," Ada said. "Thank you." She followed Marion back into the kitchen, where Marion fished out a styrofoam container filled with a variety of creamy gelato. She dropped the container unceremoniously on the table and pulled out two spoons.

"This is hazelnut, lemon, raspberry, and apricot. I like chocolate but they never get it. When Carla lived with us she'd buy it for me, but she went back to Milan. Too bad for me. No one else can stand to look after us." She handed Ada a spoon. "We'll eat it like this, so we don't have to wash any dishes."

Ada sat next to her and dug into the fragrant apricot gelato speckled with tiny bits of fresh fruit. Marion dragged her spoon from one end to the other until she had a long, multi-colored curl of gelato, which she slurped off the spoon with gusto. She puckered her mouth and licked her lips. "The lemon's good."

Inspired by Marion's suddenly companionable air, Ada decided to ask the question. "Don't you remember me from Gisele's?"

Marion groaned. "From the German Giraffe's apartment? Yeess . . . But I wanted to make Michel introduce you." She gave Ada a sly look. "Didn't you see how he hates it, introducing me?"

"I don't know." They ate in silence for a few moments.

"Maybe we can eat it all," Marion said after a bit. "We won't leave any for them."

"That's an awful lot to eat."

Marion snorted in annoyance. "It is. But I wish we could do it."

"What's Michel doing up there?"

Marion looked at Ada as if she were stupid. "Keeping her company, what do you think? Pouring the tea. Drawing the shades. Doing what he's supposed to do, when he's not ignoring us, pretending he doesn't know us." Her tone turned surly again. "A lot of things need to be done here, you know. And he's never home."

"Ah." There seemed nothing more to say.

Marion stuck her spoon deep into the container, brought up a huge hunk of gelato, and uttered a contented little grunt as it slid down her gullet. "American?" she asked after she'd pulled the spoon out of her mouth.

"*Sì*. Yes."

"On vacation?"

"I've been studying in Florence."

"I speak English," Marion said, and then, just like her brother, broke into nearly perfect English. "We used to live in Los Angeles and Berkeley."

"I'm from upstate New York."

"My father liked it there, but my mother hated it. She hated California."

"Did you like it?"

She shrugged. "I don't remember. I was too little."

"I heard that Michel is going back to the United States."

"With his big important job. He can't get far enough away, I guess." Now she stuck a finger in the gelato and thoughtfully dug up a chunk of hazelnut, which she popped into her mouth and sucked off her finger with a smack. "I knew you knew him, by the way. That very first day at that bar. He was hiding from me, wasn't he?"

"I did not know him. But yes, I think he was hiding."

She pursed her lips and looked Ada up and down. "So it was the guy you were with. He's the one that knew him."

"No, neither of us knew him."

"Well, you do now, I'd say."

Ada heard a loud thump upstairs and a door slammed. She and Marion looked at each other. "I think he's coming," Ada said.

"Not yet." Marion smirked.

And it was, in fact, another fifteen minutes or more before they heard the footsteps on the stairs, and then Michel appeared at the kitchen door, the gold earring gone and his hair still wet and slicked back, giving him the disconcerting look of a skinned rabbit. He'd changed into fresh clothes but still looked rumpled, as if he'd thrown them on in haste. And in fact he now seemed rushed and distracted.

"Want some?" Marion held out the styrofoam container with her sticky hands. He recoiled with an expression of profound irritation that surprised Ada, but seemed to make little impression on Marion, who in fact snickered in the same bratty way Ada had once sneered when she wanted to annoy Emily. "Calm down," she drawled, "we didn't go anywhere. And gelato won't hurt your figure or give you spots."

"You need to bring down the dishes," he said, as if he hadn't heard her.

"What dishes?"

"The ones under the bed. Under the bed. That need to be washed."

"You were just up there, you bring them down." Marion spooned gelato into her mouth with a leisurely, insolent gesture.

"I'm not going back up now. She's sleeping."

"Then she can bring them down. She can wash them too, if she won't have anyone replace Carla."

"I'll talk to Carla."

"I told you. She went back to Milan." Now Marion turned to Ada with a cheery, frozen expression. "You need a job? We can't survive without the nanny."

"And I told you I'd talk to her and she'll be back. Let's go, Ada," said Michel, his voice unfamiliar and sharp.

"Before she wakes up and reels him back in."

"And I will pick up the prescription, since you haven't."

"She doesn't need any prescription, Michel, don't be so stupid."

"I know what she needs."

Silence hung in the air as they faced each other down.

"Well, don't let *me* interfere," Marion finally said, her tone bored.

"Let's go," Michel repeated with an impatient gesture, as if Ada were the one prolonging the scene.

"Nice to talk to you," Ada told Marion, who gave her an impudent smirk.

"I love meeting my brother's friends." Marion's bulbous nostrils flared. Apart from the eyes, there was no family resemblance at all, except the sense of something sizzling underneath. And below that, something small and quiet crouching deep inside. Even the weird mother had that.

"Let's go," Michel repeated, his tone even more brusque.

"Good gelato," Ada said to Marion in parting. Marion gave Ada a thumbs up, and on an impulse Ada stuck out her tongue and winked as they went out the door. Marion's face went from surprised to offended to complicit in a matter of seconds. "I'll do a portrait of you next time!" Ada called, and Marion's eyes widened as the door closed behind them.

"Why did you tell her that?" Michel demanded as they hurried outside.

"Why not? Everyone likes to have their portrait done, don't they?"

He ran his hand through his hair in a frustrated gesture and said nothing. But he quickened his pace enough that Ada felt like a dachshund trotting alongside him. And because he had neglected to call a cab to take them back, she had to jog with him like that till she grew sweaty.

She tried to break the silence. "Your mother is sick?"

"She gets headaches."

"You look alike."

Silence.

"Marion doesn't look like either of you."

"She looks like our father."

"Where is he?"

He glanced at her with a flash of irritation. "In Paris. With his new family. I told you that."

"What does he do?"

"He's a scientist."

"Rocket science?" Ada thought that might make him smile, but he only pinched his lips tighter.

"Genetics."

And that was the last thing he said till they walked all the way down, armpits and foreheads damp with sweat, and he left her at the door of her unlocked apartment. Ada wanted to touch him, but he was inaccessible now, as if he were locked behind a pane of glass.

"Do you want to come in?" she asked.

"I have errands."

"All right, then."

She watched him as he slipped across the street, his gait smooth and unhurried. He had that loose look again.

TWENTY

Cristian told her he planned to return that weekend.

"Bring the key," Ada said, "so we'll both have one, just in case." She hoped it sounded like an afterthought.

"Just in case what?"

"I don't know, in case we need it. So we don't have to leave the door open if one of us goes out. So we can both get back in if we need to. You know." She would tell him about the key when he arrived, then they'd make a copy, and everything would be fine.

Just before he hung up, she added the second piece of the story. "Cristian, do you remember that day in the bar when we saw that guy wearing eye makeup? The tall woman with red hair? Do you remember them?"

"Maybe." Cristian sounded doubtful.

"I met her! The woman! I saw her at the beach one day. She introduced me to that guy too, and she invited me to her house."

"Wait, I remember. Those people were strange. They were both strange."

"Well," Ada said, dignified, "she was very nice to me."

But Cristian wasn't interested. "We'll go out for pizza on Saturday night, then we'll have an *affogato* somewhere. Is that good? I missed you."

"That's good, yes. Do you want to sleep in your parents' room?"

"In their bed?" He sounded squeamish. "I don't know. Let's decide when I arrive."

"Okay, ciao."

"Ciao, *bella*, see you soon."

That night, while Ada sprawled across the big bed in her T-shirt, bare toes poking out from under the white sheet as she ate salami and bread, she heard Michel swing himself up on the balcony.

"Hey." She shook the salami at him. "You didn't even try the front door."

He stood cautiously just inside the room, hair a little tousled but otherwise showing no sign of balcony athletics. He was wearing eyeliner again, smoky smudges that gave him a sultry look.

"I thought you might be asleep."

"I am not asleep."

He stood poised, as if ready to dive back off the balcony. "Gisele is not happy with me."

"She kicked you out, so here you are?"

"Here I am." He sounded resigned.

"All right, come in." She flopped back down and pulled the sheet over her head. "You can't come anymore after Saturday, I won't have the apartment to myself." She peeked out at him over the sheet.

He sat on a little wooden chair across from her, crossed one ankle over his knee and wrapped his arms around himself. "They're coming back?"

"Cristian is coming back."

"Cristian."

"That's his name, yes."

"Your occasional model."

"You could be my model. I could do you right now, sitting in that chair." Ada sat up, holding the sheet across her chest. "I really want to." She could not read his expression. She leaned toward him, let the sheet drop away. "I want to draw you, Michel."

"Ada wants to draw me," he echoed. He looked pained, almost ill.

She wanted to slap him. "It makes you sick just to think about it? So never mind then. Forget it."

Ada covered her head with the sheet again, rolled over and drew her knees to her chest. They were both silent. She could feel her own hot breath filling the air under the sheet, lying moist and heavy on her skin. Then she heard the chair creak and Michel's quiet footsteps. Then silence again. She waited under the sheet for a few minutes longer, then peeked out. He was gone. She rolled off the bed and padded over to the empty balcony. The fountain spattered fitfully in the dark. A noisy Vespa rattled past and faded away on the cobblestones. She went into the dark kitchen and flipped on the light, gazed at the new dishes she'd left in the sink and the mess she had to clean before Cristian arrived. Then, on a hunch, she tiptoed to the little room with the twin beds and turned on the light. Michel was in Cristian's bed, his clothes neatly folded on the floor next to him. Motionless, he blinked at her with the eyes of a silent film star.

"Michel, what the fuck are you doing in here?"

"I thought it was all right if I stayed."

"In that stupid little bed by yourself?"

"I didn't know where you wanted me."

With an exasperated groan, Ada marched over and stood glowering at him. "You know exactly where I want you."

He turned away from her. "I suppose I do."

"And you're not staying in here." She tried to pull the sheet off him, but he clung to it, wrapped himself tightly and tucked his head into his chest so she couldn't see his face, just the shiny black hair tumbling on the pillow, a glimpse of his coppery neck.

"Are you kicking me out?" The pillow smothered his voice.

"No, I'm kicking you in, I'm kicking you into the other bed, stupid. What's the matter with you?"

His shoulders relaxed and he loosened his grip on the sheet. "All right," he said meekly. "I'll be there in a minute. Would you turn the light out, please?"

Ada reached down and pulled his hair away, then kissed him on the neck. "You have sixty seconds. I'll turn the light out and then you have sixty seconds."

"Mmm." He nodded. "All right. Thank you." As she switched the light off and left the room, he rolled over. "Would you turn your light out too, please?"

"Yes, Michel. Lights out in all the rooms."

"Thank you."

Later Ada said it was too bad she couldn't see his eyes in the dark.

"Why do you want to see my eyes?"

"Well, you put eyeliner on them, you made them look beautiful. Don't you want people to see them?"

"I don't know. I stole that makeup." He lay subdued under her, his head thrown back and his breathing shallow. "I stole it from my mother."

"Ooh," she said, pinning his arms back, "I bet she'd kill you if she found out." She bit his neck hard. "Wouldn't she." Now she bit his armpit and he flinched.

"I don't know."

"Would she kill you if she knew you were here, wearing her makeup?"

He didn't answer. Ada could feel him breathing under her, undulating like a shallow wave, and she lowered her face down, almost touching his. When she came this close she could see his eyes, two dim mirrors framed in black lashes.

"Well," she said, "too bad for her. I guess you're not going home tonight."

Now he sighed and squirmed. She held him down tighter. "You're not going anywhere, Michel."

"My mama would not like this."

"I don't give a fuck what your mama likes."

"Ah!" He shook his head back and forth as if in protest, but his torso and belly grew flat and motionless again. She liked him that way. She was just about to sink her teeth into his smooth chest when he collected himself and coiled, growing tight and tense as a drawn bow. Then, with a swift ferocity that caught her off guard, he pulled both arms loose, grabbed her hips and lifted her up, suspended for a moment in the air above him, and threw her hard onto her back on the other side of the bed, where she lay shocked and gasping.

"You don't give a fuck here, only here. This is the only place it doesn't matter."

Ada bounced up to sitting, still surprised at how quickly he'd flipped her. He'd been fast as a cat and just as strong. And she'd never heard him swear.

"Holy shit. What are you talking about? What doesn't matter?"

"You're no bodyguard." Resentment crackled in his voice. She couldn't see his face clearly in the dark, so she dropped to hands and knees and edged closer, ready to spring back if he tried to grab her again. But as soon as he sensed her approaching, he rolled over on his stomach and flattened a pillow over his head. "You heard me." His voice came muffled from underneath the pillow.

"I did hear you, but I don't know what you're talking about, and I don't like talking to a person hiding his head under a pillow."

"I don't give a fuck what you like."

She thought about that for a moment. "So, you're mad because I mentioned your mother? Is that it?"

"This is the only place. This is the only place where you—where you —" He squeezed the pillow tighter over his head.

"All right, I'm going to open the shutters and let a little light in. I can barely see you in the dark. Then we can talk." He did not respond, so she went over to the balcony and cracked open the long, slatted doors so the cool street light, heatless as a firefly's underbelly, could flood in. The night air was scented with sea and musty street. The fountain gurgled. By the time she padded back to the bed, he'd pulled the pillow off his head but still lay on his stomach, face hidden in the crook of his arm. Ada sat cross-legged on the mattress, keeping a safe distance.

"You want to talk?" she asked.

"No."

"You want to go back to sleep?"

Silence.

"Why did you get mad when I mentioned your mother?"

"Never mind. I do want to go back to sleep."

"Come on, Michel, what happened?"

"Nothing. Nothing is going to happen. Everything is going to be the same."

"I'm going to touch you, is that all right?"

"Here you'll do that. Here you want to touch me. You won't do it anywhere else."

Did he mean that she offered him no public displays of affection? It was true—theirs was not an overt relationship. Maybe overt was what he wanted. But she didn't touch him.

"You know," she said, "if you're going to Washington, I've got a friend in New York City who wants to open an art gallery with me one day." She'd always told Bobby that she wasn't interested in the business end of art, but still. "New York is not so far away from Washington . . ."

He groaned and slammed the pillow back over his head.

She tried again. "So, are you going to Washington?"

"Yes. I have a job at the World Bank, all right?"

"You're joking, Michel."

"No!" He fairly shouted from under the pillow. "You don't know anything about me."

She tugged at the pillow and he jerked away from her hand.

"And what would you do at the World Bank?"

"I would be an economist, that's what."

Struck dumb, Ada stared at his naked back. It took a few moments to collect herself. "An economist. And are you going this fall?"

"I leave in a couple of weeks."

"And so—if I were in New York City? Do you understand what I'm saying?"

"That doesn't give me a safe place to sleep."

"What is that supposed to mean?"

His arms strained at the pillow, hands coiling into tight fists. The muscles in his back popped out. But he didn't say a word.

"Look, we could see each other. Not all the time, but we could see each other."

He hurled the pillow onto the floor, where it fell with a thump. Then he raised himself up on his elbows and threw his head back in a gesture of surrender. "All right, then."

But his voice gave her no comfort, and soon he sank back down on the mattress and covered his eyes with one smooth forearm.

"I'm going to touch you now." She reached out to touch his stomach. He lay perfectly still and unresponsive. She leaned over and whispered into his ear. "I don't want you to move, all right? Stay right there."

She could feel him listening. He moved not a finger.

"You stay right where you are. I'm going to draw you now, right now."

"Of course you are," he said, his voice exhausted.

They were up most of the night as Ada turned him into shadow and light, a bent elbow caught in a pool of white, face hidden except for the curve of nose and mouth, the partial sweep of jaw and neck, the flow of chest and ribcage and belly, the rest of him vague and hidden, the sheet over his hips electric, almost fluorescent. He'd calmed and relaxed by the time she was done. He seemed to be resting.

"Look," she said finally, and he let his arm slip away from his face to reach out for the drawing.

"It's me."

"It's a present. You keep it."

"There I am." His tone was contemplative. "On paper this time."

Overcome by fatigue and purged, for now, of desire, Ada nearly collapsed into the emptiness of spent passion, as if she had just spent hours in orgiastic communion. As if she had slipped under his skin and drawn him from the inside out. For a few moments she had forgotten who she was. "Now I really do need to sleep."

Michel carefully set the drawing under the bed where it would not be disturbed, and as Ada crumpled into slumber, he swung out onto the floor like a big cat and closed the balcony doors tight so not a crack of light entered, then slipped the latch firmly into place, locking them in.

TWENTY-ONE

Ada lay belly down alone under the sheets, arms spread wide, head facing the foot of the bed and nose buried in the mattress. She felt like a mandala of colored sand, brilliant grains of herself dribbling into the pattern of Michel that still rested beneath her. Her scent still mingled with his. Yet now the implacable future swept over them like the dry desert wind, scattering the colors into formless dust.

She had two days to clean it all away.

She started with the physical scouring—the crumbs and dust, the scraps of paper and trash, the mysterious sticky spots that needed to be scrubbed and cleaned. The dried milk on the kitchen floor. The brown ring in the toilet bowl that she had to scrape away, the hair and scum in the shower that she had to dislodge and wash down the drain. Then she had to collect and launder the towels and underwear scattered on the floor and hang them out to dry on the balcony. Every trace of her presence had to be erased from the big bedroom, including the fine grains of beach sand that invaded the corners.

Then there was the heavier burden of removing the sultry aura of Michel. He'd vanished with the drawing, but the taste of him lingered in the air, heavy and sweet as jasmine. Ada sat in the bedroom with it for a long time before inevitability nagged her into reluctant action.

She checked twice under all the beds for any trashy French romances. She checked for clothing and underwear. For an unfamiliar book of matches. But he had left nothing physical, not even a strand of black hair. Just those sheets that smelled like him. Hands faltering, she stripped the big bed and stuffed the sheets into the tiny washing machine. But she waited half a day to turn it on and flood them with the hot water and soap that would cleanse them, render them anonymous. She stood with her hands on the machine for a long time, feeling the metal vibrate under her fingers. Then she pulled out new ironed sheets from the cupboard. They were a completely different color, which made her uneasy. If anyone noticed, she would say that she had cleaned that apartment so thoroughly that she changed the sheets on every bed.

When it was finally done, she spent time on her own cleansing, on scrubbing her hair and scraping her legs and underarms with a new razor blade. As she smoothed sepia-colored eyeliner on her lids, Ada's shoulders began to tingle, her head to expand, and then her body seemed to lift away and slip into Michel himself, some phantom of Michel, leaning into some other mirror as he drew a line of stolen makeup across his own lids. The shock of seeing his languid reflection superimposed on her own face, the sense that he had invaded her body and was twisting against her from the inside, left her stunned, too shaken to look into the mirror again.

She met Cristian at the train station early Saturday evening, wearing her white cotton Greek pants with the drawstring and a little sleeveless red top that made her hair look paler and her cheeks rosier. She felt slinky and thin, and she smelled good too. But she began to feel jittery as the train pulled into the station, windows down to let in the air and passengers casually leaning on the glass to peer out at friends and family waiting on the platform. There was a rush and commotion of bodies inside, a glimpse of big backpacks thumping down the corridors, then the doors were flung open and they all swarmed out. Weary parents and frisky children, American and German students, a few elegant bejeweled women from the first class seats, dark, shifty-looking men in T-shirts, and then, like a mirage, Cristian himself, a duffle bag over his shoulder, looking solid and sexy in a tight shirt and jeans, curly dark hair framing his ears. Ada was glad to see him.

"Oh, I missed you. I missed having someone to talk to and I got so bored at the beach." It was almost true.

He smelled good and masculine. His neck and lips were warm, arms firm when they enveloped her. His chest was big and tough and covered with soft matted hair that peeped out of his shirt. But they pulled themselves apart, and Ada remembered why he'd been gone, so she made her voice grave as they walked to the apartment.

"I'm so sorry about your grandfather."

He made a face and shrugged. "Well, it's been hard for my mother. But he didn't suffer, he never even regained consciousness. And that's how it is, we live and then when it's time we die. That's how it is for everything. It lives and then it dies."

"Cristian, I hope you brought your key with you."

"Yes, yes, you told me ten times to bring it."

"You won't believe what happened. I had a dream a couple of nights ago, and I saw it fall into a sewer grate over near the via Garibaldi. It was so real. And then just yesterday I was walking by there, and I went to pull my ribbon out of my pocket, and the key slid out and that's what happened, it fell into the grate—"

"You lost the key down the sewer grate?"

"Yes, don't kill me! It was like the dream, it had been on my mind about that key for days. And then it happened."

"How did you get back in?"

"The shutter was unlocked on the balcony and I climbed up."

"You climbed up the balcony?"

"I had to try so many times. I thought I would die. I finally jumped high enough to grab the rails and get my leg up. I can't believe I did it. I don't think I could do it again. But I got in and opened the bolt from the inside."

"So you're saying the apartment has been unlocked since yesterday?"

"Don't kill me. It's the only thing I could do."

He sighed and shook his head. "Gypsies could have robbed you while you were gone."

"But now you're back and we can lock it again."

He wrapped an arm around her and nuzzled her neck. "We're going to lock that door and stay in there a while."

Ada slipped her hand down his back pocket and they walked in step all the way back.

He didn't want to sleep in his parents' bed. So they set up house in the little room with the twin beds, which they pushed together and used right away, ripping each other's clothes off and enjoying themselves so vigorously that Ada banged her head against the cement wall and nearly stunned herself.

"Ow!" she yelped, and Cristian instinctively clasped the top of her head and rubbed hard to relieve the sting. When their startled eyes met, they collapsed into giggling. It was fun and familiar, unmarred by moods or drama or any need for meaningful conversation.

Later they went out for pizza and beer, and since Cristian paid for everything, Ada drank extra and ordered a chocolate tartufo for dessert. They necked in the pizzeria, sly accomplices with the couple across the way who were doing the same, and ended the evening by taking their customary long walk along the seaside promenade, out to where the crowds thinned and a breath of silence emerged, and then quickly back again—Cristian didn't like the stillness. Twice they passed the bar where Ada had first seen Michel, but the table was empty, anonymous, wiped clean.

Back in the center of town, they passed a gray cement building that housed the local language school. Called the Wall Street Institute, its logo included a fluttering Union Jack juxtaposed with a baseball player batting a ball covered with the Stars and Stripes.

"You could get a job there," Cristian said. "They have one in Florence too." He stopped, and they gazed at the logo and the industrial-looking building.

"You still think I should teach English? After studying art all my life, after a year of portraiture in Florence? You think I should teach English?"

"What's so bad about teaching English? They won't ask you for a work permit and you'll make some money. That way you can stay in Rocca. My parents said you can use the apartment as long as you like. You can live here for free and teach English, and I would come visit you. You would save a lot by not paying rent. And you could still draw in your spare time."

"In my spare time." She considered the cement block edifice with its mixed message logo.

"Or you could stay in Florence. Maybe Aunt Simonetta knows someone who would rent you a cheap room. Maybe even free, if you cooked and cleaned for them. Then when I finish my exams next year we can start making plans."

The idea of cooking and cleaning for one of Aunt Simonetta's cranky lady friends made Ada's hair stand on end. Those old women made salmon-stuffed ravioli, hand-tossed pizzas with homemade tomato sauce. They waxed their marble floors and ironed their underwear.

"I'm an artist, Cristian."

"So get a permit and set up a stand outside the Uffizi. Do watercolors of the city, or portraits for the tourists. You could do that, I know you could. And remember that guy on the corner? The one who did caricatures? He had a line of people waiting."

"I'm a real artist. I was thinking New York City."

Cristian eyed her with a thoughtful expression. Silence hung between them for a moment. "Ah," he said. "So that's it."

"I'm thinking about my career."

He didn't mention that they had talked about finding a little apartment in the hills. Or Ada's idea of working under the table as a Florentine tour guide. Or the myriad other solutions she had proposed just that past spring. All the possible ways to stay in Italy and plan for their future. He took her arm and they went on walking. But doubt settled around them like a chilly shroud, silencing their conversation.

That night, from their makeshift double bed, Ada kept her ear half-cocked for the light thump of feet swinging up onto the balcony in the other room. Though she knew he would never appear. Even if he had, there was no entry—Cristian had closed and latched the shutters tight, then shut the door to his parents' bedroom. They were sealed in their own little space now, the way they had always been.

In the morning, Cristian loaded coffee into the aluminum coffeemaker, tamped it down to make it stronger, and brewed it on the stove. He went to the bakery while Ada slept and brought back the chocolate-filled pastries that she liked, as well as the same apricot-filled croissants that Gisele had tossed on the table before Michel. Perhaps he had bought them from the same bakery. Perhaps he had stood next to Gisele at the counter. Ada thought about that other morning as they ate in lazy bites, she in the chair where Michel had read his French romance, Cristian where she had leaned over to offer Michel a fig.

"I'm running out of money," she said over her coffee.

Cristian gave her that quizzical look. "I know. You told me that already."

"I have to make a decision."

"I told you, my parents said you can stay here as long as you need to."

"This place will be a ghost town in the winter. And I don't know how to teach English. I don't know anything about grammar." They'd already had this conversation, but she kept talking. "I need to find a job in my field."

Cristian rapped his fingers on the table once and set his pastry aside. "What is it, Ada? Eh? *Cosa c'è?* You look different. Something about you is changed."

To her horror, Ada began to spout tears, and it was all she could do to choke down the chocolate in her mouth. "I'm worried," she blubbered. "I have to make the right choice."

Crying made Cristian calm and efficient. He pulled up a chair next to Ada, took both her hands in his, and brought his face close to hers. "You will make the right choice," he said firmly. "But you must be clear and logical. You must be reasonable. Do you understand?"

She did not. "I've been all alone here with nothing to do but think about my future. I can't make a mistake."

"You will not make a mistake, Ada. You haven't made any mistakes yet, have you?"

She shrugged. "No one knows they've made a mistake until it happens."

"Not if you are reasonable. Not if you are serene and logical." It was an argument straight out of the Enlightenment.

"Otherwise I'll end up back in Buffalo working at the bookstore."

"Ada, *bellissima*, you are educated and intelligent. You know what to do. I'm convinced you will do the right thing."

Her own weak-kneed outburst unnerved her, but Cristian's firm confidence was even more rattling.

"I hope I do the right thing, Cristian." Ada leaned her head into his big chest and he wrapped his arms around her. "Maybe I just need some time to think. Maybe I just need some time alone."

He kissed the top of her head and ran his familiar fingers down her back. "So," he said in his organized voice, "why don't I go make a copy of this key, and you can finish your breakfast. Put a chair out on the balcony and listen to the fountain. The water sounds nice, doesn't it?"

Ada groaned. "Yes, yes. But I don't want to sit there. I don't want to sit on that balcony at all." She caught herself. "I want to sit on the front steps in the sun."

"Those steps are dirty. But all right, sit on the steps. I will get us a nice bottle of wine too, for later. How is that?"

"Good," she sniffled. She nuzzled his warm neck, her lashes and cheeks wet. "Get white wine."

They stood on the front steps and kissed before he left. Then they kissed again, and yet again, pressing up close.

"We'll take a nap this afternoon," he murmured with a frisky smile. "Eh?"

"Mmmm," Ada said. "A nap."

He brushed away a lingering tear with his thumb. "*Ciao, bellissima.* I'll be back in a little while."

Ada sank barefoot onto the warm stone steps. The sun prickled the sweat up from her scalp. Her eyes were swollen and her stomach shaky. She did not feel as if she had cried enough, but the tears stayed locked up, pushing at her from the inside. Pulling her knees to her chest, Ada clasped her hands around her shins and stared moodily out into the street.

She shot up straight when she saw Marion sidle past the house with her vagrant's walk.

"Hi, Ada," she called in the languid drawl of a California valley girl.

"Marion. Hi."

Marion stood at the base of the steps and beamed at Ada. Her black hair was tied back into a neat ponytail and she was dressed in a girlish pink cotton outfit with high-heeled white sandals. She carried a little white leather handbag over her shoulder, and she'd pushed a pair of big pink sunglasses onto her head. Her lips gleamed with a summery rose-colored gloss and her black-lined, green-shadowed eyes surveyed Ada with an exotic gaze that marked her as a member of that family on the hill.

"Is this your house?"

"This is where I'm staying, yes."

Marion gave Ada a smug smile. "My brother told me."

"Well, come on up."

Marion rushed over with undisguised eagerness, then settled beside Ada with an unceremonious plop. She laid her handbag neatly on her lap.

"It's a good thing you were out here. I wasn't supposed to knock."

"Oh? What were you supposed to do?"

A sly look flitted across her face. "You said you would draw me. And my brother told me you really are an artist. He said you really do know how to draw. And I'm going to Paris soon. I won't be here much longer."

"Paris?"

She sighed and smiled, fingering the gold clasp on her little white handbag. "My mother kicked me out. I'm going to live with my father and his wife Claire and my half-sister."

"You're kicked out now?"

"Well, not exactly right now." She delicately fiddled with the ponytail. "But my mother is going to Washington with my brother, and she wouldn't want me spoiling their little party." A mean glint came into her eye. "And I wouldn't go anyway. I'm sick of them both. So she said go live with your father if you think we're so bad. And I said fine, and he's going to let me stay with him and Claire. So I'm going to Paris where it's beautiful, where it's fabulous actually, and they can run off to Washington together and good riddance."

Her speech seemed to leave her breathless, with an odd little catch to her voice. But then she opened her mouth and gulped air, staring down at the sunny steps. "But Michel said you might draw me before I left. He showed me the picture of the cathedral with the face in the fire, and that one of you as Medusa, with snakes in your hair. I wouldn't want a creepy picture like that, but Michel was right, it really looked like you and probably you could draw me a different way."

"Did he tell you to come here?"

They eyed each other.

"Why, are you busy?" Marion smiled with her mouth. Not with her eyes.

"Well," Ada said, "I have things to do. When do you leave for Paris?"

"Soon." Her voice dripped with pleasure. "I'm leaving before they do. My father is getting the plane ticket. I think I want to fly from Nice. I want to shop for clothes in Monte Carlo first. My father goes to a lot of parties and I'll be invited, so I'll need clothes."

"All right. Maybe we can find time before you leave . . ."

"What do you mean, maybe? You told me you would draw me. Were you lying?"

Ada threw up her hands. "I can't just jump up and do a portrait on the spot."

"I'll pay you." Marion clutched her white handbag again. "I brought money."

"It's not the money." Ada turned on her calm voice, the one she used for professors and scholarship people. Her mature voice. "But I would need time, and you're leaving soon—"

"I'm going to have it framed so I can bring it to Paris." Marion spoke with a note of urgency. "My father's birthday is soon. It's going to be a present."

She could have done it, as she had done Gisele's. It would be easy. But Ada did not know how she could explain Marion to Cristian.

"Marion," she said firmly, "I'll have to check my schedule and see what I can do."

Marion looked Ada square in the eye now, thick nostrils flaring and big jaw set in the same stubborn angle as her brother's. "And I can tell you things you'd like to know. Things about my brother." Her defiant chin tilted up and the corners of her eyes narrowed. She blinked slowly, like a crouching cat. "There are things you need to know."

Ada leaned forward, silent, and took her measure. Marion blinked again, eyes fixed on Ada.

"All right," Ada said. "All right. Let's do it tomorrow."

Marion relaxed with a satisfied smirk. "Good. I knew you'd agree."

"Let's meet after lunch at the end of the promenade, where the free beach starts. There's a fish stand there. Two o'clock."

Marion licked her fingers and smoothed her ponytail again, eyes half shut as if she were about to break into a contented purr. "All right, then."

They stood at the same time. There was nothing more to say, at least not yet.

"See you tomorrow."

Marion slipped the white handbag back over a pink shoulder. "At two o'clock. Shall I say hello to Michel?"

"Sure. Hello to Michel."

She sauntered off on her little heeled sandals.

TWENTY-TWO

That night, as they lay sweating against each other in bed, Ada told Cristian she would go to the Wall Street Institute the next afternoon. "Right after lunch," she promised. "I'll see what they say." She nuzzled against his hard chest.

"Good," he said. "Good, good. Maybe it won't work, but at least you will ask."

"At least I'll ask."

"I'll come visit you. And maybe my mother will visit you some time too. I think she'd want to."

"So I can't sleep in her bed?"

"You can't sleep in her bed. You want to, don't you?"

"I don't know. Maybe. And anyway, they wouldn't be here. Come on, Cristian, she'd never know."

He chuckled, but the response was firm: "That's their room. It wouldn't be respectful."

The next day, when Cristian was in the shower, Ada packed her paper, pencils, erasers and a drawing board in a big cloth beach bag and hid them under a towel. Then she pulled off the towel—what did it matter? —drawing was what she did. But today maybe it was different. Was it suspicious? Normal? She tucked the towel back over the supplies and threw her sunglasses on top. Perhaps Cristian could have told her whether it was a good idea to draw Marion in exchange for information about her brother. Whether she should have that information. Whether she'd be sorry later. She could almost imagine asking his advice.

But Cristian was paying no attention when she left—it was a hot day and he was lounging in his swimsuit with a glass of pear nectar, waiting for his food to digest so he could go to the beach.

"I'll meet you there," Ada said. "Down by the rocks. I'm going to come back here and change first."

"Don't lose that new key."

She liked the tiny swimsuit and his big tanned chest and curly hair, and so she kissed him. "Aaar," she murmured finally, extricating herself, "I have to go or I'll be late."

"For what?" Hands up under her shirt again. "You don't have an appointment."

Giggles. Hands everywhere. "If—I—don't—go—now—aaar—I'll never get out of here."

"*Va bene*," he said with a sigh. "I'll get you later."

Ada dashed out, body still tingling.

Marion was there by the fish stand wearing the wobbly white sandals under a pair of skin tight jeans and a frilly sleeveless top. Another Paris outfit on an incongruous body. She'd pinned her hair back with two tortoiseshell barrettes. She held a cigarette at her side like a delinquent. She looked surprised to see Ada, like a person who believed she was going to be stood up.

"Ciao, Marion. Here I am."

Marion took a tug from the cigarette and composed herself. "Good, you're on time." Her tone was rude and brusque, but the young eagerness in her eyes made Ada be kind.

"Ready to make your dad a present?"

It was as if she'd stroked an anxious cat. Marion straightened her chin and gave Ada a brave smile.

"I hope so."

Ada took her to the pier. A safe distance from the free beach, it stretched out to sea from the promenade like a silvery gray plank, anchoring a little marina dotted with white-sailed pleasure craft and an occasional fishing boat. Ada liked the sound of the slapping water and the briny smell. And the light was interesting at this time of the day, when the sun was tilting towards the western horizon where Monaco and Antibes snaked into shadowy purple curves, while the invisible shore of Tuscany crouched hot and golden in the other direction, from Pisa to Livorno to Grosseto, all the way to the hills cradling the familiar domes of Florence farther inland. Marion could sit cross-legged on the smooth wood, the sea at her back, and lean against a splintered post, charcoal hair set off by mottled sapphire water. Ada would draw her straight on to catch the broad cheekbones, the smart, greedy mouth and sulky eyes. It would be an easy portrait.

"Do you look like your father?"

"I look exactly like him."

"But you have your mother's eyes and her beautiful hair."

Her eyes grew flat as a reptile's. "I don't look like her."

Ada started drawing. "I don't look like my mother either. Or my father. I'm a changeling." Marion didn't know the word. "You know, like a magical being. A fairy. Someone who doesn't belong in the family."

"A pariah," Marion offered. "That's what you call it."

About halfway through the portrait, Ada decided to add some Renaissance-style architectural details to the background that she thought would impress Marion and make the drawing grander. Her snooty features called for distant rivers and gentle rolling hills dotted with domes and spires. Ada would have put a wimple on her if she could.

As Ada grew silent and engrossed with her task, Marion's face turned into a puzzle of light and dark, angles and intersections. The matchless beauty of form. As always, the stroke of soft graphite on paper gave her a visceral thrill, like running her fingers down someone's body, along bone and tendon and pliant flesh. And yet, this time the face rolled off her pencil with such ease that it almost seemed wrong. As if she were missing something, only skimming the surface. As if she had failed to reveal the subtle geometry of this soul. Ada had a sudden unpleasant memory of Professoressa Garavoglia holding a cigarette in her bony ringed hand, lip curled with distaste. It rattled her so much that she had to stop for a moment. For an instant she forgot who she was.

Later, Ada held up the drawing for Marion to see. Marion sprang to her feet, bouncy with anticipation and impatience. When she snatched it, Ada felt a tug of regret. A queasy sensation that she'd done the girl a disservice.

"It's me!" Marion cried, triumphant. "You put hills and churches in the background."

"Renaissance style."

Marion stared at it, lips slack with desire. "My brother will hate it."

"What? Why?"

Marion lowered her eyelids and feigned a bored expression. "Oh," she said, affecting her brother's cadence, "so derivative." She giggled. "What an idiot, right? What counts is that I love it, and I'm the customer. I can't wait to show him—he didn't think you'd even do it. Probably because he thinks I'm not as perfect as him and his perfect little mama. Why draw me, when you could draw him and his mama all cozied up?" She brandished the portrait at Ada. "But what does he know, mister hot shit art lover?"

It felt physical, as if Marion had slapped her. As if Marion had slapped her twice. Ada wanted to take the drawing back and throw it into the sea. And yet she was fumbling and inarticulate, so wrung out in post-creative collapse that she lacked the strength to respond.

Marion sat down and scooted so close that their crossed knees touched. Still clutching the portrait pinned to the drawing board, she leaned over with furtive excitement. "I saw that other drawing you did. In that bed. He hid it, but I found it. He was in your bed, wasn't he? Wasn't he?"

Ada watched her, speechless.

"Do you like Michel?"

Ada opened and closed her mouth like a fish. "I do."

Marion licked her lips. "He likes you too. I can tell." She leaned away from Ada, as if to gauge her reaction. "But he's never told you about his mama, has he?" The sun was behind her head now, illuminating wisps of hair around her face and darkening her eyes into shadows. Too much time had passed. The afternoon had slipped away.

"Is she sick?" Ada asked. It was hard to pull the words from her throat.

"She'll never let you have him."

"What?"

Marion drew so close that Ada could see the enlarged pores around her nose. "He's hers." Her face looked hard and foxy. "I told you I knew something about my brother. Are you listening?"

Ada's breath grew shallow. When she reached up to push her hair from her face, her hand shook.

"But he let you do that drawing of him. The drawing in that bed." Her voice came out fast and breathy, as if she had rehearsed the words. "If he let you do that, something could happen. Something that hasn't happened before. But now they're going to Washington, just the two of them, and nothing different will happen unless you come for him. I think he wants you to. Do you understand? Are you listening?"

Ada could not articulate one single word.

"Do you understand?" Marion repeated with a hint of urgency. "Maybe you should come for him. He likes you. I know he does." She stared into her lap. "Maybe I do too."

Ada felt her spine collapsing.

Marion drew back as if she'd caught a whiff of sewage. "I know he's an idiot! I know he's disgusting! All right? I know it!"

Ada collected herself, clasping her hands together to stop the shaking. "I don't believe you."

Marion's mouth twisted. She ran a hand across her eyes. "He used to make me breakfast when we were little. When she wouldn't. He made me toast and hot chocolate. He still does, sometimes. He can make American pancakes in animal shapes, giraffes and elephants with blueberry eyes." Her voice was hollow. "I don't care whether you believe me. Come over and see for yourself. And then you can decide what to do."

Ada opened her mouth, but she was mute, struck dumb as a stone.

Marion sighed with sudden impatience, her face settling into a hard mask. "Do you want me to pay for this drawing or what?"

"No," Ada blurted. "No." She fumbled for words. "It's—it's my going away present. Let me unclip it and roll it up for you."

Marion took the drawing with delicate fingers, as if she feared she might crush it, and held it close to her chest. "I don't care whether you have that boyfriend. Come anyway."

By the time Ada got to the free beach it was late afternoon. The crowds had thinned, and only a few scattered clumps of people still sprawled in the slanting sun, or sat up with their shirts on, getting ready to pack up and drift back to their homes or lodgings, their kitchens or trattoria plans for the evening. Ada wandered down to the shore in a half-hearted search for Cristian, though she knew he wouldn't be there. Her brain still felt stretched and beaten, her body tingling with Marion's words. She wanted to fall asleep under an umbrella and have a dream.

But she went back to the apartment instead, where she found Cristian, now fully clothed, sitting on a chair out on the balcony reading a comic book, which he slapped shut when he saw her.

"Well, well, there you are."

"I didn't find you at the beach."

"I left an hour ago. And the language school said you were never there."

Ada slid down to sit cross-legged on the tiles. "I changed my mind. I don't want to work there. I've been drawing all afternoon. I was down at the pier and I lost track of time."

"So while you lost track of time, I had a visit from a couple of friends of yours. Both of them wearing too much makeup. And one of them—what is he, a pickpocket, a gypsy?—he brought me something for you." He stood up, fished in his back pocket, and pulled out the key to the apartment. He dangled it in front of her. "*Ecco*. Recognize this?"

"*Porca puttana!*" Ada gasped. "Where did he get that?"

"You tell me. He said he'd been meaning to bring it over. And I don't think he lives down the sewer grate. *Che cazzo,* what the fuck, Ada, what the fuck were you talking about, what really happened with that key?"

"I can't believe it. Holy fucking shit, I can't believe it. I didn't know he had it. I don't know where he found it."

Cristian tossed the key up and snapped it back into his fist in one sharp, belligerent motion. Ada had never seen him so angry.

"And I don't like him. I don't like him. I wouldn't want him in my house. Fucking gypsies, they'd rob you blind."

"He's not a gypsy."

"He looks like a fucking gypsy. He looks like he's dressed up for fucking Carnival. And he had my key. You gave him my key."

"I did not give him your key."

"So where did he get it?"

Ada covered her eyes with her hands. "I don't know where he got it!" A panicked parade of images whizzed through her mind. Maybe he'd picked it up on the street outside the Casa Bianca. Maybe it fell out of her pocket that first night at Gisele's. Maybe he slipped his hand in and took it. Perhaps he'd intended to rob her and been foiled by her poverty. Or perhaps he'd gotten just what he wanted. And perhaps, perhaps, now he wanted more.

"So what's going on? I've been gone for two weeks and now all of a sudden everything stinks. You tell me you're going to apply for a job and then you disappear all afternoon. I waited for you at the beach. All of a sudden your plans are changed, you can't decide what you want anymore. These slimy people come nosing around and one of them's got my key and I can tell he's looking for you. *Porca madonna*, Ada, what is this?"

"I don't know. I don't know what it is. Those people—where did they go?"

"How should I know? I didn't invite them in for tea."

"All right. All right. I need to go—sort this out." Ada hauled herself back up to her feet and leaned against the wrought iron railing. The sound of the water nymph fountain pattering softly on stone calmed her.

Cristian collected himself. Later she would learn about men like him—it was not their nature to fight, and they especially disliked battles with words. They liked simplicity and transparency. They found her attractive because they thought she was exotic. And maybe she was, compared to them. But the attraction would only be temporary. In the end, they would make their families with less complex women, with women who never lose the key.

"Ada." He clasped her face in his hands. He smelled good and familiar. She wanted to kiss him, but she didn't. "Ada. You have to tell me what's going on. I know something is going on. I don't know what it is, but I know it's something. Will you tell me?"

She embraced him, but they were both shivering away from each other like two opposing magnets.

"I'm going to find them," she said. "I want to know where he got that key. I want to know why he kept it."

"Do you want me to go with you?"

She did not.

So Cristian kissed the top of her head, and he asked her no more questions, and he let her go.

The Muse

TO THE SPRING

Sylvia Gilbertson

TWENTY-THREE

Gisele was home alone in a tiny red skirt, wearing no makeup. Her lashes were washed-out, almost transparent, her eyes pale and northern and foreign. She'd answered the door immediately, as if she were expecting the visit, and now she drew a cigarette to colorless lips.

"He's not here," she said.

"So where is he?"

Gisele threw up her hands, ran pallid fingers through prickly hair. "I'm sorry, all right? I didn't know he was going to do that. I didn't know he had your key. He said you wanted us to stop by. "

"He is full of shit. Where is he? Is he here?"

"No, no, he went home. We picked up a prescription for his mother and he was going to take it home."

Ada pointed her finger at Gisele. "He better not be here. You better not be covering for him."

Gisele took a fierce tug from the cigarette. "I'm sick of this. Everyone thinks I know what he's doing. Everyone thinks I know what he's thinking. Everyone thinks I know where he is. Well damn it, I don't know any more than you do, all right? " She jabbed the smoky cigarette at Ada. "What I know is that he left. I think he was going home. He had the prescription. And that's it. This is how it is with him. I've known him for years, and you just have to take him as he is."

"I'll take him as he is, all right. If you see him before I do, you tell him I'm looking for him. You tell him I'll be waiting for him when he gets home. Tell him I'll find him."

Halfway down the stairs, Ada stopped. Gisele leaned over the landing, fiery hair poking up all around her head and pale face. She curled her hands around the railing and stared down at Ada, silent.

With no money for a taxi, Ada had to walk all the way up the hill. Twilight gathered in the street corners, seeping into the store fronts and staining the horizon pearl and silver. Little puffs of heat still wafted from the sidewalk, and the approaching dusk was a relief, like a splash of cool water on the neck. Ada was bare-armed, wearing her orange summer skirt. Her unbraided hair tumbled against her shoulders, delicate and still sun-warmed, and the skirt grazed her naked legs. Every cell felt alive and alert, long-dormant synapses sizzling like sparklers. The shock jolted her forward, plunging her toward the future.

The lavender house lay silent behind the gate, but lights were on upstairs and down. The heady scent of jasmine drifted out to the street. Ada pressed the bell and held it down. She let go and pressed again. And then again. And then she waited. And then pressed again. For the first time, she noticed the camera focused on her from the top of the gate. She pressed the bell again. Somewhere it had to be making noise.

The gate clanked suddenly with a whir and a sigh, then opened in a long, slow-motion inward glide. Ada was able to slip in before the gate stopped moving. She was on the cobblestone drive now, surrounded by slim dark poplars and bristling bushes, the shadowy sentinels of the rich. She skittered up the drive to the house, wondering if anyone would be there to greet her. Wondering who had seen her and let her in.

The big double doors were thrown open before she reached them. Out stepped Marion, transformed back into the slovenly teenager Ada remembered. Her neat ponytail was twisted out of place, probably when she carelessly pulled a sweatshirt over her head, and she was barefoot in a pair of ripped and wrinkled jeans. She surveyed Ada with cool bemusement.

"You didn't have to ring so many times. It takes a while to get to the door from my room."

"Is he here?"

Marion gave Ada a devilish smile.

"I believe he just might be home. But he's on medical duty. You want to finish that gelato? We'll have time."

"I want to see him."

"I told you, he's busy. You'll have to wait. It could be a while. It could be all night."

"Marion! This isn't a joke."

Marion crooked her finger at Ada and headed into the kitchen, which was as silent and spotless as the last time, but now with silky pink tea roses in the crystal vase. She flopped onto a chair and propped her feet up on another one.

"There is no way," she said, "that I am going up there to get him."

Ada folded her arms and reflected, then slammed her fist down on the table next to Marion. The shock traveled all the way up to her elbow like a jolt of electricity. Marion jumped and lost the cool expression.

"I need to talk to your brother and I'm not waiting all night to do it. You wanted me to come over, and now I'm here. That's what you wanted, isn't it? So go up there and get him. Or do you want me to go find him myself?"

Marion swung her feet to the ground, bare toes slapping on the tiles.

"She has a migraine," she said, as if addressing a stupid child. "He is taking care of it. Sometimes he needs all night to take care of it."

"Not tonight he won't." Ada marched out into the hallway and found her way back to the silent living room with the leather furniture. The curtains were drawn, and just one small lamp glowed on a burnished teak table in a corner. The staircase lay at the other end, bathed in shadow, though its walls glittered dimly with Oriental tapestries. The air was dead and breathless, almost as if the house were abandoned. Ada put her foot on the first step and peered up, but the stairs curved away into darkness and she saw no light above.

"Michel," she said, but her voice dropped with a thud. She kicked the step, then stamped on it, then smacked her hand hard against the rail. It shook something loose in her. "Michel!" It came out louder now. "Michel! Come down here!"

Nothing but silence above her.

"Michel! You need to come down now!"

The whole house seemed frozen and listening, but there was no response.

"If you don't come down, I'm coming up!" Ada advanced two

tentative steps. Only inky blackness lay ahead.

"Michel?" She climbed a little further, till the darkness began to envelop her. The tapestries were Indian. She could see the languorous blue form of Krishna surrounded by maidens.

"All right, Michel, I'm coming up. Do you hear me?"

Ada didn't want to ascend those stairs, so she made noise. She thumped her feet against the wood molding and pounded a fist against the wall. She cleared her throat and coughed. But she was halfway up now. The light was gone and the silence complete.

"Michel." Her voice sounded closer, muffled by the narrow channel of stairs, and seemed to funnel upward. "I'm coming up."

Then she heard a door open and close above her. She drew in her breath and froze. Seconds ticked by.

"Michel?" she called out again, quieter this time. She heard quick footsteps above her. As she squinted into the darkness, Michel suddenly appeared at the top of the stairs.

"Get down here," she said.

He threaded his stealthy way down the steps till they were face to face. His clothes were rumpled and his hair awry. He looked like someone who'd just escaped a massacre. Or witnessed hand-to-hand combat.

"What are you doing here?" He spoke in a tense whisper.

"And you, what were you doing at my apartment with my key?"

He made a small, helpless gesture. "Not now." Yet he leaned toward her. She could feel the force of his aura bending toward her, opening. And it gave her the courage to grab him by the shoulders and give him a rough shake. Caught by surprise, he snapped to attention.

"Now," Ada said. "Right now. And what are you doing up there, anyway?"

His eyes grew hostile, then blank, and he tensed away from her, as if preparing to scuttle back into the darkness. Ada jumped at him and yanked his hair hard. His blank expression vanished as a little knot of hair ripped away, but now panic seemed to take its place.

"You are coming with me," Ada said. "Now." She clung to the hair with her fist, twining her fingers around it, and he put his arms up like a man surrendering. "Downstairs," Ada said. "We're going outside now." Some softness in her wanted to let go of his hair—he looked like a starving wild animal, an earthquake victim. But something else—some reptilian instinct, some sense of red alert, would not let her release him until the danger was past, until they had flown out the door and into the street. So she dragged him by the hair down the stairs. She herself felt like a savage little beast, spitting with anger as she pulled him out of his territory onto her own turf. Where he would have to play by her rules.

By the time they reached the bottom of the stairs, the magnetic allure of the danger above had already weakened. Ada let go, though she shoved him from behind, her hand slapping so hard between his shoulder blades that he stumbled forward in surprise. Yet he had stopped protesting. He had stopped speaking or hesitating or reacting at all.

She did not know if Marion saw them leaving. They went past the kitchen, Ada pressing him from behind, but Ada had forgotten Marion by then. Perhaps she watched them slip out the door and away. Perhaps she went to the window and watched them scamper past the slow gates creaking open to let two furtive figures through. Perhaps she watched them vanish into the dark.

The snap went out of Ada as soon as they rounded the corner that put his house out of sight. She felt breathless, as if she'd fallen down a long flight of steps, and when she brushed against Michel, she felt his arm shaking. Then she realized that his whole body was shivering. She grabbed his forearm and they stopped in the black shade of a brooding tree.

"What is happening?" she asked.

He placed his palms over his eyes for one long moment, then slid them over his temples and down the back of his head and neck, as if he were trying to pop his skull open.

"Let's go to Gisele's," he said.

Gisele wasn't home. Ada saw that Michel had a key for Gisele's place too, or at least he knew where she'd hidden it within a little crevice in the building's façade. The first thing Michel did was retreat to the bathroom. When he finally reemerged, his hair was combed, his clothing straightened, and he had the fresh wet look of someone who has just washed his face.

"Better?" Ada had curled up on the orange sofa to contemplate the glittery comet of glass shards streaking across the wall. She had been glad of the closed shutters, the neatly ordered bookshelves, the clean floor, the heavy, enclosed air. The sense of refuge. But the sight of Michel, standing there in the doorway looking like a deer about to bolt, made her skittish again. And he still wasn't speaking.

She tried one more time. "Why did you steal my key? You got me in a lot of trouble."

Head down, he folded his arms and wandered into the living room. But he kept his distance. "You got me in a lot of trouble too," he said into the floor.

"I don't think so. I think I might have gotten you out of trouble."

He glanced at her and scowled. "You don't know anything."

"You want a bodyguard or not? Make up your mind."

He backed up to the wall across from her and slid down, folding up on the floor into something resembling exhaustion. Then he stretched his legs out, let his arms flop, tilted his head back, and closed his eyes with a great sigh.

"You should take me away."

"That's what Marion told me."

His eyes flew open.

"She said you'd want me to."

Ada couldn't tell whether he was laughing or crying. "Ah," he finally responded. "Little sister, little sister. That's why you came, then."

"She said I'm supposed to take you away from your mother. And that you would want me to do that."

Now his face grew hooded, his mouth mean and stubborn. Ada waited for an answer. He looked at her with the remoteness of a Byzantine fresco, silent and glittering and flat.

"You want me to take you away from your mother, Michel?"

His face became impassive. But he averted his eyes. The pall of silence hung denser, cloaked him in gray. Ada stretched out on the orange sofa, her arm draped over the seat back, and watched him stew. She remembered what Cristian had said that first time they had ever seen him.

"You're just a big mama's boy? I'm supposed to tear you from her arms?"

"Shut *up*."

Finally she could hear the fury. It was a relief, like clear cold winter air whipping across her face. Perhaps it felt that way to him too.

"I don't believe Marion." Though she was not sure what she

believed anymore.

He raised his eyebrows in mock surprise. "Really."

She saw him standing disheveled at the top of the stairs, his shirttail out, hair on end, the distance in his eyes and the panic at seeing her there. The absolute silence in the darkness above him. And now, as he collapsed on the floor before her, he curled into a ball and bent his head so she could not see his face. He shrank into himself.

"Michel."

Ada lurched off the sofa onto the floor. Leaning back on her heels, she scrutinized him hunched up like a child against the wall. Then she crawled over and sat before him, hands on his feet in their ridiculous dress shoes. He looked at her then, unraveling before her like loose yarn.

And Ada abandoned all reason. Like a lovesick putto hovering over the adored one, Ada put her hands on his head and breathed him in. And then she melted, turned liquid, flowed into him like a trickling stream into the mother river. She swelled like a wild mountain brook after the rain.

"Tell me what you were doing up there."

"You'll save me," he said.

"Tell me what I'm saving you from."

"I'm a good son. She's all alone."

She tried to lift his head to look at him, but he wouldn't let her. He did let her keep her hands on him. He let her move close and slip them down the back of his neck and under his collar, though his breath felt tight and ragged.

"So," she whispered in his ear, "I'm going to save you from being a good son."

His whole body shuddered. But now he raised his head and looked at her, their noses just inches apart. His eyes were clear and cool.

"I don't think so." He grew limp, sliding out of her grasp and collapsing onto the floor in a heap.

Ada did not heed his words. Instead, she took in his image. She saw the life punched out of him, the spectacle of his surrender, as if it were one of those giant passionate canvases of ancient battlefields. As if she could step into the painting and take him prisoner, carry him off like a sack of golden plunder. As if he really had capitulated to her.

Michel lay in silence for a few moments. Then, unexpectedly, he rolled over on his back and threw his arms up over his head in an almost casual gesture, as if he'd been relaxing on the floor instead of flirting with disintegration.

"Do you believe in luck?" he asked. His sweet coy look made her want to jump on him.

"I believe in planning."

"Well, I just realized that I have something." He fished into his back pocket. "Look at what I have. My bank card. This is luck." Still stretched out on the floor, he waved it at Ada with a radiant smile. "I can get money with this."

"Money for what, Michel?"

"I can get train tickets with this."

"And who's going to use the train tickets?"

"My bodyguard and I."

Ada contemplated him in silence.

"You and I," he said, chastened.

"And where would we be going?"

"A secret place. A place you'll like."

She thought about that. If she went home tonight, she could still salvage the vacation home in Rocca, perhaps a chilly shared apartment in Florence, perhaps, one day, a stone house in the hills of Tuscany. The doors were still open. The past two weeks could be considered an aberration. The vine that was rooted in her heart, snaking, wrapping around that elusive man on the floor, could still be plucked out and left behind. Could it not?

Yet beauty gushed from him like a fountain, an abundance offered to slake all thirst if she would but partake of it. If she would but risk allowing it to course through her, to saturate her until it spilled out to quench the dry lands and bring the fallow fields to life. If she would but drink, drink, drink.

And she could not put that possibility back on the shelf. Not this time.

She moved over and sat on top of him, hands pressing hard on his shoulders. He grew wary and vacant again, as if playing dead, so she leaned over into his face and gave him a little shake.

"Michel," she said, "if you don't make this worth my while, I'm going to kill you. I'll rip your head off. Do you understand?"

He looked worried. "You'll see. Ada, you'll see." Then, in a much smaller, distant voice, he added, "It isn't that far. New York City and Washington." He squeezed his eyes shut and expelled a little sigh. As if he meant it. As if, at that moment, he meant it.

So she kissed him, and he even kissed her back, that time.

TWENTY-FOUR

His plan was to take her to Valsesia, a mountainous, verdant region between Milan and Turin that was cloaked in forests and traversed by veins of burbling streams. There, in an abandoned village near a place called Monte Fenera, where the ground had once been tilled and cattle had once grazed, he owned a tiny stone cottage without proper heat or electricity. He owned it free and clear.

He spoke of it with the seductive tongue of a sorcerer. Words spilling from him like ripe fruit, he described waterfalls sliding like liquid glass from rocky cliffs padded with brilliant green moss, and the lilting cries of cuckoos that echoed from the hills and valleys in the spring. The coltsfoot and butterbur that lined the riverbanks, the sweet cicely that sprang up in the mottled shade, the woodland floors speckled with wild cyclamen and black hellebore in late winter and early spring. The amanita muscaria mushroom—that red and white spotted hallucinogenic poison of the wise women and children's fairy tales—grew in secret places there. And the land itself was old, its energy buried deep. It had turned away from humans long ago, perhaps because it had seen too much blood. Witches had been burned there, battles fought, serfs worked to death, partisans and fascists hunted and killed in mountain valleys and high alpine meadows.

It was almost like listening to the back-to-the-land version of Marion's breathless hymn to Paris.

"So." Ada picked her words carefully. "How long a trip will this be?"

Michel just raised his brows and looked perplexed, as if he had not considered the matter. As if it were of no importance. As if he had decided not to go to Washington, and they were standing still in time and needed to make no further plans ever again. Or perhaps he remembered the hypnotic dance floor in that dark country town, the electronic version of a two hundred year old hut in a witchy mountain valley—perhaps he knew the matter was already settled.

And, of course, it was. The strange journey beckoned like some sweet sylvan incubus. Like the disembodied voice of a painted canvas calling her to the dark wellspring below. To the voice on the wind above. To the source.

And Ada, who had embraced the chilly victory of technique in her war on insignificance, who had implemented her battle plan with the fierce desperate cunning of a fox in the trap, for the first time abandoned her ruse, or her senses, softened and twisted the paw in some untried way and found that it miraculously slipped free, making the whole vast forest suddenly accessible, all its ripe offerings spilled before her like a luscious still life—the beauty of the fluttering leaves, the possibility of the changing seasons, the mystery of the waxing and waning moons, and the shining eyes of its secret inhabitants, her unseen companions along the way. Beyond victory, beyond defeat.

And now unchained, giddy with the scent of revolution, Ada returned to the apartment and let herself in, that one last time, with the now unneeded key that Cristian had made for her, and a tale of mystical mountains on her lips.

Cristian was waiting in the kitchen, sprawled on one chair with legs propped up on another as he watched one of those Italian variety shows full of busty starlets with indifferent talent. Ada was grateful for the noise.

"Ciao, Ada."

"Ciao, Cristian."

There was a silence. She sat down at the table across from him. She had touched Michel's fig-stained hand from that chair. Now Cristian sat in his place, all anger drained away.

"So, did you get things straightened out?"

Ada hesitated. "Well, I don't know where he found the key. I'm not sure if he found it in the street or if he took it out of my pocket. And I don't know why he brought it here."

Impatience and disbelief flitted across Cristian's face, but Ada could see that he was trying to be reasonable.

"Well, all right. But—what have you been doing with these people that someone can steal your key?"

"It doesn't matter, Cristian. They could have stolen my key and I wouldn't have known it. But listen—now I have a chance to find out, to figure things out, because this person—this person has invited me to visit a part of Italy I've never seen, in the mountains —"

"What person? What are you talking about?"

"The one with the key—his name is Michel."

Cristian sat up straight. "Wait. You're going somewhere with *him?*"

"Well, I have an invitation, it's important—"

Cristian leaned forward, resting his elbows on the table, and peered at her as if she were some exotic species of insect.

"I don't believe it. No, I don't believe it."

Ada felt naked and dissected. "Just for a few days," she offered faintly.

"Come here." He reached out to take her wrists, pulling her closer to him. His hands were big and familiar, his touch warm but not insistent. Something started to rise up and catch in her throat. It stole her breath, made it hard to talk. It locked down her body. Looking him in the eye was almost excruciating. She opened her mouth to speak, but there was nothing to say.

"Ada."

She shut her jaw tight and held it back.

"Ada. What happened? I wasn't gone that long."

She could see his straight black lashes, the faint stubble on his cheeks, the creases in his familiar lips. She could see the question in his eyes. She owed him an answer.

"I don't know what happened." It came out as little more than a jagged whisper. She could not stand to look at him anymore, so she closed her eyes and squeezed back every tear she might have permitted herself or deserved. She gave herself nothing.

"Are you coming back?" He drew closer to kiss a closed eyelid.

Ada had to look at him now. "I don't know what I'm doing. I don't know, Cristian."

"I do. I know. It's because he looks like one of those statues you love. Like one of those paintings. He makes you think of art."

She thought of Donatello's perfect David. Of Botticelli's Venus and Mars. The sweet promise in Bathsheba's eyes.

And when she packed her bag, she didn't forget her drawing supplies.

"Probably just a few days," she told Cristian at the door.

"Keep the key," he said, "so you can pick up your things later."

His expression was impenetrable, but she felt no judgment from him. He never once made her feel guilty.

TWENTY-FIVE

Ada returned to Gisele's apartment to find that Gisele was back. Flamenco music and rose-scented incense now swirled through the apartment, but Gisele stood stiff and tense at the kitchen door, cigarette in hand, wearing a pair of yellow-heeled sandals that made her tower over both Ada and Michel. It looked like she'd just run nervous fingers through her springy red hair. Apparently Michel had not been content with his ablutions, for he had taken a shower and changed his clothes. He looked damp and clean, T-shirt clinging to wet skin and hair shiny, almost dripping. Up close, he smelled sweet.

"You came back," Michel said.

"Of course I came back," Ada snapped. "And this better be worth it."

Then she burst into tears. She threw her things to the floor and rushed out to the little balcony where she could have her back to them. Big tears plopped down to the street below her. She kicked the wrought iron rails and hurt her toe. Then she gathered herself and rubbed her eyes hard with the heels of her hands till they were dry. But when she felt Gisele's tentative fingers on her shoulder, her throat choked up again.

"You don't have to go with him." Gisele handed Ada a little cloth handkerchief with a white crocheted border.

"I have a nice boyfriend."

Gisele took a long drag on her cigarette, blowing smoke through her nose. "Well. If it's a nice boyfriend you want."

Ada gazed at the pretty scented handkerchief. "I don't want to use

152

this."

"Pah, that's what it's for. I use them, I wash them, I iron them, I put them in the drawer with a bag of lavender. That's what they're for. Blow your nose."

So Ada did. "Do you think I should go? Would you go if you were me?"

Gisele flung the cigarette off the balcony into the street, long red nails glinting. Her mouth twisting into an enigmatic expression, she turned to face Ada.

"Of course I'd go. I know about that place of his, I've seen pictures of it. I remember when he bought it. What do you think? Of course I'd go."

Ada stared down into the street. Rocca was a nice town. It had a clean and rocky sea, rugged stone reefs and beaches of shiny black pebbles glistening in sunlight and water. It would be a nice town to return to in the summer. Having an apartment in Rocca would make a lot of people envious. Ada's sister Emily, for whom even a condo in Alabama was out of reach, would chew up her liver in envy at the little apartment on the via Cavour.

But perhaps Ada was being offered a villa in Rocca, not an apartment, and a cottage in the mountains too. Plus Eros himself in her bed, popping her synapses like firecrackers.

Ada wondered if she could ever bring Michel to the house in Buffalo. The front steps were crumbling. The screen on the door was deformed and let in mosquitoes. There was the velvet painting. Her father watching "Wheel of Fortune." Her mother's baked sweet potatoes with marshmallows and brown sugar.

"Well," she said, still sniffling, "maybe I just have bad taste in men."

Gisele pursed her lips and squinted at Ada. "*Ja*, well, it depends on what you like, no? Some people like red pepper, some don't."

TWENTY-SIX

The very next day they piled onto the train and headed in the direction of Monte Rosa, toward the French border in the mountains. They sat across from each other in the car, each with a separate window, but Ada stretched her leg out so it touched Michel's, and he let her leave it there. He lowered his head and watched her, mouth solemn, but said nothing. She put on her sunglasses and took cover, though she kept her leg against his. Through the protection of the dark glasses, she stole an occasional furtive look. He was always watching her. Guard or guardian, she no longer knew. Finally he closed his eyes and went to sleep, his face transformed into the guileless visage of a contented child.

By late afternoon they had arrived in a small, semi-abandoned train station with just two tracks. Big stone planters held roses and weeds. A pair of bored teenagers slouched on a cement bench in the chilly shade. Oversized white and silver clouds blotted out the sun, then drifted past as the rocky green landscape exploded with light and warmth, till another mass of clouds quenched it.

"Look," said Michel. "We are in the Valsesia."

"It's cold."

"It's clean."

A damp breeze prickled Ada's bare arms. The smell was different. It was grass and dirt and river. "Where are we going?"

Michel looked relaxed and pleased with himself. "We must find a taxi. Then we walk."

He had told her to wear walking shoes with socks and long pants.

154

Now she added a sweatshirt. Sun and shade scudded past as they wandered out of the tiny station. A middle-aged couple wearing hiking boots and backpacks strolled past, and a group of wind-burned young men ate salami sandwiches on the station steps. Then they got in a taxi and left it all behind, skirting by little chalet-shaped timbered houses dotted with boxes of scarlet geraniums, bound for a place where the trains did not go.

The road soon turned narrow and winding, flanked by craggy cliffs soaked with rivulets of running water. Michel opened the taxi window and threw his arm out into the cool, moist air. The wind tossed his hair from his face. He tilted his head up and watched the sky. As they rounded a bend, Ada saw gray-green mountains loom into sight. Drooping pines spiked up toward the sky, blue as any Madonna's robe. A cluster of big black birds circled overhead. The taxi's tires hissed on wet pavement.

"How far is it?"

Michel turned to her with the face of a pilgrim. "Soon we'll be there."

The taxi entered a little hamlet called Fonte, passing old stone houses with chickens out front pecking the dirt. An elderly man with a cane, his crinkled eyes shaded by a fedora, made his delicate way along the road. A sturdy woman in an apron carrying a cloth shopping bag marched across the cobblestone square towards a little general store. The taxi left them in front of a whitewashed church. Swallows dipped and raced around the little bell tower as they stepped out, and a big bumblebee hummed past Ada's nose.

The hamlet was named after the spring behind the church. Flat, narrow stone steps steeped in the shade of drooping fairy tale pines ascended to a shadowy little shrine built over water that bubbled up, sighing, from deep below the earth. Someone had left flowers and votive candles, and a little portrait of a Madonna hung in there too. They could kneel and put their hands in the gurgling water, so cold it made Ada's fingers clench. But Michel brought it to his lips and drank, saying it was miraculous water that cured many ailments. Ada watched him, warming her hands in her armpits.

Afterwards they went to the little general store and bought cheese, salami, prosciutto, fruit, bread, greens, vegetables, wine, water and chocolate, and loaded them into their bags. Ada felt like a pack animal.

"Now," Michel said, "we walk."

The little road past the church and the spring soon faded into a wide track, then narrowed further into a grassy trail that led into a beech wood. A noisy stream burbled somewhere just out of sight. Sometimes water welled up from the ground itself, carried by underground springs. Giant burdock plants sprang up, and spikes of tall horsetail pierced the shade. The hamlet of Fonte vanished behind them. Trees closed in and birds heralded their progress with cries of alarm and fluttering wings. The rushing stream grew nearer, and then they came upon an old wooden footbridge almost touching the water. It creaked and cracked as they crossed. Water cascaded down rocks, some worn smooth and some still raw and sharp from a recent tumble down the mountain. The water was a waxy, translucent green, like the sea. Ada could see every pebble in the stream bed, the glint of every shifting eddy. As they stepped to the other side, ferny fronds of sweet cicely hung thick and soft, and the ground was littered with little beechnuts. Ada's arms and shoulders ached from the weight of the groceries, but she raced to keep up with Michel. He was a dancer in these woods, or maybe some light and delicate animal. And like a dancer, an animal, he moved with a grace that she did not want to disturb.

They had walked like that for over a half hour when he stopped and turned. Ada trotted up, panting, and dropped her bag of bread, peaches, and wine to the ground. Her forehead was damp with sweat.

"Five more minutes," he said. "It's just up ahead, near the stream. Can you hear it now?"

Now that she was still, not breathing so loud, not stumbling so noisily along the moist and stony path, Ada could indeed hear the faint rush of water again. "I hear it."

"It's the same stream. It's curving back toward us." He looked up into the trees. "Have you ever heard of the Wild Hunt?"

The back of her neck prickled. The trees were silent, their smooth trunks soaring skyward and branches outstretched like supplicating arms. "The Wild Hunt," she repeated. Her voice felt muffled, suffocated.

"Ghost riders. Spirits. The old people say when they ride at night, you must lock the doors to protect your children, or they will steal them and take them to the underworld."

Ada swallowed. "It's a strange forest."

Michel took a deep breath, face calm and guileless. "Yes. A good forest."

He walked with less urgency now, but still with the poised, catlike gait she had seen the night he glided across that dance floor into the crowd. As if he were in his own territory again. As if he were home. The sound of water grew louder off to the right, and then suddenly the stream was visible once more, a little wider here, a little less choked with rocks. And then the path itself broadened into a clearing filled with papery white birches and small alders and willow trees. Sun streamed down, illuminating a little cluster of ruined stone buildings with collapsed wooden beams. The stream rushed by, just barely out of sight, but the scent of cold water was almost palpable.

"Look." Michel pointed to the end of the clearing.

Off in the mottled shadows Ada could see an intact terracotta tile roof over rough stone walls.

"My house."

Weeds had grown up, but the ground around the house was bare and cleared, revealing a dark metal door with a big padlock. Dark metal coverings blotted out the windows. Michel produced a big key ring and unlocked the metal door, which swung open to reveal a thick wooden door behind it. This one took a long, old-fashioned key and a sharp tug, and then they fumbled in chilly darkness until he pulled open the shutters. Lemony sunlight flooded in with wafts of warmer air, the scent of mountain summer and water.

It was tiny, just two rooms. But there was a little black wood-burning stove, a propane stove for cooking, a small porcelain sink, an alcove hiding what looked like a real toilet, and an old-fashioned bed with ancient wooden headboard and chaste white linens. Set off by a plush, voluptuous scarlet and blue Persian rug on the bare cement floor. And decadent brocade tapestries nailed into the stone walls. With beeswax tapers and fat rose-colored candles in tarnished brass holders. No electricity. A fly buzzed lazily through the screenless window.

"No hot water," said Michel. "But it doesn't matter in the summer. And look, you pour in this bucket of water and flush the toilet that way. And then you fill it up again. The water comes from the stream."

Sweat drying to a chill on her back, Ada sank into the little sofa in the room that served as kitchen, parlor and dining room. A puff of

157

dust rose up around her hips. Michel frowned, went into the bedroom and emerged with a large green Indian coverlet shot with gold threads.

"Get up."

He draped the coverlet over the sofa, tucked it in, smoothed it, and stood back to survey the result.

"Better. Now you can sit."

Ada sat. And she really did want to jump on him now, but before she knew it he was out the door with a pair of scissors, gone to cut flowers. He came back with what looked like a mass of Queen Anne's lace. Producing a blood red crystal vase, he filled it with water from the little sink.

"The only water is from this sink. But don't drink it."

He set the vase of flowers on the old wooden table. They caught a shaft of brilliant sunlight and glittered, pure snow on rubies, like the light in a Vermeer. The colors soaked into Ada's eyes, filled her head till she thought she might burst with their glory and abundance. They splashed inside her, washing through like the tides. Ada threw her head back and let them flow, from head to heart to hands to all the secret places, the hidden repositories of her art. As if from some great distance, a passionate woodland bird trilled. Leaves sighed, grasses hissed.

"Oh," she whispered. "Oh, oh."

When she looked up, Michel was sitting at the table on the other side of the room, watching her, his face docile as a cat's. "You like my little house."

"Yeah, Michel. I like your little house."

TWENTY-SEVEN

Ada had no experience with the completeness of night in the woods. When the sun set, the air grew chill and damp. The sky cleared into a huge black dome pricked with stars. An owl hooted somewhere in the shadows, and the nearby rush of the stream took on a foreign, disembodied cadence. The candlelight distorted their faces.

As Ada peered out the window in hopes of glimpsing the moon, she saw faint lights off in the trees, bobbing through the woods like people holding flashlights along some hidden sylvan path.

"Michel, someone's coming!"

He turned his placid gaze to the woods. "No," he said. "They are the fairy lights. Spirits of the land, maybe. They never come near."

Ada thought about the Wild Hunt.

Late that night Michel woke her with a high, unfamiliar cry. Ada shot up in bed and saw moonlight pooled outside the window, but the room was steeped in inky darkness. Michel thrashed next to her, one smooth arm flailing at some invisible foe.

"Michel. Michel!"

When she touched him he flinched as if burned. "Who is it, who is it?"

"It's me, Ada. You're dreaming."

He quieted, and she could tell he was awake now. She laid her hand on his chest and felt his heart thrumming like a bird's.

"Ada," he said.

"Just me."

"Ada. My bodyguard."

"What am I guarding you from?"

But she already knew.

He was gone when she woke again. Cool sunlight was streaming in the open window where silver moon and fairy lights had danced the night before. The woods were alive with birds. Everything felt damp with morning. When Ada rolled out of bed, even the thick Persian rug felt drained of warmth against her bare feet. She had to scurry for shoes and socks and a sweatshirt. Half of a little pot of coffee stood in the kitchen, but rather than risk exploding the propane cooker, she poured it cold into a cup and took it outside to drink. It was a relief to step on the grass and feel the sun on her neck, the warmth of the day to come.

Michel caught her by surprise when he finally reappeared, emerging from the trees without cracking a single branch. Gone were his dandified city shoes, his dress shirt and formal trousers. He'd not even opted for the T-shirts that clung to him so nicely. He looked like an old farmer now, clothed in sensible work gear for the country. Though he didn't move like a crotchety farmer. It was still clear that her boy knew how to dance.

He was holding a little white paper bag loaded with fat butter croissants, which he waved under Ada's nose like a satisfied cat. "Breakfast," he said.

She grabbed a fistful of his shirt collar and pulled. "What's this old flannel thing?"

His expression didn't change, except for a subdued sparkle at the corners of his eyes, but he let Ada drag him toward her. "These are my mountain clothes."

"They sure are. I can't tell what's under them anymore."

He whipped his arm around her waist and pulled her hard against him. "Can you tell now?"

"Oh!" Ada gasped. "What's the mountain air done to you?"

"It makes me strong." Then he released his grip and strutted into the house with his bag of croissants. "Fresh coffee?" he called. There was the metallic sound of the coffeepot on the counter, and then the unexpected delight of Michel humming in the kitchen.

That afternoon they went into the woods. Succumbing to life without mirrors, Ada tied her hair off her face and wrapped a black bandana around her neck to catch the sweat and grime. She wore the same wrinkled T-shirt from the day before, along with grubby socks and the soiled sneakers she'd worn on the plane to Florence, abandoned ever since Cristian bought her new Italian shoes. Her jeans had manifested mysterious stains and her fingernails had grown grimy. After so many years of cultivating the sleek look of a specialist in Renaissance portraiture, she now felt more like a house painter. And as she followed Michel through the trees, along a narrow trail that snaked past the stream with its chill, glasslike odor, she felt as if she were tailing a stranger. A sexy stranger indeed, but not the person who let her twist and turn him to meet her pleasure, who yielded when she pulled his hair, who allowed himself to be bitten. Who let himself be molded to her desires like some indolent Persian boy. This new man, this foreign person, moved like a big cat, hips swaying with the confident, slinking stride of the predator. Now he had demands of his own. Ada could almost smell them, taste them as they curled around his body, drifting out to tickle her skin like little flickering tongues. She wanted to draw him as Eros, naked and erect and alive. But she said not a word, and she kept her hands and her thoughts to herself.

The path began an ascent through scattered rocks and boulders, straight tall ash trees standing firm as sentinels, and more of the graceful beeches, branches poised high and arching like dancers. They left the stream behind, its bubbling sighs fading as they continued. Then the trees opened and brilliant sunlight poured down, yet without the piercing heat of beach and sand and lowland. Tallish grasses fluttered softly beside big gray rocks whose stern surfaces were softened and muted by summer's fleeting warmth.

"Where are we going?" Ada finally asked. To her own ears, her voice sounded smaller than usual.

Michel stopped and turned, eyes caught in the shadow of the sun, expression veiled. There was a little bead of sweat at his temple. "You'll just have to wait and see," he said. His lips parted, as full of promise as the mouth of a Greek statue. Any other time she might have knocked him down and made him kiss her. This time he just turned around, and on they trudged.

The trees continued to thin, and now they walked on tall, slippery grasses, the path faded to a mere soft indentation before them, like an animal trail. The ground sloped discretely to the right till it became an edge bordered by grass and prickly plants, then dropped off into a steep, rocky cliff. It made Ada nervous to walk so close to that edge.

161

The sun felt warmer here, less filtered, more powerful. She wiped her face with the bandana. Her armpits had grown damp and a little rivulet of sweat dribbled down the middle of her back.

Michel stopped and raised one hand in the air, finger pointed up. "Listen," he said without turning around.

Ada listened. She could hear it now, the tinkling of water again. But the sound was smaller than the stream, more like a fountain. A little like the water nymph in Rocca.

"I hear it."

"Keep listening."

They proceeded in the direction of the splashing water. The path turned to dirt again and curved away from the cliff into the filtered shade of more beech trees. They passed a silvery gray, triangular-shaped rock adorned by a lump of animal scat, then the path abruptly widened into a rocky glade. The sound of water leaped out at them, and she saw what looked like a little pool. Water bubbled within it and trickled softly around it, rising from the ground in gentle rivulets, each with its own timbre, like a chorus of silvery voices. A green hazelnut bush sprang from the water, roots buried below the transparent pool.

Ada became aware of a buzzing in her ears. It grew louder, and then the air pressure changed. High humming filled her head, which now felt as if muffled in cotton. Michel turned to face her again, face mild and hopeful and quizzical.

"My ears are ringing," she said. "My head feels weird."

Relief flooded his face. "Yes."

They stood in absolute silence for a long time. Bird wings fluttered in the forest. Small flying insects glided past. The water whispered and the disembodied little voices sang in their ears. Ada watched the colors shift, the green leaves grow brilliant and emerald, the patch of sky above them transform to almost cobalt blue. The tree trunks sharpened, flattened, and became two-dimensional, as if painted onto a giant canvas installation in some avant-garde outdoor museum.

A sudden rush of wind brought wispy tatters of mist skittering from an unseen rocky crevice. Like a damp cloud, the mist muted sun and sky, brought a chill to the air. Leaves fluttered and hissed as the treetops swayed. The sweat on Ada's neck and back turned clammy.

"Is it going to storm?" She wrapped her arms around her

shoulders.

Michel sat on the ground next to the spring. Gorged on water and shade, the broad flat leaves of a lady's mantle quivered in a silvery, jade green mass just behind him. A big black bird swept across the sky overhead, croaking as it vanished into the trees. Michel closed his eyes and sank onto his back, one hand dangling almost in the water.

"They don't want us here," he said.

"Who?"

A sharp little needle of rain stung her arm, then a sudden barrage of tiny hailstones clattered down, plopping like pebbles into the pool and battering her head with muted fury.

"Time to go," said Michel, and they took off running the way they had come, past the silver-white rock with the animal scat and following the path as it widened and twisted through the trees. The hail stopped and the wind calmed, but the shrill voices still hummed in Ada's head. She felt strange and disoriented, though a certain tension had lifted, as if the air pressure had changed. They crashed ahead, leaving cracked twigs and broken branches in their wake.

"Michel," she gasped. "What was that?"

He stopped, breathing a little hard himself, yet suffused with almost beatific tranquility. "The guardians of that place. They don't like humans. They don't like us." He turned a peaceful gaze to their surroundings. "Now we're lost."

Ada looked around. Nothing was familiar. They had followed the path, but now they were among different trees, spaced more widely apart and rolling up and down gullies and clefts, rooted in a dry, brown, leaf-covered earth. The humming had stopped, and Ada's ears felt as if they'd popped and normal hearing had been restored. The air had grown soft, gentled with new warmth. Pale sunlight filtered down. A little bird trilled over their heads, its yellow beak open, delicate throat pulsing with song. His face placid as a child's, Michel eyed the bird, and then he slumped into a graceful heap at the foot of a tree.

"Let's sit and be lost for a while."

So she sank down next to him on the soft matted leaves and leaned her head back to share the tree trunk with him.

"Why are we lost? What was that place?"

But the flat stillness of the woods seemed to curb his already indifferent appetite for words. Ada didn't press him. She too felt silenced and bemused by the calm and brooding woods. As the minutes ticked by, it became hard to keep her eyes open. Their heads bobbled together, shoulders and thighs relaxed into each other, and they surrendered to sleep.

Ada was awakened by the touch of Michel's thumb tracing her cheekbone and the line of her jaw. Opening her eyes to his impassive gaze startled her. "Sleeping Beauty," he said, but no romance echoed in his voice.

"Did you just give me the magic kiss?"

"I did not."

"Then you'd better do it. You'd better give me a good one."

His eyes were not exactly unfriendly. Not exactly sad. Not exactly anything that she could understand. She grabbed him and kissed him the way she wanted to be kissed, and as always, he let her do as she liked. He surrendered to her like water. Yet uneasiness made her want to drag something more from him.

"How long before you go to Washington?"

"We leave next week."

"We?" She kept her voice light and teasing. "You and your mama?"

Hands gentle and firm on her shoulders, he pushed her away.

"Yes," he said. "Me and my mama."

Their eyes locked. But he'd become opaque as tinted glass.

"Mamas don't like me much."

"They like me," he said, expressionless.

"And do you like them?"

"Sometimes."

"Michel, why did you bring me here? Why did you steal my key? Why did you crawl up my balcony?"

"Look," he said. "Look at those beech trees uprooted by a storm. Like arms and legs. Muscles, tendons. Look how beautiful."

Ada looked at the trees ripped from the ground, tumbled crown downwards on the steep and stony slope. It must have happened in the spring—the first whorls of buds had already unfurled to expose pale green leaves that were now dry and disintegrating. But the silvery bark was still smooth and taut, rippling like Michelangelo's strong and slinky forearms and thighs. The dappled sunlight spattered them with mottled shadows that drew out their grain, their resplendent curves. They were as hard and beautiful as sex.

"Every time I get lost here," Michel said, "I find something like that. Something beautiful."

Ada remembered coming up the via De' Cerretani for the first time, stepping out into the piazza as the famous cathedral of Florence rose before her with its iconic dome, flanked by the baptistery with its renowned doors and the spectacular bell tower, all swarming with gaping tourists. How she had wanted to press herself up against the history and the mystery. She had wanted to be ironed into it all, like a scarlet leaf in wax paper. She had wanted to take it in her mouth and eat it and make it part of her own bloodstream.

So she understood these things, she who had shared that moment on the piazza with no one. She who had kept it all for herself, hoarded it like some delectable treat to be consumed alone. She understood that she was being offered a piece of another's beauty, that she had been deemed worthy to sample it.

"All right," she said. "All right." And when she reached around his shoulders to embrace him, he yielded. Or at least he didn't pull away.

They stayed lost for a long time. Finally, ambling aimlessly through brush and dried leaves and trees that were no longer sentient, they glimpsed their abandoned hamlet far below, and decided to skid and slide down the steep ravines and gullies straight as the crow flies, with no path to guide them. Ada broke her nails and ended up with dirt and leaves tangled in her hair, and Michel caught his shirt in brambles that covered him with hundreds of little brown stickers like a mangy dog. The seats of their pants were stiff with dust and grime by the time they finally reached the bottom, their faces smudged with sweat and dirt. The sun had arced over to the west and begun to slip behind the hills as they drank from the stream near the hut. Ada's knees quivered in fatigue, but the rest of her exploded with color and sound, with the shape of the forest. She could feel that night's dreams already incubating in her head.

"I'm a city girl," she gasped, cold water running down her face and arms. "I've never done anything like this."

"So you'll remember, then."

So she would remember.

They went to bed dirty and defiant. It was the first time Ada had let someone see her naked with dirt in her crevices and sweat stinking her armpits, though as Michel slithered across the mattress like a dark

165

mountain viper, deliberately griming the sheets, it occurred to her that maybe this was not so new to him.

Still, candlelight was forgiving and two soiled partners were better than one. Michel seemed positively grateful when she flattened him down in the pillows on the soft woolen mattress and explored the pungent smell of woods and soil on his skin.

"I am your bodyguard. No one gets in my way."

"No one," He surrendered his body. "No one, no one."

"All this is for me."

"The woods and the moon."

"The candlelight. And you in it. All mine. You understand?"

But by that time he no longer had words. Ada was glad of it, proud that she had driven him beyond language, to that pure state where they were nothing but a pattern of beautiful flesh and muscle. As perfect as the entwining limbs of two beech trees.

The candles guttered out as they slept. The moon rose and set. Venus twinkled in the purple sky and then vanished. Much later, birds cheeped in a drowsy choir that gradually crescendoed into a bright and boisterous orchestra. The sun rose cool and pale, then gathered force and heat to spill across the hills and valleys in a sparkling golden flood. Ada woke once, but turned her back to the gathering day and wrapped Michel in her arms and legs, pressing herself against him as if he himself were the Gates of Paradise.

He refused to wake. Like a rag doll, he lay limp and unresisting, totally unconscious. He might stir and twist when she touched him, but he remained in stubborn sleep against the day. Ada left him in peace for as long as she could, but finally she began tugging at his hair, running her fingers around his ear, tickling his nose, nipping his chin.

"Michel," she teased, "Michel, it's almost time for lunch. Michel, I'm hungry, what are you going to give me?" When he continued to hunker down, she hissed into his ear. "Psst, psst, Michel, pretty boy, wake up."

With a sudden gasp, he shot up on his elbows.

"Hey!" Ada said. "Good morning, it's me."

He stared at her, blank, and then, emerging from some secret world, gave a huge groan and flopped onto his stomach, sheltering his head in his arms. Ada sat cross-legged next to him.

"Michel."

Silence.

"Did I scare you?"

He gave a tiny whimper, so unexpected, so raw, that she felt sick and embarrassed. She wanted to touch him but refrained, just as she would fear to touch some wild wounded creature lying by the side of the road. Afraid it might bite her. Afraid there might be maggots. And ashamed of her revulsion. So she just sat and watched him shake.

Finally he calmed. She could see his shoulders soften and relax, and he pulled his arms away from his head. She waited. By the time he rolled over, she had composed her face into what she hoped signaled understanding. Though that was not what she felt at all.

"I'm sorry I woke you up like that."

She watched him lower the shields through sheer force of will. She still could not bring herself to touch him, though perhaps he would have let her. And the import of her own intentions washed over her like a dark wave. She was no bodyguard.

He looked up at the whitewashed ceiling with its ancient wooden beams blackened with wood smoke from long-dead fires. "Sometimes you don't know if what's coming is good or bad. If somebody wakes you when you're sleeping. You don't know."

"It was just me."

He folded his arms over his eyes again. "You can grow to love your obligations." He sounded thoughtful, almost bemused.

"What are your obligations, Michel?"

Silence.

"Should I kidnap you?"

Silence.

"Should I decide what you're going to do? What's going to happen?"

He snapped his arms away from his face and turned toward Ada, mouth tight and resentful. "You're asking me?"

Ada leaned over him and shook a grimy fist. "You make me want to punch you, you know that? Except I think you'd like it. And yes, I'm asking you."

His eyes filled. Ada had the sudden disconcerting impression that she was arguing with a little boy. She wanted to slap him. And perhaps that was the shelter he sought. But she didn't give him what he wanted that morning. She waited for an answer instead.

"I brought you here," he said. "Even though I hardly know you."

"I dumped my boyfriend for you. Even though I hardly know you."

They lay in stiff, sad silence for a long time, listening to the cicadas and the summer breeze rustling the trees outside. Michel stirred first. "We got the bed dirty. Let's go wash, and then we'll walk to Fonte for lunch." He stretched out his arms to her, and she let him pull her close. The sweet smile softened her. He was doing his best.

The water was cold enough to take the breath away; Ada gasped when he poured it on the nape of her neck. He'd thrown a towel in with them, and they took turns scrubbing each other. It felt good to wash the sweat and grime away, and eventually the heat of the day, drizzling down through the canopy of trees, softened the shock, and they lolled in the water like drowsy fish.

"We're like the water babies," Ada said. He had never read the book. "They were dirty little chimney sweeps and ragamuffin children who drowned in the stream, but the fairies washed all the dirt away, and they were reborn in the water with new fresh skin."

"To start over."

"In a better life."

Michel closed his eyes and let his face sink under the shallow water. His hair fanned out around his head like seaweed. He pulled up his arms to float behind him and let his whole body rock for a few moments before he surfaced to breathe. "I was imagining what it was like to be taken by the fairies and washed."

"How was it?"

"I think I'd rather not have to drown."

They floated side by side in silence. "Well," Ada said after awhile, "it's a pretty moralistic book in the end."

"Ah. That would not be appropriate for me. Would it."

"You look nice and clean anyway, even without drowning." And she slid against him like a smooth trout, touching his chilly wet skin under the limpid water.

They brought a cloth bag of empty bottles to Fonte that they would fill at the spring after they ate. But first they bought half a tray of warm pizza at the little general store, and a bag of soft apricots. A wan-faced woman who spoke the local dialect sliced the pizza and piled the apricots into the bag. She addressed Michel by name and ignored Ada entirely. He was grave and polite, and her tired wrinkles faded into a smile as they left.

They sat on a bench near the spring and ate. Cars occasionally pulled up, and people, sometimes entire families, emerged with whole cases of empty bottles. Intent on their task, they filled bottle after bottle, plugged them with used corks or plastic caps, and loaded them back into their cases, boxes or bags. A few elderly townsfolk appeared on foot, carrying one, perhaps two empty green glass bottles that they filled along with the rest. In their homely print aprons or blue work overalls, they took their healing water and trudged away. A few greeted Michel like kind grandparents. The old men acknowledged Ada, sometimes with a gruff nod, but the old women's eyes were hard. Ada tried to look friendly and harmless and small, but they weren't fooled.

"I'm an orphan to them," Michel said. "They like to see me alone."

They filled up their own bottles.

"Drink some," he told her. "This is famous water, good for the body and soul."

Ada took a swig. It was cold and bright.

They drank sat by side, filling their throats with clear water and feeling the warmth of their bodies against each other as they passed a bottle back and forth, Michel's dusky hand to Ada's pale one.

"Somebody will give us a ride to the train station," he said eventually.

It made her heart hurt.

"When?"

"Oh, probably tomorrow. That's what I think."

"And then?"

"Then it's time to pack and get ready for the trip. We have a lot to do."

"We do?"

"My mama and I."

Ada wondered if Cristian would have her back. What kind of believable story she could tell him about this trip and this person. She imagined how she would do it—we thought he looked like a mama's boy, but listen to this. He needed someone to talk to so he could sort out his feelings. I don't know why he trusted me—I tried to help. But now I'm back, see? It was all innocent, I was just trying to do a good deed. He was too messed up, it wasn't any use. I tried.

"I guess I have a lot to do too," she said.

Michel leaned back on the bench and stared up at the sky, eyes narrowed. "Well. Come to my house one more time then, and I will introduce you to her properly."

"I've met her, remember? She doesn't like me."

"No, I'll take care of it. You come one more time. She'll play the piano for us. I want you to hear it."

"And after the show you send me packing?"

"Come," he pleaded. "Please, I want you to come." He set the bottle down and took her hands. He held on tight. But he didn't look her in the eye. "Please. She's had a hard life. It's not her fault. I'm all she has. Please."

"Look at me, Michel. I hate it when you won't look at me."

Obedient, he raised his eyes. But she could read nothing in them.

"All right," she said. "All right."

And that last night in the whitewashed room with the Oriental carpets, watching Michel's body arch in the dancing light of the candles, Ada let herself be ensnared by the power of his form, a living work of art that slid through her like a river of color and music. Like great Dionysus himself, the god of dangerous desires. She grappled with him gladly that night, heedless of the risk. She tangled with Michel's new ravenous self and they struggled, rolling beyond the strictures of language and thought and fear, all awareness focused on their own straining muscles, the slap of skin on skin, the gasp of breath and the hot smell of intimate flesh. She let him take her closer and closer to the edge, till they tottered on the brink of the terrifying foreign beauty of the maenad consuming her god. Then he pulled her back and let her play with another form of beauty, the wolfish, galloping rider of the Wild Hunt, the secret man she had never tasted before, coming for her from the dark woods.

That last night in the old forest, she herself felt like a canvas laden with paint and color, changing and shifting under the artist's driven hand. Permeated with another's life force, exploding with another's vision. Marked forever.

TWENTY-EIGHT

A big blond farm boy who smelled like cows drove them back to the train station. He and Michel sat in the front seat and talked about cheese and the boy's family as if they were old friends. Ada hunched in the back with the bags. The breezy way they talked about local life made her queasy. It irritated her that Michel understood the mountain dialect while she did not. And she didn't like some smelly cowherd in a work shirt having shinier, fairer hair than her own, and such casual familiarity with her hard-earned and slippery treasure.

Still, the handsome peasant was gallant enough to open the back door for her at the station, and give her hand a formal shake in his big scratchy paw. He and Michel exchanged a rough little squeeze of each other's forearms, but Ada saw how Michel's fingers slipped round the boy's big elbow.

As the hay-strewn Fiat made its sedate way from the station square and puttered out of sight, Ada stole a glimpse at Michel, but his face revealed nothing. Still, he noticed her looking.

"I bought my little house from his family," he said. "They didn't want to sell it at first. But now we have become friends. Enrico, he likes the rugs in the bedroom. And he comes by the little house sometimes, to check on it. To be sure everything is safe."

"I'll bet he does."

"Yes," he said. "He does." He slung the bag over his shoulder. "Is there anything else you want to know about my house?"

They narrowed their eyes at each other. "I'd like to know if your mama approves of your caretaker."

171

She was sorry as soon as she said it.

"She doesn't know about my caretaker. I have never invited him to meet her. And she doesn't know about my house. I've never invited her." His voice dropped. "I invited you. All right?"

She too remembered the rugs in the bedroom, the blue and red Oriental patterns lit by candlelight that shut out the restless threat of the dark and unknown woods beyond the windowpane. The shelter of flesh against flesh, hearts cracking open like boxes of pearls. Souls splitting, sucking in the stars and comets and swirling infinite. Being both participant and witness to that. So she placed her hands on his chest, light as two bird wings, and they stood still enough for the flutter of his heart to rise against them. And then she kissed him on the cheek.

"They did a good thing to sell you that house, didn't they?"

The wariness that had twisted his mouth melted into softness. "Yes, they did. Let's go. We'll miss the train."

The return trip felt longer than the journey out, more inevitable, more inexorable. They sat across from each other, feet and ankles touching. Michel gazed out the window and said nothing at all as the train lurched forward, leaving forests and mountains and cool evenings behind, on its way back to the sunny cities of the coast.

Midway through the trip, Michel got up and went somewhere. He was gone so long that it made Ada uneasy. She sat up straighter, hands still folded in her lap, but kept her eyes on the long aisle and the swinging doors where he'd vanished, and counted the minutes. He couldn't have jumped out. Had Enrico sped ahead to the last stop and gotten on the train? Had some other stranger laid claim to him? Was he hurting himself in the bathroom? She was no bodyguard. He'd slipped out of sight once again, when she least expected it.

Ada was about to search for him when he pushed back through the doors. He'd taken the big country shirt off and was carrying it in his hand like a discarded rag. Under it he had worn the thin black T-shirt again. It made him look exposed. And he'd painted his eyes for the first time since they'd left. People looked at him as he passed, riding the rhythm of the train like a big cat, expression veiled and watchful. He tossed his head and let everyone have their fill as he moved toward Ada with a slow swagger. When he sat across from her, the passengers on the other side of the aisle looked them both up and down.

Ada's Egyptian prince gave her a demure smile.

"I wondered where you were." She leaned forward and pressed her hands on his thighs. He settled back, legs relaxing under her palms.

"I changed."

"Yes you did." She wanted to bite him, but people were looking. "You look nice."

He blinked and pouted his mouth.

"Who's it for?" She drew her thumbs along his inner thighs.

He sat there, arms at his sides.

"I know," she said. But her eyes unexpectedly brimmed, and she had to swallow it, send it back down to the hidden heart. She drew away and slumped in her seat. And ran her hands through her hair, across her face.

"Would you like to draw me?" he asked, voice small.

The woman sitting next to him was watching Ada. Jutting her chin up, Ada stared back until the woman looked away.

"I'll draw you," she said. "But I want you to hold still."

"I'll hold still." He was eager now, ready to please. He'd put the gold earring on again too. It glinted under his hair.

It didn't matter that the swaying train sometimes distorted the lines as she drew. She had him head on, trapped in his seat and eyes open, looking straight at her. She thought of turning him into the Sphinx, but he wouldn't transform—he became just Michel, looking oddly younger than his years, smaller, more anxious. And yet there was more, some hidden other thing, foreign and remote, that drifted beyond Ada even as Michel the man surrendered to her. She leaned toward him, seeking the essence. And like a willing sacrifice, he allowed her to probe the secret places, tease them out of him, open him up like a delicate blossom. Head back, never looking away, he let her in.

"I'm keeping this for myself," she told him.

"Of course," he said. "Of course, keep it, that's good, keep it. But can I see?"

Ada showed it to him, leaning forward so the nosy woman couldn't look. Michel stared at it, impassive, then took it in both hands and examined it.

"I'm sorry," he said.

Ada snatched it back. "Yeah, everyone's sorry." She slipped the portrait back in the sketchpad, tucked it into her bag, and got up and went to the bathroom, where she sat on the smelly toilet and cried. Then she rinsed and dried her face, fixed her hair, went back out to sit across from him again. They spent the rest of the trip in silence.

TWENTY-NINE

Ada didn't know where to go when the train pulled into the rustic little station at Rocca. Michel was going to contact her through Gisele, or at least that was what he said. But he was vague, distant, as flighty and uncommunicative as he'd been that first morning in Gisele's living room. He got himself a taxi outside the station and left her there.

Ada sat on the steps, her meager bag between her knees. She fingered the key to the apartment that Cristian had given her. She would have to go back for her things. It was all right if she went back. He'd given her the key if she needed it.

But she had to drag herself there. She stopped at the gelateria and ate a huge fat cone stuffed with three different kinds of gelato. She dawdled before the shop windows. She took a detour along the promenade and watched the darkening water as the sun turned liquid orange over the blue horizon, while the mountains she'd just visited now crouched in distant shadows. She started to plan the trip back to the United States and imagined herself in New York City. Just as good a place as Florence for art. Absolutely just as prestigious. Just as many opportunities. Shitty climate, though. Shorter memory too. But less sentimental, less likely to seduce one into stupid decisions. And there were good jobs there for people like her. For qualified, aggressive, talented, hungry outsiders like Ada who knew how to survive. And so now the next step was to find a travel agency and figure out the flight. It would take a little time. But she knew how to do this. She would be all right. It was good, actually, to be on her

175

own, so she could concentrate on her career and her craft. She had been sidetracked, tricked. Ada popped the tiny tip of the gelato cone in her mouth and finished it.

As twilight turned the sidewalks violet and gray, as the first lights blinked on in the windows of vacation houses and apartments, and heat finally began to leak from the air, Ada dragged herself back down the cobblestone street behind her temporary summer home. As she passed the fountain with its now water-stained nymph, she looked up and saw that all the shutters were closed tight. She couldn't see even a glimmer of light seep through. And then, when she finally turned the big key in the lock and pushed open the heavy green door, she entered a dark apartment smelling of ammonia and soap, only a few faint remnants of sun remaining.

Cristian had left. All the beds were neatly made, the perishable food gone and the refrigerator cleaned and unplugged. The kitchen table was pushed against the wall and the chairs placed upside down on it, covered with a sheet to keep off the dust. The door to his parents' bedroom was closed. The door to the room he had shared with Ada had been left ajar. He'd left an envelope on Ada's bed. Pre-stamped and addressed to the apartment in Torino, it contained a polite note telling her to wrap the key in paper and mail it before she left. Good luck, have a safe trip. Sitting with it on the bed, Ada wondered what would happen if she called.

Before she went to sleep in the little twin bed, Ada crept into the other bedroom and opened the balcony shutters a few inches. She took out Michel's portrait from the train and propped it up on the dresser in her room. She put Ada as Venus next to it. Then she slipped naked under the sheets, leaving all the doors in the house open.

She awoke too early. The sun was still mellow and watery, light slanting through the little window in pale pointed rays. The apartment felt quiet and vacant. She could hear the purr of morning traffic, the occasional growl of a motorcycle and the more high-pitched screech of fast-moving mopeds taking advantage of emptier streets. A large clanking vehicle rumbled by, maybe headed to set up a stand at the market. Ada wished she were at the Bargello museum in Florence, sitting across from Donatello's David with della Robbia ceramics gleaming on either side. Just sitting there on that big dark bench, looking.

The shower felt good, at least. There hadn't been any shower in Michel's little house, just a cramped half bath that one had to crouch in after filling it with buckets of tepid water. Floating in the stream had been nicer, but it took the warm shower in Cristian's apartment to clean her hair and leave her skin pink and fresh again. She carefully wiped down the whole shower afterward, leaving the bathroom exactly as she had found it.

Ravenous, she put on a sundress and went to the corner bar for a croissant and coffee. The bartender told her there were airports in both Genoa or Nice. "But why?" he asked. "Why would you want to leave our beautiful Riviera?"

"Because I'm stupid," Ada said, and they laughed. "I can't afford to live here, that's why, but one day I'll come back."

"Everyone wants to come back."

"I fell in love with Renaissance art," she added.

Now the bartender looked amused. "All the Americans do. But we get sick of it." He laughed. "I'd rather have a good meal with good wine. A fast red car and a government job and early retirement, that's what I want."

Ada picked up fresh rosemary and potato focaccia at the bakery and spent the day on the stone steps, leaning against the door and drawing scenes from memory. A fantasy rendering of a nightclub, someone wearing a beret. A table full of beer bottles. A cigarette burning in an ashtray. Smoke drifting. A bed with rumpled sheets, the pillow still indented. She drew until her hand cramped and she had to stop. And then she paced the floor and the silence caved in on her. Her steps echoed in the vacant kitchen, her fist smacked unheard against the bare wall. All sound seemed to implode.

Finally Ada could bear it no longer. She locked the door behind her, ran down the steps, and went to see Gisele.

Gisele buzzed her in without asking who it was, but when Ada pushed into the lobby, she was peering down from the stairwell. "Ada!" she cried.

Ada clattered up the three flights of stairs to find Gisele still standing in the hallway outside her door, arms folded and a cigarette between red-nailed fingers.

"We just got back yesterday. From the Valsesia." It scarcely sounded true now. It felt like a shadow. A fable. Something that might slip away entirely unless she recorded it in someone's memory besides her own.

"You went. I wasn't sure he'd really take you." Gisele's mouth grew wistful. "All right, come in. You want some wine?"

Ada wanted a lot of wine. They sat at the little painted table in the kitchen, the window with its ivory lace curtain opened to the sun, the hot blue sky and the salty sea breeze. Gisele served Ada white wine in a green-stemmed glass. It felt so good in Ada's mouth that she could have wept, so that first glass went down in just seconds, and Ada reached for the bottle again. Gisele eyed her without comment, then marched to the refrigerator and pulled out salami, olives, figs and bread, which she set before Ada on unmatched flowered plates.

"Eat," she said. "You can't just guzzle wine like that."

"Oh yes I can." But still, Ada ripped a bread roll in half and stuffed it down with salami. "It's the first time I've ever been to the Valsesia."

Staring into her wine glass, Gisele was silent for a few moments. "Lucky you."

Ada's throat grew thick. "Maybe."

Gisele tapped another cigarette on the table and lit it. "Well. He calls it his sanctuary. Where he goes to be alone."

"We were there for three days."

"Well. So." She dragged on the cigarette.

Ada drank half of her second glass. She could already feel it relaxing her shoulders, the back of her neck. "He wants me to see his mother. Before they go to D.C. together. That's what he said. I think that's what he said. I don't know what he wants. This mother thing— he and his mother—what—I mean, do you know—do you think— do you understand what I'm talking about?"

"Well," Gisele said, sounding brisk as a schoolteacher, "you have to understand that she's very dependent on him. They have a close relationship, but she's quite demanding. He does need to step in for his father. He's the oldest and her only son."

Ada tore at the bread. She popped an olive into her mouth. Then she picked up a soft purple fig and cradled it in her palm. "Has he ever asked you to be his bodyguard?"

"His what?"

Ada rolled the fig gently between her hands, felt its smooth, fragile skin. "Nothing. He was teasing." She put the fig back on the plate. "So, did Marion go to Paris?"

178

"Yes," Gisele said, surprised. "How did you know?"

"I saw her last week. I did her portrait. While you two were delivering the key, remember? It was for her father's birthday, for the trip to Paris. She was excited about it."

"She stopped to say good-bye. But she didn't say anything about a portrait."

"Well, Marion had a lot to say to me."

Gisele leaned back and folded up one long leg on the seat of her chair. Her bare toes had chipped pink nails. "Marion's a little crazy. They're all a little crazy in that family, but Marion will say almost anything. Who knows how long she's really going to stay in Paris."

Ada slugged back more wine. It was making her feel wiser and more confident by the minute. "You can't fool me," she said.

Gisele sighed and stabbed the cigarette out in an ashtray brimming with butts. "I have some liverwurst. Do you want some liverwurst for that bread?"

Ada did. Gisele nearly overturned her chair getting up to retrieve it from the refrigerator. Ada refilled her glass and thumped the wine bottle back on the table. Gisele slapped the liverwurst down in response.

"You know," she said, "you're not going to get into that family. I've known them for years and they won't let anyone in."

"He said his mother would play the piano for me. He said so. He said he wants me to come. And my boyfriend has left me here and gone back to Torino, thanks to you and Michel."

"Don't blame me. I didn't make you run off to his secret mountain love shack."

Ada could not begin to respond to that, so she decided to concentrate on what she better understood. "I'm going to finish this bottle."

Gisele threw up her hands in resignation. "Then you should just stay here, or you'll fall down the stairs again."

"I'm not going to fall down any stairs after just one bottle of wine."

"Then eat that liverwurst and soak it up."

She pulled out another bottle of white table wine. Ada leaned back and watched her pop it open, head now feeling pleasantly fuzzy. "I want to put on some music. Can I put on some music?"

Gisele stood up. "What do you want to hear?"

"Music. You know, music."

Cigarette hanging from the corner of her mouth like a gangster, Gisele stalked out to the living room.

"I don't want to hear Italian music," Ada called.

Gisele didn't respond. Ada could hear her riffling through albums, then the soft plop of vinyl on the turntable, the scratch of the needle. Frenetic hooligan guitars and suddenly a woman screeching in German like some operatic delinquent. Gisele cranked the volume up, then leaned in the kitchen door, cigarette in hand and a smug, quizzical expression on her face.

"Not Italian," she said.

Ada poured wine from the new bottle. Crisp little bubbles, a nice grapey smell, and now the cool feel of the wine glass on her fingers again. She washed down some liverwurst and bread. It tasted delicious, and that woman singing made her feel strong and female.

"Rowrr!" she cried. "Who is that?"

"Ignorant American," Gisele snapped. "That is Nina Hagen. She could sing Wagner if she wanted—she has the classical training—but she chose to be a punk star instead. An artist." She slapped her fist against her heart like a Roman soldier. "A true artist."

Nina snarled in a menacing crescendo. She had never dreamed of having Italian babies, never had one single girly notion in her whole ratted hair life. She sang, she howled. Ada and Gisele began to wolf the liverwurst, ripping and devouring the bread, sloshing the wine in their glasses and down their throats as fast as they could. Gisele opened a third bottle of wine.

Soon Ada could not bear to sit any longer, so she threw back the chair and stood, wine glass in hand, music blaring and ears ringing. She shimmied around the kitchen, feeling loose and dangerous and talented. She ducked and feinted her way around Gisele, who finished her wine in a gulp, pointed her empty glass at Ada like a pistol and pulled an invisible trigger, blue eyes glinting at Ada under her big Valkyrie brows.

"I feel better now," Ada said. "Nina makes me feel better."

"*Ich war schwanger, ich wollte kotzen,*" Gisele sang, but Ada could barely hear her over Nina's harsh vibrato. The walls rattled. The windowpane vibrated.

Ada loved the sound of the words. And it seemed that Gisele had been liberated and was now free to embrace her Teutonic soul. She sashayed out to the living room, where the music was even louder, and Ada followed. The music swirled around them in a muscular tornado of sound.

"Now I'm drunk," Ada said.

"And the sun's not even set."

They thought that was funny.

"I know you're not as drunk as I am."

Gisele made a face. "Of course I'm not. I'm bigger than you."

Ada twirled, then jumped and pogoed, and wine spilled down her wrist. "Oops, better finish that before I waste it." She drained the glass and then tossed it onto the orange sofa, where a few remaining drops dribbled out and stained the cloth.

"You're going to be sleeping on that sofa," Gisele said. "Get it wet and you'll be the one to suffer."

"You mean I'm staying here tonight?"

Gisele lit another cigarette. "We already had that conversation. You're not going down the stairs."

That made Ada cheerful. "Okay, I don't want to go back to the apartment anyway. I hate it there. I want to dance here." She bounced around Gisele, who swung one long white arm up over her head and jiggled her hips. She blew two big smoke rings.

"Wow, let me try that." Ada plucked the cigarette from Gisele's hand. But Ada was no smoker, not tobacco anyway, and she inhaled too much. It triggered a coughing fit that collapsed her onto the sofa, eyes watering and lungs stinging. To distract herself, she crawled off to turn up the volume. Nina howled in an impossible shrieking vibrato.

"Do people call the police for loud music here?" Ada yelled.

"I hope not," Gisele hollered back.

Ada sat on the floor with her back to the sofa, facing the wall with its comet of splintered glass, which sparkled like rhinestones in the early evening sun. She closed her eyes and let the music enter, from sex to stomach to her beating heart. It made her limp with longing. "Ah, ah, ah," she murmured. She felt dizzy with her eyes closed, but it was hard to focus even with them open. "*Porca puttana*," she said. "I did it again."

She heard a buzzing in her ears like a harsh bell and wanted it to stop, but it went on and on. Shut up, she thought irritably. Then it did and she heard a door slam, then something fell on her outstretched legs and there was a sharp pain, and she saw Gisele's long flanks sticking out of her mustard yellow skirt right on top of Ada as she scrambled and stumbled in an attempt to reach the volume control. Then the volume seemed to go down by itself, leaving Ada's ears ringing. Gisele struggled up on her heels and Ada let out a curse. She was going to have bruises on her legs again.

"You didn't even hear me. I had to let myself in."

The voice and the sight of those familiar legs, that springy predator's step, felt like a slap on the side of the head.

"It's my house, I'll play music if I like." Gisele was on her feet now, dignity regained. Ada thought she should emulate her, so she heaved herself up too.

Michel stood there in an ironed shirt, looking clean and natty and severe. He surveyed them for a moment, then went to the kitchen. Gisele and Ada exchanged looks. Ada wanted to giggle, but Gisele seemed serious, almost stricken.

"We were eating liverwurst," she called. "Do you want some?" She snatched the wine glass off the sofa and followed him. Ada heard water running, bottles clinking. Then Michel emerged alone, holding a piece of bread smeared with liverwurst in one hand, and a purple fig in the other. He ate one small, slow bite of the bread and liverwurst, chewing carefully, then popped the rest of it in his mouth and devoured it in seconds. He caressed the fig in the palm of his hand before consuming it in one bite. Gisele came out of the kitchen with a glass of bubbling water. He downed that too. She took plate and glass from his hands and returned to the kitchen. Dishes clattered in the sink.

"That was fast," Ada said. "What a pig."

He eyed her but said nothing.

"My apartment is abandoned," she continued. "It smells like fucking bleach."

"It's also locked."

"I think I'll fly from Genoa."

"We are flying from Nice."

"*Bravi*, yeah fly from the fucking Riviera."

He folded his arms and contemplated Ada. "I told her you were coming. It's been arranged for tomorrow evening."

"That's great," Ada said. "It's been arranged. I can't wait." But her lip quivered, her throat filled. "Why don't you pick me up at my fucking abandoned apartment, all right? All right? And now I have to go. Just pick me up tomorrow if it's all been fucking arranged."

He regarded her, wordless.

"Have a nice life!" Ada called into the kitchen, then she stumbled out the door, grabbed the handle with both hands and slammed it hard behind her. She clutched the banister as she made her way down, step after creeping step. Proving to herself that she wasn't drunk. Drunks would not be so careful, so reasonable.

But when Gisele rushed out onto the landing to call her back, Ada screamed up at her. "Go ahead! Go ahead! Bring him some more liverwurst! I'm done." She made her slow and crippled way down the stairs, eyes focused on her feet, on not being drunk. And when she pushed the big glass door open onto the busy street with its smell of exhaust and fish and sea, she was as relieved and liberated as she had been to leave her family in Buffalo when she was eighteen years old.

She went out to the place where she had done Marion's portrait. The sea was already dark out on the horizon, its nearer waters glinting soft gray. Boats nudged peaceably against the piers, and pretty people with dark tans and nice clothes loitered on benches. Ada sat at the end of the dock and felt tired. She had a morbid, compelling notion to do a self portrait of Ada crucified. Better yet, Ada as Venus crucified. Though self-pity was not her strong suit.

She did no self-portraits that night. She sat at the dock until it grew dark, and then she went back to the silent, sanitized apartment and fell asleep in her clothes on the twin bed. Door locked, balcony latch closed tight. Head and heart heavy and punch drunk, in sore need of sleep and repose.

The next day she arranged for a cheap stand-by flight from Genoa on Monday morning. Maybe she would have Bobby pick her up at the airport. He was doing sculpture now, working on big installations with an artists' cooperative and planning to open that gallery. He thought Ada was in Florence, but he'd adapt to changed circumstances. They would drink beer and Ada would tell him the things she loved about Italy. She'd arrange to have her own exhibit through the cooperative while she pondered her future, mulled the possibilities of New York. It would be good to get away from the Florence hothouse, back to a fast, modern American city where she could afford the gas for her car. Where knowledge of the Italian language and Florentine art was a sweet advantage. Where she could bullshit her way into opportunity over and over again. It felt like a plan.

She pulled the suitcase from under the bed and packed. She'd live out of the suitcase for her last few days. She tossed it on Cristian's bed and left it open, her sketches and portraits on the bottom where they'd stay protected. Even Ada as Venus and Michel as Michel. Then she left the front door unlocked and had a long, thorough shower. She didn't know what time Michel would come. She didn't know if he would show up at all. But she scrubbed, shaved, shampooed, and rinsed in hopeful speculation of what might be. Then she dressed in the tight red Italian pants Cristian had bought her at Stefanel, the little white cotton Italian blouse, the black patent leather sandals with heels that made her legs look long, her feet slim and pale. The sun had bleached the hair at her temples to flaxen blonde, while the rest of it bounced thick and golden on her shoulders. She put on makeup and big earrings that she'd bought at a stand off the Ponte Vecchio. That woman would not be calling her an American tonight. And Ada and that woman's son would be a divine pair, so perfect that no one could deny it. Exotic and foreign and meant to be entwined.

By the time Ada was ready, twilight was settling outside, and she had to turn on the lights. She went into the big bedroom, opened up the shutters to the balcony, and stepped out to listen to the fountain. A young couple passed by arm in arm, walking in time. Her soft chuckle and his low response drifted back as they made their brisk way into the deepening darkness. Ada wandered back inside, leaving the shutters wide open, pulled a chair off the table in the kitchen, and sat to wait, eyes on the door and ears cocked for the sound of footsteps outside.

She waited a long time. She'd thought it was a dinner invitation, but now it felt too late for that. Ada didn't want to look at the clock. Her stomach tensed and tightened. She jumped up and paced the kitchen. She put the chair back on the table and covered it with the sheet again. She paced some more. It had grown completely dark. It was evening. It was past evening. Ada finally looked at the clock and saw the worst: nine-thirty. It was night. It wasn't evening anymore. She opened the front door and peered out, as if he might be there waiting. But nothing. She rummaged through her things and fished out a handful of coins. She fingered the coins, slid them in her back pocket, and slunk out to the phone booth across the street.

Fernanda answered, and Ada tried to disguise her voice.

"It's Ada," Fernanda said as she handed the phone to Cristian.

"Ciao, Ada." His tone was a little brusque.

"I just wanted to let you know I'm back in Rocca, and I'm leaving for New York on Monday. I'll send you the key."

"All right, thanks. Have a good trip."

"I won't. I'll miss everything. I was thinking about Florence. Do you remember those red pants you bought me at Stefanel? They were so expensive."

"You looked nice in them."

"Yes, I'm wearing them now, right now. It's hot, but I wanted to wear them tonight."

He was silent.

"Well, that's all. I just wanted to tell you I was thinking about that. Thank you for that."

"Oh, Ada," he said with a big sigh.

She started to feel choked up. Then she noticed something white and shiny out of the corner of her eye. It was a taxi parked across the street. Michel had emerged and was making his way up the steps to the green door. Engine running, black smoke sputtering from the tailpipe, the cab waited like a fidgeting insect in front of the building.

"Michel!" she cried. "Michel!" She flailed an arm to get his attention. He turned, and the relief buckled Ada's knees.

"Hello?" said Cristian.

"Well anyway," she offered, but the air had gone out of the conversation. "So, thank you . . ."

"And now you have to go."

Ada signaled to Michel with one finger. One minute. Just one second.

"Yes, well . . ."

"All right, Ada. All right. Ciao, *bella*. Take care."

"Bye, Cristian. Bye, thanks. And say thanks to your parents too."

But he'd already hung up.

THIRTY

Ada took little steps across the street in her fancy sandals. Michel wore a white shirt and dinner jacket, as if he were an affluent businessman out for dinner at a big city restaurant. His hair was slicked back behind his ears. No earring, no makeup. He even sported a soft, expensive-looking black leather belt with a slim silver buckle. It was him, but it was not.

"Hello," Ada said. "Hello, hello. I'll be right there, I just need to run inside for one moment." She took the steps as fast as she could, clattered into the bedroom and rummaged through the suitcase on the bed till she found her white plastic sunglasses with the rhinestones. She put them on and examined herself in the mirror. Exactly. Then she sauntered out, locked the door, and descended, masked for the ball.

"You're late," she told him. He surveyed her without comment. She was glad he couldn't see her eyes. Serves you right, she thought. Now you can figure me out.

"It took awhile to get a cab," he offered vaguely.

Ada just tossed her head and slid in all the way to the window. He stayed on his side too, and the cab pulled away in silence. Ada could barely see behind the dark glasses, but she knew they must look impressive. The rhinestones would catch the streetlights. And the person behind the lenses would be a blank. She squinted out at the dim streets, but Michel stared straight ahead, hands folded on his lap. They did not exchange one word until they were watching the slow electric gate glide open as the taxi left them alone in the dark. Then

186

he turned to Ada with something like impatience.

"Will you take those off now?"

"Why? Are you afraid I'll embarrass you?"

He surprised her by snatching them off her face. "Please," he said. "Don't do that. Please."

"Put yourself in my shoes."

He looked down at them. "Well," he said, "they're nice shoes."

"Stop it, Michel! Don't be so stupid."

"Maybe," he added, "you should put yourself in mine."

They glared at each other.

"All right," he finally said. "I'll be in yours, you'll be in mine. And let us be kind to each other." He handed the sunglasses back. Ada slid them on top of her head, and he moved his hands to gently straighten them. "There. That's nice. You could even set them down somewhere inside later on." But his hands shook as he let go, and Ada had to straighten the sunglasses herself.

"Come on," she said. "Let's do this."

He held out his arm, and she placed her hand on his forearm as they walked to the house. As if entering a theater, a red carpet affair, steeling themselves for the flash of the camera, the brilliance, the noise.

The house smelled like flowers. There must have been a vase of tea roses somewhere, or maybe some exotic blooms from a coastal greenhouse. The large entry and hallway probing the domestic depths were dim and silent, though works of art were tastefully illuminated on each and every wall. The tiles were exotic, splashes of garden color like the steps of the villas on Capri. Ada's heartbeat made it hard for her to breathe. She clutched Michel's arm tighter and felt him tense under the expensive jacket and fine white shirt.

There was movement in the kitchen. They peered in to see a gray-haired woman, thin and dry as a stick, humming a little tune as she arranged flowers in a vase. Purple irises, just like the last time. She broke into a big smile when she saw Michel.

"Signor Michel! You are just in time."

"Hello, Carla. I would like to introduce you to my friend Ada."

Carla wiped her hands on her apron and held out firm, cool fingers for Ada to shake. "I am very pleased to meet you, Ada. Very, very pleased. I have known Michel since he was a little boy." She reached up and ruffled his hair with casual familiarity. "But you never bring your friends to visit, do you? You are a bad boy who never introduces your friends to old Carla."

"I have, though," Michel said, his voice gentle, as if speaking to his grandmother. "Look, Carla, here she is."

"Such a lovely girl. Look at that hair! A lovely girl."

Ada smiled and tried to look like a lovely, relaxed girl who met servants every day. Her sunglasses fell off her head and clattered onto the spotless tile floor. Carla swooped down to snatch them up. "I will put them on the table by the front door, where you won't forget them. Signor Michel, your mama is waiting for you in the piano room. I'll bring you a Sanbitter, yes? And for Signorina Ada?"

"A Martini & Rossi," said Michel. "With ice."

"All right. Now go, go, Signora Mireille is waiting." She bustled out with Ada's sunglasses.

Michel straightened his jacket, ran his hands down his flanks. "Are we ready?" he said. His voice was mild, expression grave. Though the amused expression in his eyes took Ada off guard.

"Are you ready?" she countered.

"One is never ready to be torn apart by his lovelies." He winked, as if joking. "Come on."

The piano room looked out over the dark expanse of the Mediterranean. It was the first thing a guest would see upon entering—a panel of glass that probably offered the best view in the house both day and night. Strands of lights sparkled up and down the curving coast, the vaster blackness of the sea in the background with faint dots of stars above, and a sliver of cold white moon hanging in the corner. Then her eye was drawn to the big grand piano, its black surface gleaming softly, the white and black keys shining in their own indoor strand of light. She never seen a piano like that close up. The beauty, the expense of such an instrument. Even the sleek piano lamp with its little black marble and crystal stand looked like a delicate museum piece. Ada wanted to touch it. But now she noticed spots of color, a big illuminated display case beyond the piano filled with things that looked like crystal eggs or paperweights, splayed before her in an erotic, lavish rush of brilliant hues and exciting shapes that begged to be touched, caressed.

Skin prickling, heart gripped by an unexpected urge to cry, Ada did not even see her at first. Clad in melon-colored silk, her dusky skin and black hair at play with the shadows, she had seemed like another ornament, hidden in an intimate alcove on the other side of the room. She was seated at a table set for three, positioned where she would have a view of the nocturnal coast and distant sea. She did not rise to meet them.

"Hello, Mama," Michel said, a chill in his voice.

No one moved. Michel's stance grew stiff. Tension rippled. Then she stood up, setting down her glass of sparkling water, and moved gracefully to approach her visitors.

"Ah," she said. "Good evening. How lovely." And she took Ada's hand and shook it, this time with a surprisingly firm grip. Ada could feel the ring on her finger as she squeezed. Then she reached up and kissed Michel on both cheeks, hands resting lightly on his shoulders. "There. Your mama has no manners sometimes. Too few visitors! Please, come sit down." She gave Ada Michel's own radiant smile, then took Ada by the elbow. "Ada, welcome to our home. I believe we've met. I apologize, I had such a migraine that time. It was hard for me to be sociable. Please forgive me."

She smelled delicious and floral. The folds of her long silk dress slipped and slid over her body as she moved, catching the light like pale orange waves. Ada could see by her eyes, by the tell-tale thickening around her waist, that she was older than she appeared at first blush, that she had borne children, but everything else about her bespoke catlike youth, the coiled, elegant intensity of her own son. Ada felt like a tacky little slut in those tight red pants.

Michel pulled out the chair for her before seating Ada. Then he removed his jacket and hung it neatly from the back of his chair. He was wearing real cufflinks, black ones that sparkled like two negative stars in the radiant white sky of his expensive shirt. He sat between them like some slinky, graceful animal.

Nervous, Ada craned her head around to look out the window. "That's a beautiful view."

"It is, isn't it?" said Mireille. "Look, do you see those lights out there, far along the coast? That's Monte Carlo. A lovely city. And then, just a little past that, that's Nice. Have you been to Nice?"

"No. I've never seen Monte Carlo either."

Mireille clapped her hands in dismay. "Well, that is quite a shame. What a pity. If there were time, I should have Michel take you there for a day. But we are leaving soon—Michel has told you? We are going to your country to live, to your own capital city with its cherry

189

trees." She smiled at Michel. "It's very exciting. We've never lived in Washington, it's a place we don't know, and we are terribly eager to discover its secrets."

"I've never been there either, actually. I'm returning to the United States myself in just a few days. To New York City."

"A very nice place. Wonderful restaurants. We bought a painting there once—do you remember, Michel?" She looked around, as if considering. "But I don't think it's here, in this house. I don't believe so. Is it, Michel? It's in Rome, isn't it?"

"Or in storage," he said carelessly. "What's this, Mama?"

"Carla's stuffed figs with gorgonzola. She knows what you like. Ada, please help yourself. Ah, here she comes with your drinks."

Carla was carrying a little tray with the vase of irises, Michel's red Sanbitter, and Ada's dark caramel-colored vermouth on the rocks. She set the vase at the end of the table before she served the drinks. The yellow and purple throats of the flowers exuded a faint perfume. Ada had never known that irises could be scented.

"There," said Carla with an air of finality. "More water for you, Signora Mireille?"

Mireille held up her slim little hand. "No thank you, Carla. I think we are settled now."

"Those figs are especially for you, Signor Michel. I don't want any leftovers, do you hear?" Carla wagged her finger at him, and he cringed in mock submission.

"I promise, I promise to eat them all."

"They should be eaten, every one. But share them. Signorina Ada, be sure that he shares them. Greedy boy!"

She hustled out, swinging the tray at her side.

Mireille and Michel exchanged amused glances. "What would we do without Carla?" Mireille sighed. "But now she has grand-nephews, and her loyalties are so divided. Michel had to charm her into coming back to Rocca with us, and now, how to convince her to travel to Washington to help us set up our new home? Even if she comes, we are not sure she will agree to stay."

"She feels sorry for you," Michel pointed out. He popped a fig into his mouth.

She tossed her head with a perfunctory wave of her hand, then leaned over to Ada with a conspiratorial air. "Without Carla," she said, "he'd eat nothing but fried fish at the beach stands. He *starves* when she's gone. He can't possibly take care of himself." She leaned back and laughed, her voice sweet as a delicate bell. "Neither of us can possibly take care of ourselves! Carla has spoilt us rotten."

"Here." Michel placed a big stuffed fig on Ada's plate.

"This is wonderful," Ada said, and then was at a loss for words.

Mireille leaned back in her chair and picked up her glass of sparkling water. She ran one hand through her hair and down the back of her neck, lips curving in an indulgent smile as she watched Ada eat.

"Michel tells me you are an artist."

"I am. A portrait artist. I've focused on Renaissance portraiture. I've just spent a year in Florence, which was very inspiring."

"How lovely. He said you had a productive stay."

"I did, and now I have to decide the direction I want to take. I could aim for a position as museum curator, or else start exhibiting my work."

"How very exciting. Perhaps we should commission you to do our portrait. Wouldn't that be nice, Michel? Wouldn't you like to have Ada do your portrait?"

Michel focused on the figs and his drink, expression innocent. Ada sipped her vermouth with a shaky hand. Carla had dipped the rim of the glass in sugar.

"No?" Mireille continued, leaning back now and tilting her chin in a little pout. "No portrait? Not even with your mama? You see, Ada? He's stubborn. He takes after his grandfather. He makes up his mind and that's the end of it."

"I am not like my grandfather."

"Well, you don't look like him, but ah, that character of yours," She crooked her finger at Ada. "Come, Ada, do you want to see a photo? Let me show you something."

She led Ada over to the display case with the crystal eggs and glass. There were photographs on the wall, from the same era Ada had glimpsed in the living room that first time. These were portraits in fancy frames. There were close-ups of a stern, unsmiling couple against a background of cultivated fields and a hot, humid sky, then photos of them each separately, taken indoors in a tropical-looking home flooded with sunlight. The man was Ada's father's age but had the air of an old-time cattle baron. Perhaps it was the jaunty clothing. Or the moustache. The woman was young and had Mireille's eyes and mouth. It was clear that Michel had inherited his looks from the female side of the family. Though there was a ghostly resemblance to the arrogant old man in the jut of the jaw, the willful expression.

"Where is this?" Ada asked. There were palm trees and big lush flowers she didn't recognize.

"This is my country, Mauritius. A little island south of Africa where I grew up. That is our sugar plantation. Michel never told you? He used to go there for holidays as a little boy."

They looked over at Michel, now slouched in his chair stuffing figs in his mouth. Mireille tapped Ada's shoulder and leaned over like a friendly high school girl.

"He's more interested in food than in his grandfather," she whispered with a little giggle.

Michel chugged his Sanbitter. "Tell her what the national bird is," he called.

Mireille tittered as if he'd told a funny joke. "It's the dodo," she said. "Though it can't be a national bird, can it? It's so very extinct. The dodo."

Ada could hear Michel's big impatient sigh all the way across the room. He stood up, glass in hand. "I'm getting another drink." He stalked out.

"He doesn't get along with his grandfather," Mireille confided.

"I didn't know he still had a grandfather."

"Ah, you see?" She shrugged, glanced at the door, then pressed her finger against her lips, as if telling a secret. "Well, I don't get along with him either." She giggled again. "No, not at all, so here we are very far away, you see?"

"And this is Michel's grandmother?"

"Oh," Mireille said with an air of dismissal. "Yes, of course. You can see the resemblance. Poor mama."

"Are there pictures of the other side of the family?" Ada scanned the photos, seeking safer territory.

"Ouf," Mireille said sharply. "They're dead. And we have enough of his father on television, don't you think?"

"Television?" So maybe his father was not a scientist. Maybe he was actually something embarrassing. A Mauritian soap opera star. A Bollywood singer. A televangelist.

Mireille eyed Ada with sweet smugness. "He hasn't told you, of course, that his father is Bruno Boccanegra. The geneticist."

Ada remembered that he'd said genetics. But she hadn't imagined that suave fellow who hosted science shows. The charming, heavy-featured man who wore a tie with an image of Munch's *The Scream*. Who made genetics fun for the masses. "That's his father?"

Mireille clapped her hands in delight. "And we can't stand him!" she cried triumphantly. "So no pictures on the wall." Now she looked at Ada with something like pity. "Oh dear Ada, I know it's true that Michel and I, we don't seem like the family of a geneticist. We've had to find our own way."

Michel returned with a full glass. Mireille pulled Ada over with their backs to him, as if they were examining the photos, and slipped her arm around Ada's waist. She smelled like gardenias. "We shan't talk about his father in front of him," she whispered. She hugged Ada a little closer. "But I am so glad he brought you here, so you would understand our lives a little better. He has stepped in to accept responsibility and takes no credit for it. He has been such an inspiration to me." She pointed to the piano. "Did you know that I compose music? All because of Michel." She smiled gently, but her eyes were smug and cold.

Ada turned to glance across the room. The fluorescent red liquid in Michel's hand looked like a portable stoplight as he stood watching them, inscrutable, from the shadows. Mireille pulled away from Ada with a silky gesture.

"We were just looking at the photos of gran-papa and gran-mama," she called. "We were talking about how hot and humid it is in Mauritius. The smell of sugarcane. My goodness, how I recall that smell." She floated back across the room at him. Motionless, he watched her approach, then submitted to a kiss on the ear. She linked her arm in his and smiled at Ada, waving as if from the deck of a ship. "There's a family resemblance, no?" Her laugh was sweet and throaty. Her eyes sparkled as she tilted her head against his shoulder and pulled close. "A pity you don't have a camera." As if synchronized, their arms slipped around each other's waists. Michel's hand rested on the curve of her hip. Interlocked, they looked at Ada with blank, benign faces.

Michel collected himself first. He took a little breath and pulled away from his mother as if burned. She must have felt it, for she darted her head around to look at him, then slid off sideways. Their hips no longer touched. They moved their arms to their sides like mannequins and gazed foolishly at Ada, as if she'd walked in on them making out.

Mireille combed her hands through her hair with the same gesture as her son. She tossed her head with a tight little smile, hurried over to the table, picked up her glass of sparkling water and drained it.

"Shall I have Carla refill our drinks, Ada? Would you like another vermouth?" But she hastened out before Ada could respond.

Michel and Ada stood across the room from each other, he still holding his full glass in front of him like a hot potato. Ada sloshed down the Martini & Rossi. "I can't believe you brought me here," she said.

He sat down, clutching his glass in both hands, staring at it like a crystal ball. "Wait."

"For what? You want me to tell you everything's all right?"

He nodded, not looking at her. "Yes." His voice was firm now. "And come and sit down here at our table."

So she went over and they sat without speaking for a few moments. Then Ada reached across the table. "Give me some of that." She took a drink of the Sanbitter. "That tastes like shit."

"But it's alcohol free. To keep my wits about me."

She threw up her hands in frustration.

"But you can see that I need to," he said. "I need to keep my wits about me. You can see that, can't you?"

In came Carla with a new tray of drinks and antipasti, this time a plate of stuffed dates wrapped in prosciutto. "For this boy who is always so hungry." She set the tray down with a flourish and swept away the empty fig plate and glasses. "Your mama tells me I am not fast enough."

"Oh," sighed Michel, eyes on the platter. "Look, Ada. Look what Carla has brought us." He lifted a date and held it out to her. "You first. I want you to try it."

Carla beamed. "He's a good boy, isn't he?" She gave him a gentle smack on the side of the head. "When he's being good."

Michel cringed and grinned like a child. "Carla, I'm always good."

Mireille rustled back in and settled down before her new glass of water. "Thank you, Carla, that is lovely."

Ada could see that everyone was waiting for her to bite into the date. And it did, in fact, meet every expectation. She thought they were going to cheer her, as if she had won a contest. Then Michel and his mother gazed at each other across the table, sipping their drinks delicately, like satiated cats, and took a collective sigh.

"Thank you, Carla," Mireille repeated, though this time her tone was dismissive. Carla dipped her head, now the efficient domestic, and swept out with the used dishes. Michel snatched up two dates and popped them into his mouth one after another. Mireille watched him eat, her eyes narrow with pleasure.

"He eats for the both of us," she told Ada with a good-natured shrug. "He's never full."

"I only eat what's good. Don't I, Mama?"

"He's got good taste, he does."

The date was filled with a creamy, spiced cheese that slid down Ada's throat in smooth abandon. She added a big drink of vermouth.

"Will you play for us?" Michel asked.

"Ouf," Mireille said carelessly. "I don't know. Ada doesn't want to hear me play the piano."

Ada took her cue. "Oh, but I do. I want to hear you play."

They looked at each other. "Anything you like," Michel said.

"He always wants me to play the piano," she said with an exasperated wave of her hand. Her charcoal tresses bounced against her trim shoulders. "Ever since he was little. I tried to teach him, but he never wanted to learn himself."

"I learned to dance, though. Didn't I?"

"Oh my. Yes, you did. Did you know that, Ada? Michel's a fine dancer. The Viennese waltz! Isn't that fun? Oh, I get dizzy going around and around."

Michel smiled, demure, under lowered lashes. Ada thought of him squeezed between those strangers on that hallucinogenic dance floor. She wanted to tell his mother. She wanted to bring her down a notch. Even though it wasn't Ada he'd been dancing with.

Mireille stood. Fingers spread wide, she ran her slim hands down her hips and thighs, though nothing needed to be smoothed. Michel leaned back as if someone had pressed hard on his chest. As if he were surrendering, opening. Ada had seen it before and thought it was for her. Mireille gave her a wink, then strolled over to her son and casually squeezed his shoulder.

"All right," she said. "Music inspired by Michel."

She was no coquette at the piano. Her delicate shoulders straightened, and her hands stretched long and strong. No fingernails

195

to click on the keys. She whipped her head back once to toss her hair, but it was an automatic gesture now, not a tease. And Ada saw that she was improvising, creating music before their eyes. That she forgot anyone was even watching her.

Michel and Ada sat, hands folded in their laps, the table separating them. They closed their eyes and listened as the room filled with the complexity of sound. It wrapped then, muffled them, pierced them. Ada knew little about such music, but this sweetness seemed to aim straight for the groin. It nearly collapsed her. When she stole a glance at Michel, his eyelashes were glistening and he was looking right back at her. He leaned over the table and stretched out his arm. Ada reached too, and they grasped each other's forearms. Then he stood, motioning her still, and padded across the room to stand behind his mother as she played. He ran one flat, gentle palm from her neck all the way down her spine. She stretched a little, like a cat, but did not stop playing. He stepped away and turned to Ada, then beckoned with that same hand. Ada tiptoed over to them. He placed a finger on his lips, then took Ada by the elbow and pointed under the piano. They got down on hands and knees and crept underneath, then lay next to each other on their backs.

Everything vibrated under the piano. Ada touched a glossy black wooden leg and felt the music coursing through it. She felt it under her hips on the parquet floor. She felt it in her skull. She felt it pulsing into her from all directions, over every inch of her body. She gave a little gasp. So did Michel. They stretched their arms above their heads and let their hands and shoulders touch, their thighs and the length of their legs, while the music shivered through them.

"It's even better this way," he whispered into her ear.

It was too exquisite to respond.

"She can't see us here," he said, voice only the barest breath.

Ada rolled over right on top of him and they lay pinned, arms still outstretched and hands flat against each other, hearing their own heartbeats merging with the music that poured through them. But he wouldn't let Ada kiss him.

"See her feet," he whispered.

Ada could, when she turned her head. She saw Mireille's bent knees beneath the pale silk, and two pretty feet in shiny little slippers, the working sinews of her ankle revealed when she pressed the pedal.

Michel embraced Ada, hands light as a moth on her shoulders.

"When I was little," he whispered, "I would try to touch her foot sometimes, that part of the arch that her slipper didn't cover. Most of the time she would kick me, but sometimes she let me do it."

Ada rested her head on his chest, and they both watched the foot.

"Now she always lets me touch her," he breathed into her ear.

Ada rolled off him and landed on the floor with a thump. One of the knees under the piano started and the music hiccupped, caught for a beat. Michel brought his fists up to his ears and squeezed his eyes shut. "Shh, shh, shh," he gasped. He curled up like a baby. One of the tails of his fine white shirt had pulled out. He'd messed his hair. A trouser leg twisted to reveal the expensive dress sock. Ada clenched one hand into a fist and pounded him hard between the shoulder blades. He coiled tighter. Music vibrated all around them; she'd returned to the keys with a vengeance. Ada slid away from Michel and stared at his tight back. Perhaps she could crawl out and slink away without being noticed. Even in her wobbly shoes.

But as soon as she eased herself up on elbows and knees, Michel unwound with a little snap of energy. He grabbed Ada's arm with surprising force. She had to sink back down again unless she wanted to get into a scuffle two feet from his mother's calves.

"Shhh," he whispered again. Ada reached out and pulled his ear hard.

"I'm done," she spat. "I can't take any more of this."

Face twisted in consternation, he straddled Ada with one leg and held her down by the shoulders. "Don't move, don't move. Please." He whispered through her hair, voice so soft she could barely hear him. "It'll be done soon, and we'll go. Ada, it'll be done soon. I promise, Ada, I promise. Don't move now."

They stared at each other, faces inches apart.

"Get off me," Ada hissed. He did. They lay sprawled side by side like two flat starfish, while Ada waited for it to be over.

She was the first one to crawl out. The room was still vibrating and her skin sizzled. Mireille sat at the keyboard looking drained. There were two spots of red on her cheeks, and her temples looked damp. Ada noticed for the first time the little wrinkles around her eyes. She gave Ada a wan smile.

"Both of you under the piano."

"Thank you," Ada said in her university voice. "That was beautiful."

Now Michel rolled out, uncurling to his full height in one seamless movement. When he ran his hands through his hair to smooth it back, Ada saw the darker moist strands at his forehead. His wary eyes. Mireille held out her hands to him with a limp, tired gesture.

"I've done it again," she said. "Would you massage them for me, please?" She slid around on the piano bench to face them, but it was Michel she was watching.

"Stand up," he said, and she did. He twisted and turned a palm, pressing it between his thumb and fingers.

"Thank you," Ada said again. "It's been an enjoyable evening. The best of luck to you in Washington."

Michel looked up at Ada sharply. "I'm going to take Ada home, Mama."

"No, I'm fine. It's no trouble for me to walk, it's a beautiful evening."

Mireille slumped closer. "This hand too. How it aches."

"I'll take you home, Ada. I'll get a cab."

"Oh dear," Mireille murmured. "I feel a migraine coming on."

"It's really not a problem," Ada said.

"Just a *minute*," Michel snapped. "I'll have Carla call the taxi."

He let go of his mother's hands and strode out. They both turned to watch him move. When he was gone, Mireille heaved a great sigh and pressed her fingers to her temples. Wordless and distracted, as if alone, she wandered over to the big picture window, now squeezing both palms against her head. She uttered a tiny groan. Ada went over to the table and downed the rest of her stale vermouth.

Michel returned, looking rumpled and agitated. "All right," he announced. "The cab will be here soon."

Mireille emitted a small sob. "It comes on so quickly."

"All right," Michel repeated. "All right. Go upstairs, and Carla will bring you the medicine."

"But my hands." She stepped towards him, holding out her arms with wrists drooping like lifeless flowers.

Michel grasped both her wrists in one swift motion, pulling them up to his chest. His back was to Ada, and she could see neither his face nor Mireille's. Whispered words flew back and forth. Mireille snatched her hands away—they flew up over her head as if rocketed from a slingshot—and she turned her back on him.

"An hour," he said, coming round to face her.

Mireille flounced over to the window, shoulders rigid, and stared out into the night. She rubbed her temples, clasped the back of her head with splayed fingers. Michel came to stand next to her. She stepped away from him, but he slipped behind her, clasped her wrists, and pulled them away from her head. She put up a grim struggle till he leaned over and said something in her ear. Then she suddenly collapsed, shoulders sagging and quivering. As if she were a recalcitrant child, he steered her back to the table, firm hands guiding her from behind, and she sank into her chair like a weary toddler.

"One hour," he repeated. This time she covered her face with her hands and emitted a tiny sob.

He looked over in Ada's direction.

"I can go back alone," she offered.

But now Mireille turned her haggard passionate face to Ada, eyes dark and glistening. "Michel will take you home. Please excuse me. It comes on so fast. Go on, Michel. Go."

He backed away from her as if from royalty. "Just an hour."

"Oh, *god*," she said, her voice breathy and weak.

"Come on, the taxi will be here soon."

"Goodnight," Ada called.

Mireille gave Ada a pallid smile, but her eyes were points of steel. "Don't let him forget the time," she said. "And Michel, tell Carla I need the ginger tea."

Shields up, prickly cold energy fairly shooting out of him, Michel strode with purpose back to the kitchen without even turning to see if Ada was following. He leaned into the doorway. "Carla," he called, polite but brusque. "She needs the ginger tea."

As Ada was catching up, Carla appeared, wiping her hands on a midnight blue dishtowel. She gave Ada a dry, speculative look before turning to Michel. "What else?" she asked, with the take-charge tone of a nurse.

He threw up his hands in a limp gesture. "I don't know. I have to take Ada home."

"I can get home by myself," Ada repeated, and they both swung to her with sharp, offended eyes.

"Of course Michel will take you home."

"I told you I'd take you home."

Then they returned to the matter at hand.

"Get her upstairs if you can," Michel said. "I'll be back."

Carla gave a big, exasperated sigh. "Take your friend home. Everything will be fine." She suddenly shook a skinny finger at him. "Everybody must relax!"

Michel broke into a big, unexpected smile and threw an arm around her bony shoulders in a lopsided embrace. "You're right. You're always right."

She ducked away and shooed them off. "Go on, you two! That taxi is waiting."

But there was no relaxing on the way back. They sat squeezed against their opposite windows while Michel engaged the driver in pointless small talk. When the cab pulled up in front of the dark apartment, the chill and lonely stone steps, he didn't move to get out.

"Well," Ada said, "thanks for the interesting evening."

He sat over on his side as if paralyzed, mumbling some formality Ada could not hear.

"Goodnight, Michel." But before she closed the door on him, she leaned back in. "You don't need any damn bodyguard. Enjoy your headache duty."

She slammed the door and marched up the steps without looking back. She heard the taxi pull away, the sound of the engine fading as it turned the corner and left her behind. She wished she were leaving the next morning. She wished he had gotten out of that taxi.

THIRTY-ONE

Her self-portraits stared at her from the portfolio when she pulled it out again. Ada as the perfect Aphrodite, Medusa, Mary. All odes to Michelangelo and Raphael, to the long-dead world of the Florentine Renaissance. She stared at them, arms folded. She kicked off a shoe and threw it at the wall, where it clattered against the painted cement. Then she threw the other one.

She stayed up all night and drew herself as a bodyguard toting a machine gun. She added a Viet Cong bandana like Rambo, a camouflage vest. But it wasn't right. As the sun rose behind the shutters, she rummaged through her materials and fished out a red pencil. She added a big red bloody heart hanging out of her chest next to the black and white gun. It was enough to let her sleep for a while, till her tight pants pinched so much that she had to sit up and peel them off her legs. Then she went back to sleep and didn't get up till afternoon, throat parched and head clogged and heavy. She drank a liter of water from one of the green glass bottles left in the kitchen, then wandered back into the bedroom and stared at the bodyguard drawing. Stupid and obvious as some kindergarten scribble, it failed to rise to the occasion. Something writhed in her groin.

She pulled off the rest of her clothes and tried to lift the hair off her neck. The water she had just drunk seemed to transform instantly into dripping sweat. She threw herself down on the narrow bed and burst into tears.

"Stupid, stupid, stupid," she spat, and whipped the pillow to the floor. "Stupid."

Something was happening to her stomach. It twisted and fluttered as if she were on a rollercoaster, at that moment where the little cart reaches the top of the loop, far above the carnival grounds, and is just about to careen down and make its occupants scream in terror and delight. Ada flipped around on the bed, but the sensation would not stop. And something roiled around in her head too, something encroaching on her brain that felt like color and emotion. The color of emotion. It was orange and big and vibrating to music, flattening her, consuming her, screwing her. She realized she was still crying, but the way one cries when the pain has become exquisite. When it is too beautiful to bear.

She rolled off the bed and lay naked on the floor. The cool tiles pressed against her buttocks and the backs of her thighs, but her forehead still burned. She flung her arms up and closed her eyes. The voluptuous orange sound was bearing down on her. Then she could see it next to her, the gleaming black shape of a piano leg looming out of the color. The squirming source of music above her. A cosmic web revealed. And the world tilted.

Pencils weren't right for it. Not enough color. Oil would have been best, but that had never been her preferred medium. Pastels would have to do. She needed orange, she needed flames and galaxies and the crazy black leg of a grand piano. But it was impossible to express this magnificent fire rising up from the base of her spine, spewing like a fountain all the way up her back and out through the top of her head. One lifetime would not be enough.

She lost track of time. The shadows came and went. Street noise ebbed and flowed. She wore the fire-colored sticks down to a nub before she finally gave up. Then she slept again and dreamed of swirling silver shadows soaked in traveling colors. When she woke she thought she was in her childhood living room. She wanted to paint the giant colors right before her eyes. The mystery of them. Their primal shapes. She pulled out the pastels and tried to reproduce the rude and vital glory. It was impossible but she had to begin the work. She bent naked over the paper and let the raw color pour out.

Later she felt shaky. She went to the sink, stuck her head under the faucet and drank. She found a can of tuna and ate it with her hands, running a finger around the empty tin to get the last of the oil and bits of meat. She rubbed her greasy hands over her breasts and belly and flanks to clean them. She felt weak and swollen, as if she had been through an orgy. And what day was it, anyway?

She pulled on a sundress without any underwear, with the idea of going out to ask the day and time at the corner newsstand. She nearly stumbled over a small gold foil gift bag on the doorstep, which she picked up and carried across the street with her like a little handbag. It was four o'clock and her flight was the next day. She stood out in the street for a few seconds, blinking at the light as the piercing turquoise sky filled her eyes and settled like lust between her thighs. The stone steps to the apartment across the road shone in a complicated pattern of green and gold. The door blazed emerald. She'd forgotten her shoes and the pavement was hot and sun-soaked. A cranky signora in a housedress pushed past her; she'd been blocking the way. Ada scurried across the street with the crowd, feeling the hot asphalt with its dangerous shards of junk and broken glass, and skipped back up the steps into the cooler, dim apartment where the colors did not seep into her with such fervor. Jittery yet filled with bright excitement, she slipped down on the kitchen floor against the wall. She let the little bag drop between her knees and she stared at it, surprised. It glittered like some pretty little treasure chest.

Ada pulled it open. Inside was a package wrapped in tissue paper, which she retrieved with a delicate hand. A smaller bundle, heavy for its size, fell out—a sheet of white paper taped around something. She unwrapped it to find four keys. A big, smooth, old-fashioned Italian key and a gold padlock key hung on a chain labeled "Fonte." The third key had a little white tag looped through it which bore the typewritten word "Rocca" and the numbers of a combination lock. The fourth looked like a typical American house key. On the sheet of paper wrapped around the keys was a Washington, D.C. address and telephone number written in a small, elegant script. Ada let it all drop in a little pile between her legs and sat limp for a long time.

AT THE SOURCE

Sylvia Gilbertson

THIRTY-TWO

It is the night of the winter solstice. The north wind carries the scent of Canada, its cold breath freezing the lakes and rivers. City fountains are dry and silent. Now the only moving water is underground, trickling secretly through the veins of the earth. I know it's there. I know I'll get to drink it again when the light returns. When it finally brings the thaw.

But now it's dark and frigid here in the heart of winter. The wheel of the year has stopped and I wait. Once again I've rented a little retreat room at a country monastery so I can keep my one night vigil. Tomorrow the wheel reverses direction, and imperceptibly at first, the days will begin to lengthen. One morning I'll wake up to hear the drip drip drip of melting ice and I'll go outside to paint the watery spring light. I can almost feel it pattering around in my brain, this sweet memory of the future. I can smell the colors waiting to spring from my fingers. It's what I want to dream of tonight.

And I want to be left alone.

It's not fair that tonight of all nights, Michel has decided to breeze into town before he heads off to Paris for Christmas. I haven't even seen him in nearly five years, not since his mother's death. I don't know if he still has the apartment in D.C. And anyway, it was Bobby he contacted, not me.

So I'm going to ignore the visit. This is my time to forget business and work for a day and a night. To slip away from the gallery by early afternoon and wander into my fallow garden, bristling with the dry canes of last summer's bee balm. I'll watch the sun blink out just past four, and the temperature will drop and the evening wind will rise, scrubbing the sky clean and black and pricked with stars. I'll scurry back into the house and pack my things, including the special memento I bring every year, the symbol of my own artistic birth. It's my traditional gift to the brand new sun.

And Michel, of all people, doesn't have any right to rob me of my ritual.

"It's just dinner," Bobby says. "He told me to be sure you'd be there."

"So I'm just supposed to hop to it and change my plans?"

"Come on, Ada. And he's going to stop by the gallery before we go out. We might even make another sale."

"You can handle that. I don't have to be there. And if he wants to see me, he knows where to reach me."

"He wants to see you. Come on, just for a little while."

It's always like this. When I put Michel on the gallery's mailing list years ago, it was just a way of telling him I was still alive. That I'd made something of myself. I never expected any response. Then he showed up out of nowhere one day when I was out of town, Bobby sold him some interesting collage work, and they were suddenly great friends. Now whenever he reappears, everyone drops what they're doing. Every fucking artist he's ever met. They all want his attention, even when he's not buying. They think he's fun and cute. They flirt with him. He flirts with them. And he and I haven't had a private conversation for so many years that I've forgotten what it was like. Almost.

So I double down on the decision not to cancel my plans. I agree only to go out with everyone for a little dinner and conversation before I make a graceful exit to my night of solitude. After all, I'm not one of Michel's moonstruck fans. He's got Bobby for that.

I meet them at a Laotian restaurant. Everybody from the gallery is there. Bobby, the chatty businessman, is friends with them all. I judge their work, but I'm not interested in their personal lives. Anyway, most of them are scared of me—under normal circumstances we would never dream of having dinner together. But now, of course, Michel's in town.

And in fact there he is, right in the middle of the table, holding court and charming the whole lot of them. He's looking quite fine, with rakish hair and a slim silver band on his wrist. He's got to know how nicely it glints in the soft light. He's acting like a big shot in his low-key, beguiling way, because he used to live in Laos and knows more about the food than we do. In fact, he's popping a morsel of something into his mouth in a familiar way that muddles my brain. I remember eating figs together.

I stride to the table as jauntily as I can. I've worn my intimidating Frida Kahlo shirt, and her baleful Mexican scowl under that black unibrow feels just right tonight. Michel sees me and his chin tilts up, stubborn and tense. We barely greet each other, and I deliberately avoid talking to him, though I listen with everyone else as he tells his exciting tales.

"I can't stay late," I explain after declining a beer. "I'm going on a personal retreat tonight at a monastery out in the hills."

"A monastery?" Michel says mildly, though I can see that he's curious.

"Yes," I respond in the breezy, no-nonsense tone I use to cut off conversation. "Tonight's the solstice and I like to spend it there by myself. I read the tarot cards, write in my journal, meditate, walk the grounds. I like the silence." I sense their reserved, instinctive respect. Nobody knows jack shit about the solstice but me, so I can say whatever I like.

"Ada," says Bobby, always more daring, "you should read the cards for us."

"Well, maybe some other time. This really isn't the right place, in the middle of a restaurant as if it were a parlor game."

Michel gives me a bemused look.

I hate it when he does this. They may not realize it, but I've known him longer than anyone here, and I recognize this coy and shallow game. The possibly unconscious flirting, even now. He only does it because he can. Because he is still awfully cute.

"Don't worry," I say, my voice too loud and teasing. "I won't read your cards and reveal your secrets to the world."

He delicately sips his silly drink. Everyone else has ordered beer, and Bobby is even drinking it out of the bottle, but Michel is having something red with a little yellow umbrella in it, a real girly drink to go with his official, native-level, mouth-searing hot Laotian food. I don't know how he still gets away with it.

"So," he inquires, "why do you do this silent monastery retreat?"

As if he barely knew me. As if it's okay to have this conversation in front of a bunch of ambitious thirty-somethings who have no idea.

But I am as calm and mature and boring as befits my age. "It feels right for the season, I think. It's supposed to be a holiday, we're all supposed to be cheerful and active and shopping for presents, but really, it's cold and dark and we should be resting and contemplating the night." The echo of these platitudes is so embarrassing that I wish I'd never mentioned the retreat at all. Why did I do that? This is a private date with myself, just me and the friendly dark, meeting for our annual winter rendezvous. I, who have never wanted for a man in my life, sleep alone with real relief this one night, and it is nobody's business but my own.

I pick at a papaya salad that is far too spicy for me, though I'm going to eat it simply to prove that I can. I just know that after all the food and drink Michel's ordered, at the end of the meal Bobby will put it on the gallery card as an entertainment expense, while everyone else will have to fend for himself.

Now Michel's acting as if I hadn't said anything of the slightest interest. He has shifted his attention from me and is offering samples of food to everyone else. Of course they eagerly take the bait, gently pulling morsels from his chopsticks as he feeds them like baby birds. And of course it is too fiery for anyone to taste anything, and they are all so impressed with his tolerance for such fierce stuff. I want to groan, but he actually does seem hopeful that they will appreciate it as much as he does. His concern for their happiness does seem sincere. This is why you can forgive people like him over and over again.

Bobby likes to drink, so he orders a couple more beers, which inspires others to do the same. Michel drinks another two of the red things, and I stick with sparkling water, which seems to make my mouth burn even more. But as I sit back and withdraw from the conversation, I do begin to appreciate how well he's orchestrated this occasion, how thorough and irrevocable he is. How once again I am forced to watch others helplessly lavishing their attentions on this inexplicable object of their desire. One of them—is her name Maggie? Molly?—wants to sip his drink, and he lets her lean over so that her smooth shoulder grazes his. His expression is mild and distant, but she doesn't notice. I try to catch his eye but he makes sure not to look. Still, when her hand slips too intimately onto his, he moves away in a smooth and inoffensive gesture to suggest yet another unfamiliar dish to delight us all, and I'm swept with a stupid, unexpected urge to protect him. He really does aim to please.

"Well," I finally say, as we sit around empty plates and drained bottles, "time for me to retreat into solitude." Bobby turns over the check and we all take a look at it, except for Michel, who is rummaging through the pockets of his sexy leather jacket. He pulls out a two euro coin and holds it up.

"I can't find anything else." He looks somewhat abashed. "I know I have a credit card somewhere . . ."

"I've got it," Bobby says briskly. I wonder if he's in love with Michel. He pulls out a credit card, and I watch Michel's eyes grow soft. I sigh as Bobby puts Michel's bill on the gallery account, while the rest of them pay up. Bobby's going to give him a ride back to the hotel, and I don't even want to know what happens after that.

But as I stand up to go, wrapping a jade green scarf around my neck, Michel catches my eye.

"Is that Thai silk?" He reaches out to touch it. There is a little gleam of grease on his lip, and now he does look like he's had a few.

"I believe it is."

"Very nice quality," he remarks. "And pretty with your hair."

I look at him with sudden suspicion. "Thank you. I've covered the gray rather well, don't you think?"

Some emotion flits across his face and is gone. "I believe my hotel is in the direction of your monastery," he says.

Bobby starts to shake his head—I can see the "no" forming on his lips—and then he catches himself. I don't look him in the eye, though I can feel him watching me.

"You need a ride?" I say. Michel looks sheepish but doesn't respond. "I'll give you a ride, Michel."

The relief on his face surprises me.

Outside, the night air is sharp and clammy, and we don't linger long. Still, everyone clusters around Michel like a pack of bodyguards as they wait their turn to hug and touch him goodbye. That young artist—Molly? Maggie?—clings to him just a moment too long. He is gracious and blank. Finally, he and Bobby give each other a slappy male embrace that's just a tad too affectionate, and Michel murmurs hesitant thanks for the meal. And then the official evening is over and it is time to retreat to our respective vehicles. Michel follows me to my car, hands in his pockets, maybe fingering the odd currency he has brought for the night. I can't be mad that he ripped off the gallery for dinner. He's a good customer, after all. He paid a lot of money for some of my experimental work long before the critics noticed it.

As I pull out of the parking lot, Michel reaches over and switches on my music, as if he were in his own car. Then he slips a manicured hand into his pocket and turns off his cell phone.

"I hope this isn't too inconvenient for you," he says.

"I don't mind. After all, I'm just going to twenty-four hours of silence and a bag of pistachios."

He has no comment. We drive in silence, the music solid between us, and he stares out the window.

"So," I finally say, "how have you been?"

He shakes his head, non-committal. "Not bad."

"I heard about your mother. I'm sorry."

He makes a little sound but says nothing.

"Did you keep the place in D.C.?"

He nods slowly. "Yes. Yes. Everything is still there." He leans his head back and I think I see his chest heave in and out.

"Which way am I going for your hotel?"

It's nowhere near my monastery, but I say nothing and try to drive slow. The silence settles once again.

I make another effort. "So, are you still in touch with Gisele?"

"Who?"

"Gisele. The big red-headed German girl in Rocca."

"Oh. She's living in Prato. She married an Italian and has two children. Two or three, I don't know." He hesitates. "She's quite a good photographer. She had her own exhibit a few years ago."

I'm dead sure that Michel was part of her exhibit, captured in every possible pose.

The conversation dwindles, rootless. I am having trouble concentrating on the road.

"Well," I say, "it's been a long time." Now I wish I hadn't offered him a ride. I feel like a cab driver. The hired help.

"I think I told you the wrong way," Michel remarks after a minute. "I think I got turned around."

"So where am I going?"

"Go back. Turn around and go back, I think we have to go—oh, east, I think."

"What's the name of your hotel?"

He sighs. "I don't know. I don't remember." I glance over at him, eyes narrowed, and I see him run his hands across his face.

"Where are those cards of yours, anyway?" he blurts.

I don't know why hot shot Mr. Boccanegra from the World Bank would be interested in my tarot cards. "You think they'll tell you where your hotel is?" I ask. But I gesture to my bag in the back seat, and he turns around to root through it till he comes up with the little yellow brocade pouch that holds my cards. It looks fragile and funny in his clumsy hands.

"Michel, you're not going to ask me to read the cards for you, are you?"

"No, no, I don't want to know anything," he responds absently, fumbling with the drawstring. "My life is challenging enough without knowing what's going to happen next." Now he's got the bag open and is pulling the cards out, though what he thinks he can see in the dark car is beyond me.

"Well, they don't tell you the future, you know. They're just a tool to stimulate your intuition."

"Ah, intuition."

"And you probably don't need tools for that. You seem perfectly capable of floating out into the ozone on your own."

"I do?" He sounds pleased with my judgment, probably because he knows it adds to his mystique. I imagine he gets some enjoyment from telling people what he does for a living. Being considered ditzy can only make him more interesting and enigmatic, of course, and Michel is all about smoke and mirrors.

"Yes, you do. You know that already, Michel, c'mon." I am now driving aimlessly up and down parallel boulevards and avenues, heading nowhere at all.

He holds up a card and peers at it.

"Are there monks at your monastery? Do they know about these cards?"

"I don't know, I never saw any last year, just a guy at the reception. I didn't tell him I was bringing tarot cards with me. And anyhow, he'll be gone now. I'll have to let myself in—I have a special combination to open the door."

He perks up at that. "Really? So you're all alone in there."

A hiccup of silence hangs in the air between us. I want to take in my breath but my heart is beating too fast. I can actually feel it like a little fist inside me rapping at my breastbone. For a split second I think I may faint.

"Unsupervised," I say. "Maybe there are other seekers of solitude in there, but I don't know them. I never saw anyone at all last year."

"This card says The Tower."

"Does it." I'm trying to focus on the road, but I have no idea where we're going.

"Ada," he says, "are they falling off this tower or are they jumping?"

"Well," I respond in the calm voice I would use for a child, "that depends. It's being struck by lightning. Its foundations are being shaken. What do you think they're doing?"

He squints at the card in the dark. "I don't know!" he cries plaintively. "I don't know what they should be doing." He lowers the card and leans back with a sigh. "I don't know. And you don't have time to explain anything because you're going to an abandoned monastery."

"Michel, it's not abandoned." I hesitate. Out of the corner of my eye I can see him looking at me, hand clutching the card. "You want an after hours tour? A tarot demo?" I feel queasy, shot back in time. Like I've asked him up to see my portraits. Ada as Venus. Or Medusa. Or the Virgin Mary.

But then he gives me that sweet smile. "That would be fantastique. If it's not too inconvenient, of course." He tucks the card back into the pouch and tries, unsuccessfully, to tie the drawstring back into its original little bow. I know he's going to end up tangling it into some kind of crazy knot.

"Okey dokey," I say. "We'll go tour the monastery then." And now, finally, I know where I'm going. We'll think about finding the hotel later. Michel cranks up the music again—it is good Brazilian— and now it's too loud to talk, so the pressure is off. I still can't believe I'm taking him with me, though my heart has slowed a little by now. He, on the other hand, seems perfectly relaxed, albeit a bit remote. He might even fall asleep if we drove far enough.

I get onto the highway and zip out into the country as fast as I can before he has a chance to change his mind. It grows darker. Icy fields slip by. I glimpse his black silhouette, his profile, from the corner of my eye. It's cold.

I finally cruise up to the dark parking lot. There is only one other car there, crouched by itself in a far corner looking like it hasn't moved in a long time. I park on the other side of the lot, near the entrance.

"Oooh," says Michel in a soft voice, "this is very monkish."

And indeed it is. As we step out of the car, me hauling my bag over my shoulder with its candles, cards, incense, journal and change of clothes, we are both struck by the silent, heavy air and the star-spackled sky. There is no moon. Wind wafts gently across the stubbly frozen grasses. They hiss like little serpents.

"There are paths out there," I say to him. My voice falls like lead, as if we were in a sealed chamber. "There are miles of paths on the grounds, and two big ponds with nesting birds. Do you want to take a walk in the dark?"

"Mmm," he responds, hands in pockets, breeze ruffling his hair. I look again—are there streaks of gray? I have already seen the lines around his eyes, noted his heavier step and his newly clumsy hands. Probably he's seen the same in me. It's a killer, time. It drains us all in the end, even the most beautiful. Yet right now he's not paying any attention to me. And I think he's completely unaware of himself too. I watch him furtively as he stands tousled and alone, and I wonder what he is thinking, what is transfixing him, here in this lonely place.

"Okay," I say, still softly. "Let's take my things up first and then we'll go for a walk."

When he turns to me, it is as if the starlight sparkles in his eyes. It is like gazing into water or an open portal. He looks totally foreign at this moment. I feel I have stumbled onto some sacred place where I have not been invited. And I fearfully wait for the spirit voices to hum, for the hail to fall. But then he tosses his head and wipes the hair out of his face, and the familiar Michel pops back into place.

"Okay," he says. "I wish I had a camera."

He does not think to help me with my bag as I fumble with the combination to the door. I'm kind of glad—I'm not ready for any more strangeness just yet, as if this were not weird enough, really, the two of us creeping in through the front door to the silent reception room with its empty desk and lowered lights, the computer vacant and dark, everything neat and orderly, and a bill and room key waiting for me on the counter. I stuff them into my coat pocket and up we go to the long, dim corridor of retreat rooms.

"Here it is," I say, and push the unlocked door open. You don't really need a key in this place. We click on the light to reveal my little sanctuary. I have my own bath and shower, a twin bed with a plain wooden cross over it—no freaky dying gods hanging from it, thankfully—and a desk with a lamp. The window looks to the north, though it's too dark to see the lawns and the trees, the rolling hills covered with flaming maples in autumn, populated by deer and maybe even black bears.

I drop my bag at the foot of the bed and try to think of something plucky to say. There are a couple of chairs, so at least we don't have to sit on the bed. When I turn to Michel, his eyes look panicky.

"They're restoring the land out there," is all I can think to tell him. "But you can't see it now. Did you still want to take a walk?"

He folds his arms and leans up against the wall next to the door, as if he plans to bolt. "Is that what you want to do?"

I throw my coat onto the bed. "I don't know." Yes, he is definitely going gray. I can see it clearly as he swipes his hair back, revealing his temples.

"I suppose you hate me."

Feeling exhausted, I sink onto the chair. "Close the door, will you? Unless you're planning to run out."

"I'm not running." He kicks the door closed but stays hunched against the wall in his elegant jacket. It's made for aesthetics, not protection.

"What do you want, Michel?"

It was one thing to see that look on his face thirty years ago. It is entirely different now, infinitely more painful.

"I didn't want to go back to that hotel by myself," he responds, averting his eyes.

"Oh baby," I say, my voice harsher than I anticipated, "I doubt that you have ever had to go back to your hotel by yourself."

"You do hate me." There is such certainty in his voice; he really has no idea.

"Take your fucking jacket off, at least. And get away from that door."

Later on, squeezed together in the dark with the curtains open to let in the starlight, he asks me to smack him, and I refuse.

"Otherwise I can't feel anything," he whispers. "It's like spices in your food, that's all." But I can feel his wild and frightened heart under my hand. I can almost hear it.

"I don't want to," I say. We are both crying.

"All right," he answers, after a long silence. Then, unexpectedly, he gives me that radiant smile and curls up against me like a puppy. His hair is soft and sweet-smelling. "My bodyguard."

I know he means to be kind and generous, but I am not worthy, I who have shirked my duty. I who have protected no one. Who just took what she needed and moved on.

"Michel," I say, my lips against his ear. "I want to show you something."

He grows still and listening.

I don't want to turn the light on—I don't look as good naked as I used to, and I'm afraid he won't either—but there's no choice. I rummage through my bag on the floor. He's sitting up now, blinking, the sheet pulled around his hips, as I find what I'm looking for and squeeze back next to him.

We bend our heads over a shabby little foil bag that still glints faintly in a few spots. Maybe he doesn't remember. But when I open it and pull out the keys, he takes in his breath. I drop the keys in his hand and he holds them, palm outstretched.

"You never used them," he said. "You never came."

"And you never used my key either, did you? Even though you stole it from me just for fun. And then you made sure I could never use it again."

He closes his eyes for a moment, as if to steady himself. "I don't want you to be sorry."

The unexpected compassion in his voice—for me?—for himself?—makes me want to collapse, to disintegrate, but I don't move. Instead, I open my mouth and take two deep breaths before I tell him the rest. "I want you to see this too."

It's wrinkled and stained, but when I unfold the paper, the swirling orange is still there, the crazy tilting leg and the music-filled piano above, vibrating with color and sound.

Michel holds it in both hands and stares at it for a long time. "You're right," he finally says. "It was orange under there."

Awkward, I fumble for words. "That night—I don't know what happened. My work changed after that. It all changed."

But this seems to cause some heaving grief in him that I did not intend. When he looks at me, his face has transformed, he has cracked open. I can't look, can't stand to see it, but still, hard and childless woman that I am, I follow some subterranean instinct and wrap my arms around him. He lets go of the paper and it slides off the mattress. The unused keys drop from his hand too. They slip behind the bed and are lost.

It's just me and my muse now. A brief interlude of beauty. A cold drink from the hidden spring. A gift.

ABOUT THE AUTHOR

Sylvia Gilbertson was born in Gary, Indiana. A former civil litigator, she left the practice of law to study medicinal herbs and wild plants, eventually moving to the mountains of northern Italy, where she and her husband raised their family. She is now a freelance legal translator in Madison, Wisconsin. Her short fiction has appeared in Wisconsin People and Ideas, the magazine of the Wisconsin Academy of Sciences, Arts and Letters, and Black Heart Magazine.

www.SylviaGilbertson.wordpress.com

www.ingramcontent.com/pod-product-compliance
Lightning Source LLC
Chambersburg PA
CBHW050042180626
46810CB00002B/853